A SMOKE TREE SERIES NOVEL

WOMAN
OF THE
DESERT
MOON

GARY J. GEORGE

Cover Design by 100Covers.com
Interior Design by FormattedBooks.com

For my dearest Ginny

Everything remains exactly as it was.
I am I, and you are you,
and the old life that we lived so fondly together is untouched, unchanged.
Whatever we were to each other, that we are still.

Death is nothing at all
Henry Scott-Holland

I'm nobody! Who are you?
Are you nobody, too?
Then there's a pair of us – don't tell
They'd banish us, you know.

Emily Elizabeth Dickinson

Contents

Prologue

THE CREATION OF THE MOJAVE DESERT

A reviewer commenting on the earlier books in the Smoke Tree series wrote that the desert is as essential to those books as the human characters. That is more than usually true about this novel. The Mojave Desert and the Providence Mountains, in particular, shape the life of Woman of the Desert Moon.

In the creation story of the Chemehuevi, the entire world was once water. Ocean Woman, Wolf, Mountain Lion, and Coyote floated on the water in a boat of woven reeds for a span of time so vast the human mind cannot comprehend it. Finally, Ocean Woman grew weary of seafaring. She scraped dead skin from her body and cast it upon the brine, where it turned to land.

When there was sufficient land to support her, Ocean Woman stepped from the reed boat and lay down, facing the sky. Using her arms and legs, she stretched the land, north and south and east and west. She sent Wolf running north and south to see if there were enough land. She sent Coyote east and west on the same mission. Wolf, always serious and reliable, returned first. Coyote, a dawdling trickster, took much longer. When he finally came back and said, "it fits," Ocean Woman created *Tuumontcokowi,* the Chemehuevi people, to walk upon the land.

Geologists tell a different story, and yet, and yet... please, read on.

The Mojave Desert has not always been a desert; it has not even always been where it is today. Three hundred million years ago, the massive tectonic plate geologists call Pangaea contained the earth's entire visible landmass. The rest of the world was ocean. Pangaea and the floor of the ocean that stretched away from it on all sides were contiguous parts of a fifty-mile thick crust that spanned the globe.

The bottom of the crust rested on the earth's mantle. The temperature where crust and mantle met was seventeen hundred degrees Fahrenheit. That intense heat created plasticity, which allowed Pangaea to "float" on the mantle. Ten thousand-degree heat from the boundary between the inner and outer core of the planet flared into the churning, burning mantle and probed Panagea for a weakness.

Two hundred million years ago, the heat found a flaw. Pangaea fractured into two tectonic plates. The new southern plate, containing what would someday be Africa, South America, Antarctica, India, and Australia, split off from the northern plate made up of present-day North America and Eurasia.

For the next fifty million years, the section of the North American plate containing the land that would someday be the Mojave Desert drifted on the viscous mantle in an arc across the equator beneath the shallow, warm waters of an ancient sea. Billions of primitive marine organisms lived and died in those waters, and their remains accumulated on the seabed.

One hundred and forty-five million years ago, another fracture created an additional tectonic plate. The new plate formed the floor of what would become the Atlantic ocean, and the floor began to spread. The movement fractured the plate containing North America and Eurasia into two pieces, pushing the North American plate west. Island arcs and other land collided with North America as it moved and became part of the larger landmass.

Eventually, the North American plate smashed into a much bigger crustal object: The Farallon plate. The Farallon was an oceanic plate. Oceanic plates are colder, denser, and more basaltic than continental plates; therefore, the Farallon dove beneath the lighter North American plate. After the collision, both structures continued moving, the Farallon eastward beneath the lighter plate; North America westward over the Farallon. Geologists call that process tectonic subduction.

As the plates moved, gigantic chunks of ocean crust were scraped from the Farallon and welded to North America by the heat generated in the collisions. The language of geology, which fluctuates between the pedantic and the poetic, calls such events "dockings." "Sutures" are the places where the dockings are welded to their new location, and the enormous chunks of land are "terranes."

The first major terrane from the Farallon docked at the present-day American Midwest. That docking sutured a new landmass to the North American continent that extended from the Midwest to present-day eastern Utah. The docking of the second significant terrane added the land from Utah to Nevada.

Forty million years ago, the third and final major docking began, suturing California to the western edge of Nevada. The heat of the suturing created a volcanic arc. Activity within the arc trapped a massive chunk of fiery material, an igneous intrusion, between the plates. The intrusion cooled and formed an enormous granite batholith. Heat below the batholith thrust it to the surface, where it became the Siera Nevada, the largest mountain range in the continental United States.

West of the new range, a valley covered by an inland sea lay trapped between the Sierra Nevada and the coastal ranges that were the final fragments of the subducting Farallon. Erosion gradually stripped the volcanic cover from the Sierras and dumped the material into the valley from the east. Similar erosive forces acting on the coastal mountains deposited their accumulations into the valley from the west. The combined deposits eventually filled the valley and displaced the inland sea, leaving behind the continental basin known as the San Joaquin Valley.

By thirty million years ago, the entire Farallon plate was beneath the North American plate and diving deeper into the mantle. Subduction ended. With the Farallon out of the way, an even bigger plate, the Pacific, struck North America a glancing blow as it moved northeast while North America was moving southwest. The collision created the San Andreas Fault.

But while the subduction of the Farallon had ended, its effects had not. Although the entirety of the plate was beneath North America, the two structures were still grinding against one another at the crust/mantle boundary. The resulting intense heat formed a dome under Nevada. Great blocks of granitic crustal gneiss full of silica and metal oxides floated on the plasticity of the dome. The dome crowned. The superheated crust above the crown stretched east to west and increased the width of North America by thirty percent.

In reaction to the extreme east/west stretching, the dense blocks of gneiss rotated, rose, and tilted in parallel rows aligned north to south. The upthrust tops became mountain peaks. The land between the ranges sank to form basins. As the mountains rose, they began to weather and erode. Rock fractured by the erosion rolled down the mountainsides and filled the basins with residue. The result was the basin and range country that forms the deserts of Nevada, Arizona, and southeastern California.

This pull-apart fracturing, known as rifting, is still underway in the Great Basin Desert of Nevada. The powerful rifting also continues in the Northern Mojave Desert, including Death Valley, where the fracturing is so violent the highest and lowest points south of the Canadian border are less than eighty miles apart.

The Southeastern Mojave Desert is different. While pull-apart fracturing was underway there, two major faults, the San Andreas to the west and the Garlock to the east, squeezed the Southeastern Mojave. Therefore, the basins and ranges are not uniform. While the Providence, the Piutes, the Old Woman Mountains, the Dead Mountains, and the Sacramentos trend north/south like their cousins in the Great Basin, some, like the Bristols, the Clippers, the Bullions, and the Marble Mountains, align southeast to northwest. And a few, the Granites, the Midhills, the Pintos, and the Coxcombs, run due east and west. It is as if a toddler had carefully lined up a few Jack Straws in parallel rows before losing interest and scattering the remainder with a casual flick of the wrist.

During the rifting in the Southeastern Mojave, the block that became the Providence Mountains flipped over as it rose and tilted. The seabed material that had once been the bottom of the block became the top of the range. The billions of dead marine organisms that had accumulated fifty million years before had been resting on the crust/mantle boundary ever since, and heating and compression had turned them into limestone and dolomite: sedimentary carbonate rock.

Water seeped through the limestone at the top of the Providence Mountains and absorbed the natural residue of the decayed organisms: carbon dioxide. Water and carbon dioxide combined, forming carbonic acid. The acid slowly ate channels through the limestone. The channels widened and met and created the caverns sacred to the Chemehuevi.

— Chapter 1 —

JANUARY 1973
The Plane

Mason Leferenge streaked less than two hundred feet above the ground as he piloted his Aero Commander above the southwest-to-northeast trending desert wash. As he flew, his eyes constantly shifted from the desert to the attitude indicator, also known as the artificial horizon, which allowed Mason to keep the speeding plane from becoming a dusty fireball on the desert floor.

His loader, Francisco Velasquez, sat behind him and to his right. Although this was the loader's tenth run with Mason, he never allowed any loader to sit in the co-pilot's seat for fear he might inadvertently brush the yoke or touch the rudder pedals.

Having Francisco back there reminded Mason of his time in 1962 as an Air Force pilot flying for Operation Farm Gate in Vietnam. Officially, his flights were "combat training sorties." Unofficially, the US Air Force was bombing the hell out of the Viet Cong in support of the Diem regime's Strategic Hamlet Program. Mason flew a B-26 Invader, a twin-engine propeller-driven bomber on loan from the CIA in Taiwan. To maintain the "advisor" fiction, he had to carry one Vietnamese National, any national he could scrounge up, on his bombing missions. The Vietnamese National, sometimes a politician but sometimes a clerk or even a janitor at the airfield, sat on a pull-down seat behind Mason's navigator. The totality of the guidance advisor Mason provided was, *"Đừng động vào bất cứ thứ gì!"* ("Don't touch anything!")

"We must be getting close," came the lightly-accented English of Francisco Velasquez over Mason's headphones.

"Yeah. We're just about to Yucca. Keep your eyes peeled for the landing strip."

Their unregistered, illegal flight had started in the early evening hours of January nineteenth, at an airfield near Badiraguato, the gateway to the Golden Triangle where the states of Sinaloa, Chihuahua, and Durango meet. The ground crew packed the plane with marijuana, methamphetamines, PCP, Mexican "black tar" heroin, and the most precious cargo of all, bricks of cocaine from a cartel in Colombia.

When they finished, Francisco had to climb over cargo to wedge himself behind a co-pilot's seat occupied by a bale of marijuana. The overloaded plane struggled to get off the ground.

Before midnight, Mason landed at a remote airstrip in the state of Sonora. He refueled and immediately took off again, crossing the US border just southeast of San Miguel, Arizona, not long after midnight and before the rising of the waning moon. He flew so low he and Francisco could almost smell the creosote flashing by beneath them.

They passed Cholic, Cowlic, and Pisinemo before crossing the Papago Reservation and ducking into the gap east of Sand Tank Mountains but close enough to Table Top Mountain to avoid the easternmost edge of the Air Force gunnery range. Then they sped north and passed east of Gila Bend before sliding west into the low valley separating the northeast end of the Haucuvar Mountains from the Bill Williams River. That brought them to the drainage between the Hualapai and Black Mountains.

"See anything, Francisco? They should have heard us by now and powered the generator to light the landing strip."

"Nothing."

They flew on.

"Wait, there's a red light," said Francisco.

"Blinking?"

"Yes."

"How many times?"

"Three. Okay, three again."

"Uh oh!. That means the strip is under surveillance."

"Local cops?"

"No. Bureau of Narcotics and Dangerous Drugs. They don't even tell the locals what they're doing, much less invite them to the party."

"Now what?"

"We divert. Head for the backup site," Mason said as he banked to the left.

"Where's that?"

"Landing strip in the middle of the Mojave. They loaded us so heavy; we've barely got enough fuel to get there."

"Is it a good place to land?"

Mason finished the turn, flew south back over Yucca, and headed west, following Sacramento Wash.

"No more talking for a bit. A little dicey flying coming up."

South of Topock, he slotted the Commander between The Needles and the Chemehuevi Mountains as he swooped low over the Colorado River, holding the ship barely above the water through the devil's elbow area before emerging to skim Lake Havasu.

"Okay. No more white knuckle stuff."

Francisco exhaled so loudly Mason could hear him over the intercom. "*Gracias a Dios.*"

"Yeah, same here," replied Mason.

"This backup strip we're going to, is it long enough for this plane to land and take off again?"

"Relax, Francisco. It's good. Built by Army engineers. Desert Strike, nineteen sixty-four, but deteriorated just enough to make me miss the plane I used to fly for Air America."

"Is that like American Airlines?"

Mason's laughter echoed in the headsets.

"Oh, my, Francisco. How the spooks would love to hear you say that!. No, Air America is the CIA's private airline. I flew different planes for them, but the best was the Pilatus Turbo Porter. What a sweet aircraft! Only needs two hundred yards to take off. Now, don't get me wrong, Francisco, I love my Aero, but the main reason I got it was it has the same high-wing design as the Pilatus."

"Why was the high wing important?"

"Cause Rangers and Green Berets were going out the doors on low-altitude jumps into Laos. On their way to help the Hmong."

"What's a 'mong?'"

"Laotian hill people. Fierce. Independent as hell. At war with the Pathet Lao, and hated the People's Army of Vietnam troops who were in their country keeping the Ho Chi Minh Trail open."

"I didn't know the US Army was in Laos."

"Officially, it wasn't. Thus, Air America. But by the way, Francisco, why are you so nervous about this diversion? You've always been a cool dude."

"Because this is my last trip. I've got my money and my phony papers. When we land in Corona, I'm heading for the coast."

"And then?"

"Disappear."

"Well, you'll be able to. Your English is excellent."

"It should be. Studied it in high school and then at the University of San Carlos."

"Guatemala?" asked Mason, surprise in his voice.

"Yes."

"Question for you, Francisco."

"Go ahead."

"If you're from Guatemala, how did you get in with the cartel? I thought they don't use anyone on that end of the operation who isn't from Sinaloa."

"They like my Engish, I guess. Thought it might come in handy."

"Has it ever?"

Francisco laughed. "It will once we land in Corona."

Mason turned west off the lake and skirted the south end of the Chemehuevi Mountains before turning northwest to fly just above Chemehuevi Valley."

"Why did you leave Guatemala?"

"The civil war."

"You must have been just a kid when it started."

"Yeah, 1960. I made a run for it."

"So you went north."

4

"Hoping to get to the US someday."

"And got on with the cartel?"

"I was out of money, and a job's a job, Mason."

"Well, you're getting out at the right time. This gig's not going to last."

"Why not?"

"Aerostats."

"What are those?"

"Big ass balloons. Look like the Goodyear blimp, but bigger than a 747."

"But surely you can fly faster than those."

"I could Francisco if they flew, but they don't. They're tethered to the ground."

"How long is the tether?"

"Thousands of feet, and it's more important than the blimp."

"Why? Do they think planes will run into it and crash?"

"No. The tether carries the power for a radar system hanging from the blimp that can look over a hundred miles into Mexico. Can't fly faster than radar, Francisco."

"Don't they have radar now?"

"Sure. That's why we fly so low coming over the border. But those are air traffic control radars."

"Why don't they spot us?"

"They're set well back from the border, and they're aimed up and out because the commercial planes are at thirty to forty thousand feet. Couple that with the curvature of the earth, and you get a big radar shadow. The shadow we hide in when we cross."

"Why aren't these aerostats up already?"

"Federal bureaucracy, Francisco. The federal budget is a zero-sum game. To add money for aerostats to Customs and the Bureau of Narcotics and Dangerous Drugs, you have to steal it from somewhere else."

Mason slid into the gap separating the Sacramento and Piute Mountains and then banked left to fly just above the Santa Fe tracks.

"Who would they steal it from?"

"In this case, the Defense Department, and more specifically, the Air Force. Added to the loss of money, the Air Force hates to give up control of anything that gets more than a few feet off the ground. Hell, they're still mad about the Army getting helicopters and keeping the Caribou."

Below them, the tracks gleamed in the light from a third-quarter moon now rising higher in the sky behind them. Mason followed the tracks to Fenner before veering due west across the Clipper Valley.

"I don't know how long it will take Customs and the Bureau to get their toys, Francisco, but when they do, no more flights. That's why I've been doubling and tripling up. Socking away money before the gravy train grinds to a halt."

Mason turned southwest to avoid Hidden Hill and flared above Granite Pass before heading straight north toward Kelso. The Providence Mountains were to the east; the Devil's Playground on the west.

"Okay, that's Kelso down there. I'm going to turn northeast above the Union Pacific rail line. We'll be over the airstrip in a minute. It's right next to the tracks. Watch for a vehicle. When you spot it, I'll fly by and then circle back. The backup crew won't be expecting us, so they'll need time to power up the lights."

The phone had rung at eight o'clock the previous evening in Felix Abrigado's tiny rented house in El Monte, California. Waiting every night for an eight o'clock call was a key component of Felix's job. If it rang, he had strict instructions not to pick it up until the tenth ring. That was so the gravelly voice on the other end of the line would know Felix was answering and not someone else.

Felix had been born in Delano, California, in 1953 to migrant agricultural workers from Los Mochis, Mexico. Although his parents were not American citizens, Felix became one at the moment of his birth. In 1953, nobody cared about children who would someday be known as "anchor babies." What farmers in Kern County cared about was getting their grapes harvested.

On his eighteenth birthday, Felix walked across the Bridge of the Americas into Texas, his carefully folded birth certificate in his pocket. No one paid any attention to him. He was just one of many brown faces. In El Paso, he hopped a freight, and less than thirty-six hours later, he was in California. Felix made his way to El Monte, where he had relatives.

Felix spoke little English but was fluent in cars. As a youngster, he had tinkered with small engines at a shop in Los Mochis and then repaired farm machinery. In El Monte, Felix soon found work at a garage. Felix lived a quiet life, and even though he sent money home to his mother and father, he saved enough to move out of his uncle's home and rent a tiny house. He wanted to meet a girl, so he started night school to improve his English. Meanwhile, his reputation as a man who knew his way around a high-performance engine began to grow.

One day when Felix was working on a tricked-out Chevy Chevelle SS, he heard a voice behind him say, "I hear you're the best in the San Gabriel Valley. Is that so?"

Felix stood up and turned to see a sharply-dressed man with coal-black eyes that seemed to have no bottom.

"I don't know about that."

"Well, that's what I hear. And you'd better be because if you screw up my ride, they'll be dragging the San Gabriel River for your body."

"And if I don't screw it up?"

The man broke into a broad grin. His capped teeth flashed, but his eyes did not join in on the merriment.

"That's what I like, a man with confidence! Come on, take a look at my *carro.*"

"Better check with my boss. The owner of this Chevy wants to pick it up before we close today."

The smile disappeared.

'Already did, *güey.* Somebody else can work on this punk-ass Chevy. Look over at the office window."

When Felix turned his head, he saw his boss gesturing toward the front of the garage and nodding his head. Felix dropped the rag he was holding and followed the man who was already walking away.

There was a '58 Thunderbird on the parking apron. It was such a deep and dazzling black it looked as if the paint job had swallowed the midnight sun. The simulated wheel spokes and center spinner caps winked in the sunlight. The roof had been channeled; the chassis raked.

"Like it?" asked the man.

"It's beautiful."

"The engine is original. Too weak. I've got a 351 Cleveland in a crate. Has the 4V head. Got twin four-barrels for it, too. And a tranny that will fit with four on the floor. The question is, can you shoehorn all that into my ride?"

"Won't be easy."

"Didn't ask if it was easy. Asked if you could do it."

"Yeah. Take a lot of different parts and lots of cutting and welding, though. That's more money."

'The money is nothing. Whatever it takes, do it. And *vato*? If you do good, couple extra C-notes for you on the side. I'm Mateo Valdez."

Felix extended his hand. "Felix Abrigado."

Mateo ignored the hand and walked away.

Two weeks later, the job was done. Mateo arrived and took the Thunderbird for a shake-down ride. He returned all smiles.

"Perfecto," he said as he stuck three folded one hundred dollar bills into Felix's shirt pocket. *"Realmente eres el mejor del valle."*

"Gracis por el dinero y el cumplido."

Mateo stared at him for a moment.

"There's something about your accent. Where are you from?"

"Born in Delano. Grew up in Mexico."

"Where in Mexico?"

"Los Mochis."

This time Mateo's smile reached his eyes.

"Damn, a homeboy, I thought you sounded familiar. How long you been in El Monte?"

"Year and a half."

"Your parents still in Los Mochis?"

"They are."

"You send them money like a good *hijo*?"

"I do."

"Homes; how'd you like to send them some real money?"

And just like that, Felix Abrigado became part of the horizontal drug distribution operation run from Badiraguato. It was a clever delivery system, full of cut-outs. Low-level employees knew only one or two people, so they could give away little of importance if arrested.

And the pay! *¡Madre de Dios!* Felix wasn't even into the big money yet, but he had already quit his job because he was making more in a week than he had in two months twisting wrenches. And the phone only rang once a week or even less! Of course, he had to stop going to night school: it interfered with being next to his phone at eight o'clock every night.

Felix worked the backup sites, riding to them with the owner of the gravelly voice. Because he had been to several more than once, Felix thought perhaps he had been to all of them. There were two east of highway 395 north of Adelanto. One east of Boron. One west of Blythe and one just northeast of Kelso.

When Felix picked up the phone after the tenth ring, the voice said, "Kelso. Ten minutes." It was always like that. Just the place and "ten minutes." But something was different tonight. The man had slurred the words.

It was more than ten minutes before the bug-eyed Ford Econoline careened to a stop in front of his house, sending a trash can flying down the street. Neighborhood dogs barked.

Felix pulled open the passenger door.

"You drive; I'm too drunk," said his boss as he pushed open his door and fell to the street.

Felix hurried to help him. His reward was shoes splattered with alcohol and spicy food when the man threw up. Felix jumped back. When his boss stopped spewing, Felix helped him around the van to the passenger door and boosted him inside.

"*¡Manejar!*" the man yelled.

By the time Felix reached the 10 Freeway, his boss was snoring, head tilted at an angle against the window. Felix had never driven the van to the sites before but had memorized each route. And Felix knew what to do if a plane ever came to a backup location. Set out the lights on both sides of the landing zone. Off-load the product from the aircraft into the Econoline. Pick up the lights when the plane leaves. Drive to Highway 395. At four corners, take Highway 58 to Tehachapi. Drive down the pass. Find the dirt road beyond the fruit stand to the middle of an orange grove. Help the two men waiting there transfer the product to another van. Drive away. Get paid. Two thousand dollars instead of five hundred!

Felix's snoring companion didn't wake up when he left the 10 Freeway to climb Cajon Pass, but when Felix turned off the highway at Baker to take Kelbaker Road, the snoring stopped. The man sat up and looked around.

"Pull over, man, I gotta pee."

"Let me get a little way out of town."

"*Ese,* you think I care if somebody sees my *verga*? Pull over before I piss my pants, and I make you change my underwear."

Felix steered onto the shoulder.

Forty minutes later, they bumped over the railroad crossing in Kelso and took the right-of-way road paralleling the tracks. At Hayden siding, Felix angled off the dirt road onto the west end of the landing strip. He parked, turned off the ignition, and rolled down his window. The only sound was the ticking of the engine as it cooled in the chilly air of early morning.

"You did good driving us here. We're on schedule."

It was the first time the man had ever said anything complimentary to Felix. Maybe this would be the night the man told Felix his name.

"Don't matter, though. Plane won't come here anyway, but God help us if it did and we weren't here. *Ahora me voy a volver a dormir.*"

He did just that and left Felix alone with his thoughts as a jasper moon rose through a faint haze of opalescent clouds clinging to the ridges of the Midhills and spread a soft glow over the unforgiving landscape.

The man was still snoring when an airplane swooped low over the van.

"There's a van down there by the tracks."

"That's our guys."

Mason swooped down to let the backup crew know it was time to light up the strip.

"What the hell?" shouted Felix's boss as he lurched from sleep.

"Plane just went over," said Felix. "We'd better set out the lights."

The man groaned.

Felix, thinking his boss was hungover, said, "Never mind, I'll get them."

The man groaned again.

"*Ese,* I had such a load on; I forgot to put them in the van."

Felix heard fear in the man's voice. It was catching.

"What do we do?"

"We got the headlights and the spotlights on both sides. Start the engine."

Felix cranked the starter and turned on the headlights.

"Angle your spotlight out past where the headlights reach," said the man as he worked the one on his side.

"Now what?"

"I've got another spot. It plugs into the cigarette lighter. I'll get on the roof with it."

"Okay."

"There's a jack under your seat. Prop it against the brake pedal so the brake lights will stay on when you get out. Tells the pilot where the landing strip starts."

"I'm getting out?"

The man was digging beneath his seat.

"Take these flashlights. Run out past where the lights reach and put one every thirty yards. Set them so they shine to the right."

Felix climbed out and got the jack. He propped it against the brake and then ran to the other side of the van. When the man handed him three flashlights, his hands were shaking.

"*¡Ve! ¡Ve! ¡Tan rápido como puedas!*"

Felix ran.

Mason brought the Aero Commander back around. The van's headlights were on, as were two spotlights. One man was sprinting to the east, and one was climbing onto the roof.

"Somebody screwed the pooch," said Mason. "There should be two sets of lights about ten feet apart on each side of that strip. Six lights on each side, with reflectors between the lights."

"Maybe the guy who's running has them."

"Couldn't carry all that stuff. Jesus! I should have stayed with Air America."

Mason banked again and began to climb.

"Let's see what we're up against. There's a couple rolls of toilet paper down by your feet. Throw them out, and I'll make a circle so we can see what the wind's doing out there."

The plane turned a slow circle as the two men watched the unfurling toilet paper flutter earthward in the moonlight.

"Crap!"

"What?"

"I thought the wind blew out of the north all winter here."

"And it's not?"

"This strip runs southwest to northeast. The wind is coming out of the southwest. Looks like maybe twenty-five knots."

"And that's bad?"

"It's terrible. You always want to land into the wind. And if you have to land with a tailwind, one stronger than twenty knots is a real problem. In normal circumstances, you wouldn't even try it."

"Maybe they could move the van. We could land the other direction."

"And how do we tell them that? You think I'm a skywriter?"

"What are we going to do?"

"We've got no choice. We're almost out of fuel. We're going to have to make a black hole landing."

"That doesn't sound good."

"It isn't, but it's all we've got. The running guy put down a couple of dim lights. Flashlights, maybe. But not near enough lights down there. That means no depth perception. Makes everything look like a pool of black ink. Gives the illusion you're higher than you really are."

"But you know that, right? And you're an experienced pilot."

"Francisco, what a pilot knows logically and what his eyes tell his brain are two very different things, but we've got no choice. If we try to fly to the airfield in Dagget or the one in Barstow, we won't make it before running out of fuel.

Hang onto your sombrero, *compadre.* We're going in."

Felix was placing the flashlights when the sound from the airplane changed. What the heck? Was it leaving?

He turned and tilted his face to the sky. Streamers of something white were drifting toward the railroad tracks. The plane turned away and flew toward Kelso but then turned again and began to drop toward the landing strip.

He could see his boss on top of the van, sweeping a spotlight in an arc across the strip. The pilot of the plane turned on his landing lights, backlighting him.

It's going to land, thought Felix, *and I don't want to be standing here when it does.* He sprinted toward the tracks and then stopped to watch. Everything seemed fine until the plane suddenly tilted and dipped toward the van and struck his boss, catapulting him off the roof. The man and the spotlight spun in different directions.

The airplane righted itself and continued to descend. It passed Felix, touched down awkwardly, bounced hard, and then skidded at a skewed angle, losing speed rapidly. The engines shut down. The plane ran off the south side of the airstrip into the desert, and the tail rose abruptly before subsiding. The aircraft came to rest with its left wing canted.

Mason, survivor of other crash landings, stayed calm. Francisco did not. He gibbered in Spanish. Mason had no idea what he was saying but assumed it had something to do with the poor bastard the nose gear had sent flying.

Mason removed his headphones and sniffed the air as he unbuckled his harness. He couldn't smell fuel. *Good thing we were almost empty.* He twisted in his seat to look at Francisco, jammed against the bale of marijuana in the co-pilot's seat by the bales behind him.

Well, he thought. *He must be okay. He's still talking.* Mason searched through his memory for his few words of Spanish.

"Francisco," he shouted, "*¡Cállate!*"

Francisco halted mid-phrase and stared at him.

"We've got to get out of here."

Francisco tried to move. "*Dios mios,* I'm stuck," he screamed.

Mason climbed out and dropped to the ground, landing awkwardly. He got to his feet and ran to help Francisco. The right wing, though badly damaged, had kept the door from jamming against the ground. Mason pulled it open and leaned in. He pushed against the bale of marijuana pinning his loader, and Francisco managed to scramble out. The two men were walking down the landing strip when Felix ran toward them.

"That guy's dead," he said, gesturing toward the van.

"I'm sure he is," said Mason. "There's blood all over the nose gear."

Francisco, forgetting his English again, launched into something in Spanish. Felix replied in the same language, and soon the two were involved in a panicked, hand-waving discussion.

Mason put his hands on his hips and leaned back, looking into the night sky. Hercules labored on the eastern horizon, and Hydra snaked across the southwestern sky.

Well, thought Mason, as the discussion got louder, *this is getting us nowhere.* He called up the Spanish word he had used before.

"¡Cállate!"

Both men turned to face him, faces illuminated by the waxy glow of the moon now riding higher in the eastern sky.

"That plane isn't going anywhere, so you'd both better be thinking about what you're going to do."

"Shouldn't we unload the stuff and put it in the van?" asked Felix.

"What's your name?" asked Mason. But before Felix could answer, Mason waved his hand. "Never mind, I don't want to know, so I'll just call you 'kid.' Kid, you're going to load a fortune in illegal drugs into a van and drive away from a dead man and the wrecked plane that killed him?"

Neither Felix nor Francisco replied.

"I suggest you figure out how to get away from here without driving a vehicle that can be traced to the scene of a crime. Now, I'm heading south, and I don't want company."

"What do you think I should do, Mason," asked Francisco.

Mason winced at the mention of his name but did not comment on the lapse.

14

"Well, if you walk up the hill beside those tracks, eventually, a train moving even slower than you're walking will come along. I'd get away from the tracks until the engine goes by so the engineer doesn't see you and then climb on. It will take you to Las Vegas."

"Anything else?" asked Felix.

"Yeah, get off before it gets into town," said Mason over his shoulder as he walked off into the desert night.

Felix and Francisco watched him for a moment before turning toward the railroad tracks.

As the three men departed, they were making very different plans.

Mason Leferenge, well aware the wrecked Aero Commander would be traced to him, was mourning the loss of his plane and his home in Palm Springs. He would miss the Spanish-style house sheltered in the shadow of Mount San Jacinto a few blocks off Palm Cayon Drive. He would miss the Mexican food at Las Casuelas and his desert hikes, especially the Lykken trail on the side of Mount San Jacinto and the long trek to Agua Alta Spring in the Santa Rosa Mountains.

At least he still had his bolt-hole in Wonder Valley, built on land bought under an assumed name in preparation for a day like this. It was pretty much vandalism and theft-proof: built of concrete blocks with a metal roof and a solid-steel door with triple deadbolts. It looked like a public utility building of some kind and was often mistaken for one. The cable running to the roof reinforced that look, but the line connected to a pump in a well, providing water for the indoor plumbing. Built atop a six-inch-thick concrete slab, the place was rodent-proof, too. It had to be because inside were cabinets full of dried food. There was also a freezer full of meat.

Mason planned to lie low for a few weeks and then make his way to Canada, where he had stashed money in several banks. From there, he would fly to Switzerland, where he kept a numbered account with more money, a lot more. He intended to live out his life in the Alps as quietly as possible, with occasional forays into Italy and the south of France.

Francisco was the least worried of the three. He was carrying everything he needed. It was a substantial amount, and he had no roots:

no family in the states or anywhere else and no friends expecting him. He was thinking Pacific Northwest. Green, cool and wet might make for a nice change.

Felix was the most worried. With family still in Los Mochis, he couldn't simply disappear, but perhaps the crashed plane near a dead man and a van abandoned in the desert would merit a good news story.

Felix didn't even have a phone number for the dead man sprawled on the airstrip, and he had no way to contact Mateo Valdez. However, he was sure Mateo would come for him when the product didn't arrive in Bakersfield. Felix hoped a high-profile news story would keep him from being blamed for the plane crash and lost drugs. That might save his life and the lives of his parents.

— **Chapter 2** —

JANUARY 1973
Woman of the Desert Moon

*T*he *waning moon was almost overhead as the slow-moving Union Pacific freight* crawled up the grade between Kelso and Cima in the pre-dawn gray of winter. The head-end brakeman saw it first. A van, driver's side door open wide. The brake lights appeared to be burning, although it was hard to be sure in the early-morning light. But there was no doubt the headlights were on. The brakeman pointed out the van to the engineer, who glanced over and said, "So what?"

"Just seems odd. And there's something that looks like a bundle of clothes in front of it, but maybe it's a person."

"Nah," said the hoghead, after another quick look.

Nothing more was said. The freight labored on, diesel engines thrumming at full-throttle, vibrating the steel floor as they powered the generators making the electricity that turned the steel wheels.

That is, nothing was said until the brakeman saw the airplane skewed at an angle in the desert. It was just off the south side of the asphalt once spread across the desert to create a temporary runway. The twin-engine plane was canted sideways, one wing higher than the other, the tail higher than the nose.

Harvey Wyskoski didn't bother with the engineer this time. He keyed his handheld radio, breaking squelch twice.

"Yeah, Harvey," came the voice of the conductor.

Woke him up, Harvey thought.

"Mark, in a few minutes, you're going to come up on a van parked on the old landing strip at Hayden. Headlights are on, and something's lying in front of it. Might be a bundle of old clothes, but could be a body. A little farther up the hill, you'll see an airplane in the desert south of the strip."

"Okay."

The conductor and rear-end brakeman stood on the rear platform of the caboose and stared at the van as the train crawled slowly past.

"What do you think?" Mark asked the brakeman.

"Don't look like a body to me."

It was barely above freezing at 2,500 feet, so the two men went back inside the crummy to watch out the window until they saw the wrecked airplane. When it came into view, they returned to the platform.

"What do you think now?" asked Mark.

"Might have been an emergency landing."

"Except for that van. I make it a drug plane."

"Might well be."

"And that means that could have been a body back there."

"It does. What should we do?"

"Sheriff's Department, I guess."

"Yeah."

"We're closer to Smoke Tree than Barstow. Substation there."

Mark keyed his handheld.

"Harvey, tell Jimmy to keep it slow when he tops the grade and heads down to Nipton. I'm going to have him stop the train when the rear end comes up on Cima."

"You got it."

When the train came to a stop with the caboose adjacent to Cima, Mark climbed down and made his way to an octagonal windowless phone booth that looked like an expanded version of a child's playhouse. He inserted a key into the padlock and snapped it open. Inside the booth, he picked up the phone and pushed a button.

"Dispatch."

"Mark Frenalt. Patch me through to the Sheriff's Department station in Smoke Tree."

When the phone rang in his bedroom, Captain Caballo, known as 'Horse' to almost everyone in the tri-state area, was grateful to be awakened from a nasty, recurring dream about a terrible day in Korea.

"Horse."

"Merle, boss. Sorry to disturb you, but I just got off the phone with a Union Pacific conductor calling from Cima. He says there's a wrecked plane off the edge of the airstrip left over from Desert Strike. Says there's a van nearby, and there might be a body not far from it."

"Who's on the midnight to eight near town, Merle?"

"Quentin."

"Call him in. Have him check to be sure the Landcruiser has a full tank. I'll be there in a few minutes."

Esperanza was already on her feet, putting on her robe.

"I'll get the coffee started. Don't want you drinking that nasty stuff that's been burning in the pot all night at the station."

"No need for you to get up, *querida.*"

"I'm already awake. You've been restless."

"Bad dream."

"I'm sorry. I should have woken you, but I wasn't sure. The usual one?"

"Yes."

Esperanza came around the bed and hugged him fiercely.

"*Mi pobre esposo.* It's been so many years."

"Over twenty."

"Do you think it will ever stop?"

"*Cuando me pusieron en el suelo.*"

"Oh, my love, I hope it's not that long."

"Me too."

She hugged him harder before heading for the kitchen.

By the time Horse had splashed water on his face, dressed, and got his .357 out of the gun safe and strapped it on, Esperanza was pouring coffee into their dented Stanley thermos.

She nodded her head toward the full mug on the counter.

There was a tap on the kitchen door. They could see Chemehuevi Joe through the glass.

"Horse reached into the cupboard for another mug.

"Come on in, Joe."

"Heard your phone ring," said Joe as he stepped inside. "Saw your lights. Sheriff stuff?"

"Yeah. A weird one. Out by Kelso. Want to come along? We might have to do some tracking. I'll get you paid for it if we do."

"Sure."

For the last two weeks, Joe had been sleeping in the Caballo's tack room by the corral. He was spending his days making adobe bricks for the new house he would build west of the corral. Carlos, Esperanza, and their adopted twins would move in when he finished. Horse's mother had finally agreed to move out of the house Horse had grown up in and move into their present home.

When Joe arrived to start the job, Esperanza had tried to persuade him to sleep in their house, but he wouldn't do it.

"Houses and me," Joe said, "don't get along."

'But you sleep in your place in the Chemehuevi's."

"Not a house. Dugout."

"Well," asked Esperanza, "what about when you stay at the place Burke left you out in the Piutes?"

"By the creek. Army cot."

"What if it rains?"

"Porch."

"And if it snows?"

"Doesn't, much."

"But when it does?"

Esperanza thought perhaps Joe almost smiled before he answered. "Sleep good in snow."

And that was all she had been able to get out of him. Frankly, she was amazed he had said that much.

Horse had said nothing. When Esperanza asked him later why he hadn't joined in, he shrugged and said, "I've never won an argument with Joe. He does what he's going to do."

"He's so stubborn."

Horse smiled. "Stubborn is way too weak a word to describe Joe Medrano."

So, Joe slept in the tack room. Slept in the tack room with the door open. Said he liked to hear what was happening outside. Like a phone ringing in the early morning hours. A phone that might get Esperanza up to make coffee. Joe dearly loved coffee.

Johnny Quentin steered the Toyota off Kelbaker Road and onto the Union Pacific right-of-way just south of the depot." He bumped along the road under a sky the blue of Chinese porcelain until he was adjacent to Hayden siding, then angled east to park behind the van on the airstrip. When he shut down the engine, the fierce wind, now reverted to its typical January pattern of ripping out of the north, growled about what it would do if it could get inside.

The three men climbed out into the grit hurtling ankle-high above the crude asphalt. They walked a semi-circle around the van. Thirty yards in front of it, they examined the crumpled body. Ants had beat them to it.

"Johnny," said Horse, "better fetch a body bag. We'll just drape it over this guy and put some rocks on top. If this scene is what I think it is, I want to leave it as much like we found it as we can. Let the Bureau of Narcotics take the lead in this deal. I'm going to have a quick look inside the van."

He and Joe approached the passenger side of the van in a new semi-circle while Johnny retraced the old one. They passed a shattered portable spotlight connected to a long cord. When they reached the open passenger door of the van, the other end of the cord, the connector, though badly bent, was still plugged into the dashboard. Horse snapped on a pair of latex gloves and opened the glove compartment. Documents inside described a van registered to Hector Delgado. He showed the registration to Joe before putting it back where he had found it.

"Unless this van is stolen, I'm guessing that's Mr. Delgado over there."

The three men arrived back at the badly damaged corpse simultaneously.

Johnny unzipped the body bag. "Let me help you," said Horse, and they spread it over the dead man. Joe had walked into the desert. He returned with some large rocks. Horse and Johnny weighed down the covering while Joe went for more. The wind ripped in frustration at the mound they had created, but the body bag stayed in place.

"Anything in the van?" asked Johnny.

"Registration. This is probably Hector Delgado from South El Monte. Joe and I found one of those portable spotlights smashed up but still plugged into the cigarette lighter. Delgado must have climbed on the roof to guide the plane. Something went wrong, and it hit him. Gear shift is in park. Emergency brake is on, but there's a jack leaning against the brake pedal, and the keys are still in the ignition. I guess it ran out of gas."

"Why would you lean a jack against the brake pedal if the emergency brake is on and the van's in park?"

"No idea. Let's go have a look at the plane."

As they walked up the side of the strip, they passed three flashlights.

"You think Hector put these out here?"

"Unlikely."

Horse and Johnny stayed on the asphalt when they reached the plane while Joe walked into the desert to examine the ground around where the plane had come to rest. He moved directly to the front of the plane and then began circling it in a series of widening arcs, pausing now and then to look more closely. When he finished, he returned to stand beside them.

"Two men. Cowboy boots jumped down from the high side. Walked around the nose. Helped a second guy out. Street shoes, smooth soles, in the back seat."

"Not the co-pilot's spot?"

"Seat's taken."

"Another body?"

Joe shook his head.

"Bale of marijuana. Left the plane. Walked to the runway. Don't know after that. I'll go figure it out"

"Okay. Johnny and I are going to take a closer look at the airplane."

The two men followed in Joe's footsteps. They looked through the open door into the plane but didn't touch anything.

"Looks like the whole plane is stuffed with drugs. Marijuana, for sure. Don't know if there's anything else. Leave it all to the Bureau."

They followed Joe's footsteps back to the strip. When they reached him, he was turning in a slow circle.

"Three men. Two, the one in street shoes, and another one in work boots went off toward the railroad tracks. I'll follow the trail later."

"Probably turn out they climbed on a train."

Joe nodded.

"Worried. Cowboy Boots."

"Why?"

"Went southwest, toward the Providence. Followed him a bit. Don't like the direction he's headed."

"Why not?"

"Woman of the desert moon." Joe pointed toward the distant mountains. "Lives up in there. Keeps to herself. Only comes out at night. Walks around."

"How long's she been back there?"

"Nineteen years, give or take."

"You never told me about her."

Joe shrugged.

"Never asked."

Horse had to smile. *That's our Joe,* he thought.

"Okay, we'd better follow him. Johnny, you drive down to the depot. Call the station. Tell them what we found. Have them call the Bureau of Narcotics and Dangerous Drugs in Vegas. Then come back and secure the scene. If the Bureau gets here before we get back, bring the Landcruiser. Where should he meet us, Joe?"

"Know the road to Cornfield Spring?"

"Yes."

"Park at the corral. Walk from there. Woman lives up the hill."

And so, the three men split up, just as three men had split up before sunrise, but this time, one went due west and two southwesterly.

Joe had been seeing woman of the desert moon for many years. He felt her terrible loneliness in the early years. Then felt her dismay when she realized loneliness was to be her constant companion. Felt her desire to be elsewhere at times, overridden by her determination never to associate with others. Never be subjected to rejection, as if she were untouchable, unfathomable, inhuman.

Joe first saw her beneath a full moon, her disfigured face etched with pale shadows. She had passed close enough that Joe could have reached out and touched her. Of course, he didn't. And, of course, she hadn't known Joe was near. No one, with one exception, ever knew Joe was near unless he wanted them to know.

Every time he saw her over the next nineteen years, it was at night. But woman of the desert moon never saw Joe. He was a phantom, a wisp of moonlight, a motionless shadow, unheard, unseen, unknown.

Joe knew solitary. Knew it because he had left home when little more than a child during the Depression after he realized his parents were starving themselves to feed him. Rode the rails. Struggled to survive day by dangerous day, the wicked, slender boning knife in his boot used a time or two in self-defense.

Returned home in his early twenties to enlist in the Army after Pearl Harbor. Returned to defend the country that had delisted his people as a tribe. Delisted them despite the reservation east of the mountains named for them. Delisted the Chemehuevi so they could have no standing to sue in court when the Bureau of Reclamation closed the flood gates on Parker Dam in 1940 and drowned their former reservation to create the reservoir they named Lake Havasu.

The Army had absorbed Joe into a wider world he never felt part of. More assassins than soldiers, he, a Mimbres Apache, and a Ute from Colorado terrorized the enemy in the Pacific islands, slipping through their lines in darkness and leaving behind silently killed soldiers. Soldiers with the Japanese character for "four" painted on their foreheads, symbolizing death because "four" is sometimes pronounced *shi:* the Japanese word for death.

Often, Joe felt a stronger connection to those he killed than to those with whom he served. Something about that momentary flare of terror in the suddenly opened eyes even as blood gushed in great gouts from a severed throat, larynx ripped speechless. Terror followed by something else. Surrender? Acceptance? Surrender to death? Acceptance of its inevitability? An inevitability Joe knew would come to him someday. An inevitability he in no way feared.

But while Joe did not fear death, he didn't want to die in the Pacific. He wanted to die in the desert and be transmuted into a landscape already a part of him. So, although Joe had no fear of the enemy, he feared the myriad of tropical diseases on every island: filariasis, malaria, dengue fever, dysentery, and hookworm.

After the war, Joe continued his solitary life, detached from others. While he often saw woman of the desert moon on his frequent rambles to listen for the whispers of his ancestors in hours of darkness, he never disturbed her, choosing instead to respect her separateness.

And then, a few years after he first saw woman of the desert moon, Joe made a friend: a new sheriff's deputy, Carlos Caballo, returned from another war, this one in Korea. A deputy, later Sergeant, then Lieutenant, and later still Captain Caballo, the Smoke Tree Substation commander.

Veterans who have experienced close combat have a look, and Carlos had that look. If you have known one of these veterans and you search your memory, you will realize you have seen it, perhaps without understanding what it was. It appears when they are in a room with other people having an ordinary conversation. Suddenly, the veterans' eyes go out of focus, and they are looking at something others cannot see. Something just beyond their skin but thousands of miles from the room. Something that happened long ago but suddenly seems more real than today. Something terrible. And because Carlos had that look, Joe felt a kinship, and they became friends.

And not long after he met Carlos, wonder of wonders, Joe made another friend. Burke Henry, blue-eyed, blonde-haired half-Kiowa Apache. Veteran of both World War Two and Korea, the deadliest warrior Joe had ever known, and the only man who knew Joe was nearby whether Joe wanted him to or not. But then Burke died. Died and left Joe the place Burke had built at the mouth of Piute Gorge along Piute Creek. And so, Joe once again had only one friend.

But then Johnny Quentin, former Ranger, returned from Vietnam. Johnny had only intended to stay in his hometown long enough to pay his respects to the mother and widow of Charlie Merriman, a fellow Ranger and a Mojave Indian. Charlie had given the last full measure of devotion to save a patrol caught outside the wire when the Viet Cong tried to breach a perimeter in the highlands of Central Vietnam.

But Johnny had stayed on in Smoke Tree. Stayed because Charlie Merriman reached out to him from beyond the grave to task him with teaching his twin sons to be warriors. Johnny was doing his best, but he knew something was missing. A conversation with Carlos Caballo led to an introduction to Chemehuevi Joe. And because Johnny Quentin had 'the look' in spades, Joe joined Johnny in his quest to honor Charlie Merriman's wish. And so, Johnny became the friend who replaced the friend Joe had lost when Burke Henry died of pancreatic cancer.

And because Joe was blessed with two friends, he often wished woman of the desert moon had at least one. Thought it would be good for her. But Joe didn't believe that decision was up to him, so he continued to respect her commitment to a life of solitude.

Cowboy Boots was easy to follow. He had made no effort to conceal his footprints or alter his course as he moved steadily southwest.

"Tell me about this woman."

"What about her?"

"Any idea where she's from?"

"First came here, little motorcycle. Nevada plate."

"You saw her on it?"

"Time or two."

"And now?"

"Triumph twin. Off-road bike."

"Why do you call her woman of the desert moon?"

"Only comes out at night."

"Even on the motorcycle?"

"Even then."

"But she rides on the highway?"

"Nope. Railroad right of way. Vegas."

There was no more talking until they reached the two-track that paralleled an abandoned aqueduct that had carried water to Kelso in the days of steam engines.

"Damn," said Joe. "Turned here. Headed straight for her."

"She stay at the spring?"

"Close enough for water. Far enough, left alone."

They joined the road as it began to climb.

26

"Hope he didn't bother that poor woman."

"When you say poor…?"

"Face twisted."

"You think that's why she's out here all alone?"

"My guess."

When they reached the foothills of the Providence, they began to see exposed, rusted sections of the aqueduct. Beyond a dilapidated corral, the road sloped downward into a wide wash."

"Hoped he'd turn," said Joe."Kept going."

The road nearly disappeared in the sand, gravel, and large rocks.

"End of the line for the Landcruiser if Johnny comes," said Horse. Joe nodded.

The footprints Cowboy Boots left behind were easy to follow through the wash, but the sand and loose gravel made for tough going. Beyond the wash, they encountered a steep section reduced to bedrock by cascading waters from countless flash floods. Horse began to feel the climb despite intense martial arts workout sessions with Johnny Quentin in the sandpit next to his home.

But it's a piece of cake for Joe, even though he's at least ten years older than I am, thought Horse as he considered the slight, hatless man moving ahead of him. A man with jet-black hair and eyes, skin the color of walnut shells and muscles of their consistency. *That's what you get,* thought Horse, as he watched Joe move with the ease of a lizard scampering up a rock slab, *when you hike twenty miles or more a day, day after day, year after year, over the desert.*

Horse had never known a man more likely to be underestimated than Chemehuevi Joe. Horse was pretty sure two Mafia hit men had once made that mistake at their peril. But they would never make that mistake again because Horse felt sure they were dead.

Fortunately, the sharp climb did not last long, and the upper road re-appeared, rocky but well-defined. Joe began to stop now and then to make sure Cowboy Boots had not left the road. Horse could not imagine how Joe could tell. All he could see was bare, blue-gray limestone.

Before them, the massive front of the Providence Mountains thrust into an electric-blue sky the color of a burnt motorcycle exhaust pipe. Single leaf pinyon pines dotted the ridgelines of deep canyons towering high above. The air was colder here, but the exertion of the climb and mild heat from a sun now directly overhead kept them warm.

Creosote, cholla, and the occasional barrel cactus yielded to yucca, catclaw, and junipers, the berries a lighter blue than the rocks. Scott's orioles, brilliant yellow beneath inky-black heads, flashed between the trees. The peculiar, climbing twitter of lesser goldfinch rose thinly from the junipers, but the pale-yellow birds themselves could not be seen. The harsh cries of flocks of scrub jays echoed in the canyons above.

The road ended, but Cowboy Boots had continued upward. Horse and Joe heard the sound of water trickling over rocks, a beautiful sound to the ears of any desert hiker.

"Wanted a drink," said Joe, understanding even as he spoke that the man they were tracking knew the desert. Knew it not from flying over it or driving across it but from walking arid places.

Water running above ground in the Mojave Desert is a rare and wonderful thing, and it creates a world of its own very different from the desert beyond its reach. Cornfield Spring was a good spring, and water ran from it into a narrow creek three hundred and sixty-five days a year. Moving up the hill, Horse and Joe came to the first of a series of small pools the tiny stream had created.

"Down on one knee, drank here."

Joe pointed to the right of the pool.

"Not dumb enough to keep climbing. Turned."

They moved west along the hillside less than a mile before reaching a door made from planks that blended into a rockface. Joe pointed at the wood, touched his finger to his lips, and spoke in a near whisper.

"Lives here. Guy shuffled around. Maybe tried to break in."

He pointed to disturbed rocks beside the crude door.

"Went away."

"Lucky for her," said Horse.

"Not lucky. Look closer."

Horse moved forward and saw four splintered holes.

"She has a gun?"

Joe nodded. "Big revolver. Magnum."

"That why you're whispering?"

Joe nodded again.

"Still in there. No footprints on top of his."

"Think she's afraid to come out?"

"Never comes out in daylight."

"I'm going to knock."

"Stand to the side."

Horse unholstered his revolver, crept to rock face beside the door, and tapped the closest plank with the butt. The response was a thunderous explosion.

"I told you last night, get away from my door!"

"Ma'am," called Horse in a calm voice once his ears stopped ringing, "I'm Captain Carlos Caballo of the San Bernardino County Sheriff's Department. Me and my friend are following the man you're referring to. Would appreciate it if you'd stop shooting."

"How do I know you are who you say you are?"

There was something unusual about her speech. A lisp? Almost imperceptible slurring?

"If you promise not to shoot again, I'll push my ID through the crack at the top of your door."

The woman took her time replying.

"All right, but step away quick as soon as you let go of it."

After Horse did as he had been told, there was a lengthy silence.

"I'm going to unbar the door, but don't try to come in until I tell you it's okay.

"That's fine."

Something scraped across the door. After that, it was several minutes before they heard the woman's voice again.

"Okay, you can come in, but only pull the door wide enough to squeeze past."

When Horse pulled the heavy door open, and he and Joe went inside, it took his eyes a while to adjust to the dim light. As they did, he saw they were inside a short tunnel. A tunnel dug by hard-rock miners early in the century. Horse never failed to be amazed at the physical and mental perseverance of such men, digging day after day through solid rock with nothing but picks and shovels. Whatever the miners had been looking for, they had given up before they got very far. The result was more like a cave than a mineshaft.

There were lighted candles on the many rocks jutting from the walls, and they illuminated the slight figure of a woman wearing a field jacket seated on what looked like an upturned soda pop crate. She was wearing a full-face motorcycle helmet with a tinted shield. A wool overcoat hung from a railroad spike driven between the rocks beside her. A stack of crates next to her had been arranged to make a simple table. Two oil lamps burned atop the table, and the smell of coal oil filled the room.

On another crate to the right side of the table, Horse could make out a camping stove of some sort: Against the back wall was a cot covered with a sleeping bag. There were two large, wooden boxes beneath the cot.

There appeared to be little else in woman of the desert moon's living quarters. Horse noted the difference between her minimalist shelter and the home in the Chemehuevi Mountains Joe had created by enlarging an existing cave.

Horse stepped toward the seated woman.

"Stop!" came the sharp command. "That's far enough."

The helmet muffled the woman's speech, but there was something else. A slight impediment?

"Just making room for Joe."

"Who is this 'Joe' person?"

"He is helping me track the man who was outside your door last night. Actually," he corrected himself, "that's not accurate. Joe is tracking the man. I'm tagging along."

"All right. Let's get this over with. Ask your questions."

Horse waited until Joe was beside him.

"Did you get a look at the man who came to your door last night?"

"Yes, I saw him."

"Outside your door."

"No. Earlier."

"How much earlier."

"I was out walking. I heard an airplane and then saw it come in for a landing."

"What time was that?"

"By the position of the moon, I'd estimate around three-thirty in the morning."

"Then what?"

"Something went wrong. The plane skidded off the runway."

"How far away were you?"

"Maybe half a mile."

"Did you walk toward it?"

"For a while."

"Did you get close enough to see how many people there were?"

"There were three of them. Two went toward the railroad. One came my direction."

"What did you do?"

"Stayed out in front of him, parallel to the direction he was moving."

"Can you describe him?"

"Not well. I can tell you he was above average height and slender."

"And then?"

"When he reached the aqueduct road and turned onto it, I stayed ahead of him and started for home. He never saw me."

"Didn't walk on the road," said Joe.

"I guess that was Tracker Man talking."

"Was."

"How do you know I didn't?"

"Pilot, cowboy boots. Tracks not on top of yours."

Woman of the desert moon fell silent as she absorbed that information. Horse did not attempt to rush her.

"How do you know which tracks are mine?"

"Seen them for years. Combat boots. Lug soles."

Her voice dropped to a whisper.

"But how do you know those tracks are mine?"

"Seen you make them."

"How? I only walk at night."

"Walk nights myself."

Woman of the desert stared silently at Joe for a long time.

"I've never seen you."

Joe nodded.

"Seen you."

"That's creepy, Tracker Man."

Horse cleared his throat.

"Don't be offended, ma'am. People don't see Joe unless he wants them to."

"At night?"

"Pretty much anytime."

"Since you know so much about me, Tracker Man, how long have I been here?"

"1954. Abandoned buildings, Vulcan Iron Mine. Moved here."

"You've seen my face?"

"Yes."

"Grotesque, isn't it?"

Joe shrugged.

"Big word."

"I'll make it easy for you. Try ugly."

"No."

"Come on, Tracker Man. If I'm not ugly, why didn't you ever try to talk to me?"

"Didn't want to."

"You didn't want to?"

"Not me. You."

"How could you know that?"

"Obvious. Sorry, big word. Try simple. Only out at night. Stay away from people."

Woman of the desert moon's voice took on an overtone of anger.

"So, have you watched me bathing in the pools up by the spring."

"No."

"You're lying," she hissed.

"No." Joe enunciated his next words precisely and delivered them hard and flat, spacing them far apart.

"It… would…not…be…right."

Lord, thought Horse, *she has offended him.*

"Which? Lying or watching me with my clothes off."

"Either."

"Sentenced to death by moonlight," thought woman of the desert moon to herself, unaware, in the manner of one who lives in absolute solitude that she had spoken the words aloud.

"What?" asked Joe.

"Nothing. I said nothing, and yet, you know what I am thinking? Do you also track people inside their minds, Mr. Tracker Man?" she said as she struggled to regain her composure. When she had, she asked another question.

"They were drug people, weren't they?"

"What makes you say that?"

"Two plus two, Sheriff Man. Van on the airstrip. Plane slides off the runway. Everybody runs away. Pilot leaves his expensive airplane. One thing I don't understand. Maybe you can explain it to me?"

"I'll try."

"Why didn't they just drive off in the van?"

"The plane crashed because it hit a man who was standing on top of the van. Killed him. Damaged the nose gear."

"So, the man who banged on my door is not only a drug smuggler; he's a killer?"

"Maybe a murderer. *People versus Ford, 1964.* California Supreme Court. Homicide during the commission of a felony constitutes second-degree murder if the felony is inherently dangerous to human life. So, it will depend on what kind of drugs are in that plane. We saw lots of marijuana, but if there's anything more dangerous, the pilot is a murderer."

"I see you know the law, Mr. Small Time Sheriff, but if you don't have any more questions for me, Id like to get my rest."

"Would you take us through what happened when the man got here?"

"He tried to break in."

"What did you do?"

"Told him to go away. Told him I had a gun."

"What did he say?"

"He laughed. Said he didn't believe me."

"And so you shot through the door?"

"Yes. Four rounds."

"Weren't you afraid you would hit him?"

"The truth?"

"It's always best."

"I was afraid I wouldn't."

"What happened next?"

"I thought he went away, but I wasn't sure."

"Did you follow him?"

"No. I knew he'd seen the spring, might have decided to hide out there."

"Thank you for your help."

"Since I've answered all my questions, I've got one."

"Go ahead."

"It's for Tracker Man. How many people have you told about me?"

"None."

"I don't believe you."

Uh oh, thought Horse, *here we go again.*

"I think you should, ma'am," he said. "Joe and I have been friends for many years, and he never said a word about you until he thought the pilot was headed toward where you live."

Her voice was quieter when she responded.

"He's kept my secret?"

"I would say so, ma'am."

"Will you?"

"I will only tell my wife and the other deputy who was with us on the airstrip. I will ask them not to tell anybody else."

"And they will do as you ask?"

"They will."

"Will you write a report about this case?

"Yes."

"And will it mention me?"

"Mention who?"

"Mention....ah, I see. Thank you, Captain Caballo. And thank you, Joe Tracker Man, for keeping my secret all these years."

"Ma'am," said Joe.

"I do have one more question," said Horse.

"Ask it."

"What's your name?"

Woman of the desert moon remained silent for a moment.

"Captain Caballo, you were kind enough to quote the law to me a moment ago: a California Supreme Court decision, I believe it was?"

"That's right."

"Let me quote a higher law to you. The United States Constitution. The Bill of Rights. Fourth Amendment. 'The right of the people to be secure in their persons will not be violated.'"

"Ma'am, I was not demanding an answer. Only wishing for one."

"Sheriff, if wishes were fishes, there'd be no room in the sea."

When it was clear those were her final words, Horse and Joe turned and left.

Outside, Joe tracked Cowboy Boots less than a quarter of a mile, then stopped and studied the sloping terrain.

"No reason to follow him farther."

"Why not?"

"Slow us down, track over hard rock. Downhill now. Know where he's going."

"Where?"

"Kelbaker Road."

Horse thought about that for a while as they walked back toward Cornfield Spring.

"So, you think he's flown over this country before."

"Sure."

"Then why did he climb up here? Why not go straight west?"

"People."

"As in…?"

"Too many. Too close. Airplane with drugs."

"And water up here."

"That, too."

"And found woman of the desert moon's place by mistake."

Joe nodded.

"Was already heading downhill. Got lucky."

"If you consider almost getting shot lucky."

Joe shook his head.

"Lucky he wasn't."

They reached the pools below Cornfield Spring and stopped for a drink.

"So we go straight down aqueduct road now?"

"Faster. Cowboy Boots way ahead."

They made their way down the steep embankment and through the boulder-strewn wash to the corral where Horse had said Johnny would have to park. No Johnny. No Landcruiser. A half-hour later, they had dropped far enough down the hill they could see the airstrip, and there was a plane parked on it.

"Cavalry has arrived," said Horse.

"Cavalry not good news for Indians," replied Joe.

Horse was so startled he almost stopped. Had Joe made a joke? Perhaps talking to the woman he had been seeing off and on for nineteen years had cheered him up.

"That woman back there, how old do you think she is?"

"Not sure. Young when she got here."

"Has anyone ever come looking for her?"

"Not here."

"Somewhere else?"

"Maybe. First couple years, man from Searchlight."

"Where did you see him?"

"Burke Henry's place, Piute Gorge. New York Mountains."

"But not down this way?"

"Never."

"How do you know he was looking for someone?"

"Binoculars. Glassed the hillsides."

"Do you know the man's name?"

"Never did."

"And he stopped?"

"Gave up, maybe."

They saw the Landcruiser coming up the road a half-hour later. Because the aqueduct road was so rocky, the usual desert dust cloud was not billowing behind it. Johnny pulled to a stop, and they climbed in.

"We saw the plane."

"Yeah. Who knew the Bureau of Narcotics had an air force."

"Did they ask you a lot of questions?"

"More than I could answer. Wanted to know what was inside the plane. I told them we had checked for bodies. Saw the marijuana but didn't dig around inside. When I left, they were pulling drugs out of the plane. Said a vehicle was on the way from Vegas to haul it away."

"Did you tell them about the two guys who had headed for the railroad?"

"I did, plus a little more. While I was waiting for them to arrive, I followed those two. Footprints stopped at the tracks. Looks like they climbed on. And, I told them you and Joe were following the pilot."

"Did you mention what Joe said about woman of the desert moon?"

"No."

"Good, because we're not going to. And Johnny?"

"Yessir."

"Don't mention her to anybody. I'll explain another time."

"Okay. So, the pilot showed up there?"

"Yeah. Knocked on her door. She told him to leave. He didn't. She blew a few holes through her door with a magnum. He left."

Johnny smiled.

"Like to have seen that. Where do you think he is now?"

"Joe tracked him a little farther west before we turned back. Joe thinks he's headed for Kelbaker Road. Let's go to Kelso."

Johnny drove toward Kelso and then turned south onto Kelbaker Road.

"Drop us just west of Vulcan Mine Road. Joe thinks he'll come off the mountain near there."

Johnny passed the eroded blacktop leading to the mine and continued south for another half a mile before Horse told him to stop.

Before he got out, Horse said, "I want you to drive up the road to Granite Pass. Cowboy Boots couldn't have walked farther than that. Maybe we'll get lucky, and you'll find him trying to hitch a ride. If you don't spot him, come on back. Joe and I will be on the shoulder trying to find the place he reached the road."

Johnny drove the fifteen miles to Granite Pass. Along the way, he saw neither a walker nor any vehicles. Horse and Joe were in the desert beside the road when he returned. Johnny parked the Landcruiser and joined them.

It was another hour before Joe found what they were looking for. The three men followed Cowboy Boots for another mile, and then the tracks ran out. Joe crossed to the opposite shoulder and walked a hundred yards in each direction.

"Caught a ride," Joe called. "Long gone."

They turned back the way they had come. When they were almost to the Toyota, an old pickup truck came rattling toward them. Horse stepped onto the roadway; badge held high. The driver stopped, and Horse walked to his door.

"Hello, Harold. What's a guy from Kessler Springs Ranch doing way over here?"

"It's a long story," the man replied, "and not worth the telling. What are you and your deputy and that other fellow doing wandering along the highway?"

"Looking for a guy."

"Have anything to do with those airplanes I saw along the railroad track?"

"It does. I don't suppose you've seen anybody walking along the road?"

"Nope."

"Okay. Thanks for stopping, and if you see a hitchhiker between here and I-40, don't pick him up."

"Okay. Take care, Horse."

The pickup drove away, gears grinding on each shift.

Horse shook his head.

"See Harold still has to double-clutch that old truck."

"Nobody getting rich, desert ranching," said Joe.

When they reached the Landcruiser, they shared the remainder of Esperanza's good coffee before driving to the airstrip to tell the feds they had not found the pilot.

That night, after the twins were in bed, Horse and Esperanza sat on the couch while Horse reviewed the unusual events of the day. When he finished, Esperanza said, *"¡Estoy tan contenta de que no te haya disparado, mi querido esposo!"*

"It wasn't for lack of trying."

"Tell me more about this woman who tried to shoot you."

"She's a puzzle, *querida.*"

"*¿Cómo?*"

"Actually, I'm not sure who's stranger, her or Joe""

"Why?"

"He told me she's been out there for almost twenty years, but he's never mentioned her."

"And that surprises you?"

"I guess it shouldn't. You know, Benjamin Franklin supposedly said, 'three can keep a secret if two of them are dead,' but he never met Joe. If he had, he would have said, 'three can keep a secret if one of them is dead and one is Joe Medrano.'"

Esperanza laughed and snuggled up against her husband.

"*Tu gracioso, Carlos. Ahora, cuéntame más sobre esta mujer*".

"She lives in a shallow mining tunnel up near Cornfield Springs. Joe says she has a motorcycle hidden nearby, and it must be about the only thing she owns, 'cause there isn't much inside where she lives."

"*¿Qué más tiene de extraño ella?*"

"Well, for one thing, she was wearing a full-face motorcycle helmet."

"Do you know why she wears it?"

Joe says her face is 'twisted.' His word. Said that's why she only goes outside at night. He calls her woman of the desert moon. He thinks he might be the only person who's ever seen her and certainly the only one who's ever seen her face."

"*¿Qué triste!* What did she say when he saw her that time?"

"She didn't know he had. Was really upset to find out."

Esperanza sat up straight.

"Wait a minute. Joe was close enough to see her face at night, and she didn't know he was there? *¿Cómo es eso posible?*"

"Because he's Joe."

"Ah, of course. And this place she lives, does she own it?"

"I doubt it."

"Who does?"

"Well, it was obviously a mining claim, but the tunnel is so short, it's clear the ore never proved out, so I'd guess the claim was never patented."

"So what happens when a mining claim doesn't work out?"

"Land reverts to the public domain. Probably owned by the Bureau of Land Management."

"Couldn't the BLM kick her out of there?"

"Maybe, if they knew she was there. But I doubt they would even care. I mean, that kind of thing happens all the time. Remember Caleb and Eunice Clovis?"

"How can I ever forget? Murdered in the terrible place they lived."

"Well, that was BLM land, and everybody in Smoke Tree knew they didn't own it, including the people at the BLM office in town. But nobody cared."

"I see. So, that happens all the time?"

"Yes. This is the Mojave. People squatting all over it. People like this woman of the desert moon."

"You think she's poor, like Caleb and Eunice?"

"One thing I've learned, *querida,* from my time with the department is that people can always surprise you. I mean, based on the stuff in that cave, she looks as poor as a dust bunny. But she must have some money. After all, she's been buying food and gas for her motorcycle for almost twenty years."

"How did she and Joe get along?"

"Not too well, at first, but she warmed to him when she found out he had never told anyone she was out there. Thanked him for it, in fact."

"Well, if you're going to be out there, you could have a worse friend than Joe."

"You could, and I get the idea he kind of checks on her, time to time."

"*¡Qué triste!*" Esperanza repeated and then leaned back against Carlos and fell silent for a long time. Horse thought she might have fallen asleep, but she spoke again.

"I wonder what she does out there?"

"Joe says she walks all over the desert at night."

"Well, that takes care of a few hours. What about the rest of the time?"

"No idea."

"I can't imagine such loneliness."

"I can't either."

"Do you think she's really been all alone out there all this time?"

"Joe says she has, and I tend to agree. She said something out loud, and I don't think she realized she had. People who are isolated for a long time often do that."

"*¿Qué dijo ella?*"

"She said, ' Sentenced to death by moonlight.'"

Esperanza shuddered.

"*Querida*, imagine Christmas and Thanksgiving and your birthday alone for nineteen years!"

"Not to mention Valentine's Day," said Horse.

Esperanza sat up and hugged him fiercely.

"I'm so glad we have each other. And the twins."

"*Yo también. Soy bendecido.*"

"*Al igual que yo, mi esposo.*"

As he was falling asleep later that night, Horse thought about the woman alone in her freezing cave on the side of the mountain. He thought he would probably never see her again.

But that's not the way things would shake out.

— Chapter 3 —

OCTOBER 1972
Jets

A rthur Ransome was happy but not overjoyed. He was outside the walls of Lewisburg Federal Prison for the first time in seven years, it was almost Halloween, and he had a cornfield to visit. Also, he was out max time; therefore, no limits on where he could live; no restrictions on associates, no parole officer to report to; no strings. His debt to society was paid in full, and Arthur Ransome was Joe Citizen again.

However, he was also an ex-con, and he wasn't sure that even his unique skills would get him a good-paying job despite his felony conviction. Arthur had plenty of time to think of his past and future on his long bus ride across the continent and plenty of room, too. He had the entire back seat to himself the whole way. Something about his prison pallor and the flat look in his greenish-gray eyes spoke to a deadly cold energy. Passengers who might otherwise have joined him turned away.

The bus may not have been the most luxurious way to travel, but it was a slice of paradise compared to his two-man cell in Lewisburg. Yes, the rear seat put him next to the bathroom, but the odors that drifted out when the door opened were mild compared to those from the toilet in that cell, especially when his first cellmate, Fat Freddie, had been on it.

"I gotta dump it, so you gotta lump it," Freddie would say with his evil grin. Were you going to complain to a three-hundred-pound felon whose massive buttocks practically swallowed the seatless, stainless steel device? Not if you wanted to live.

When Arthur climbed down from the bus in Henderson, Nevada, his first stop was a hardware store where he bought a trowel. His second stop was a drug store where he picked up a small jar of Vaseline, a pair of rubber gloves, and a package of single-edge razor blades. Then, Arthur made his way to Boulder Highway, where he set off to the east along the shoulder. The sidewalk ended when he passed the city limits. While he got an occasional glance from passing vehicles, no one looked twice at the solitary man toting a small duffle bag holding all his possessions.

It felt good to stretch out his legs after so many hours riding the dog. Even better was being in wide-open spaces after years of confinement. A long walk took him to the at-grade crossing where the Union Pacific railroad spur, constructed in 1931 to carry supplies for building Boulder Dam, bisected Boulder Highway. The tracks brought to mind something Arthur had been thinking about for a long time; something that would be important to his future.

Arthur turned away from the road and the rail line and struck out to the southwest across open desert. He skirted the base of a desert mountain range until he reached a two-track leading east into the foothills.

Arthur had turned off the two-track and walked another half-mile before he came to a spot etched indelibly in his mind: a singular rock within a semi-circle of creosote. There, he turned a slow three hundred and sixty degrees and also scanned the sky above to be sure he was utterly alone before easing his duffel to the ground and dropping to one knee. Arthur pushed aside the rock, removed the trowel from his bag, and began to dig.

In less than ten minutes, the point of the trowel struck what he was hoping to find. Arthur set to work excavating dirt until he had uncovered a gray metal box. He stood and scanned the area again before lifting it out. He opened the lid. Inside was over twenty-five thousand dollars. It was some of the money he had been able to bury once he suspected he might be under observation at work.

That long-ago uneasy feeling had led Arthur to fear he might eventually be arrested. He was sure if that happened, he would be convicted. And so, Arthur started contingency planning. His priority had been hiding money he would need when he got out of prison.

As it turned out, he was fortunate to have been so cautious and methodical; because when the feds arrested him, they seized every account he had opened and every safe deposit box he had acquired in various banks around Las Vegas. But no one knew about the funds he had buried.

Arthur was worried about recovering this first cache. There was a chance the prosecuting attorney who had put him away was aware Arthur had finished his sentence. *Probably has the date circled on his calendar,* Arthur thought.

So, the question was, did a prosecutor from the United States Attorney's Office for the District of Nevada have enough pull to order surveillance at the airport, the train depot, and the bus station for an ex-con who had gone out max time? Arthur thought it was unlikely, but not impossible. Seven years in a federal penitentiary will induce that kind of paranoia.

When Arthur had buried each stash, he knew anyone finding the metal boxes would break them open. The keys were under the money in every box. Therefore, there was no point in locking them. And Arthur had an important reason to leave the keys inside; he had looked up the search and seizure laws. He knew if he were stopped by the police for any reason while returning from retrieving the money at any location, they might be able to make a case for a cursory search.

Today, for example, it would be easy for the cops to say they had probable cause because they had received an anonymous tip about a man carrying something dangerous along the shoulder of Boulder Highway. But the metal box inside the bag? It would be locked. And while the police might be able to claim it was reasonable to have Arthur turn his pockets inside out to see if he had a key to the box, they would not find it. Not in his pockets, not in his shoes, and not on a string around his neck. Oh, he would be carrying it, all right, but not in a place they could search beside the highway. And since there was nothing in the bag that was illegal, they would have no probable cause to haul him to the station and force open the box.

Arthur locked the box. He reached into the duffel and arrayed the Vaseline, rubber gloves, razor blades, and dental floss on the ground. Cutting the thumb off one of the rubber gloves with a razor, he inserted the key and tied off the open end with dental floss. Then, he coated his creation thickly with vaseline.

Looking around one more time to be sure he was alone, he pulled down his pants and underwear. He inserted the small package into what prison slang called his 'suitcase.' After pulling up his pants, Arthur scoured his hands with dirt, put the metal box in the duffel bag, and zipped it shut. He pushed the gravelly sand back into the hole and set off to retrace his footsteps. Every fifty yards or so, he stopped to hurl an item far into the desert: first the trowel and then the drug store purchases one by one.

Arthur Ransome was born in Spencer, West Virginia, in 1939. When he was a teenager, Arthur and his friends liked to say that Spencer, the county seat of Roane County, was a great place to grow up until about the age of three. The town was so small there was only one stoplight. It hung from a wire above the intersection of State Route 33 and Market Street, adjacent to a bank that, at three stories, was one of the two most significant buildings in town. The other was the Hotel Spencer Roane at four stories. The hotel carried the full name of the famous juror from Virginia, of which each Spencer and Roane County had half. There was little else of note either in Spencer's downtown or its environs, and like many small-town teenagers, Arthur and his friends talked incessantly about getting out of the place when they graduated from high school.

Arthur's father owned a small shop just off Market Street where he made a marginal living repairing clocks and small appliances. Arthur inherited his father's mechanical aptitude and was soon taking things apart. More importantly, he could put them back together. Arthur was especially taken with airplanes and longed to disassemble one. Since that was not possible, he settled for building models and hanging them from the ceiling in his room.

In 1952, at the age of thirteen, Arthur saw his first jet plane. Probably a Lockheed Shooting Star from Shaw Air Force Base in South Carolina, the fighter blasted over Spencer, flashing silver in the summer sun. Arthur was used to the drone of small planes, but this was no propeller-driven aircraft. A jet engine thrust the gleaming airplane through the air at incredible speed. Arthur wondered how that engine worked and, at that moment, decided he would someday be a jet engine mechanic.

That desire, plus Arthur's determination to escape the drabness of Spencer, led him to the office of an Air Force recruiter two months before he graduated from high school. Since almost everybody else who walked through the door wanted to fly jets, the Technical Sergeant he talked to was delighted to meet a potential recruit who hoped to repair them. The recruiter signed Arthur up under the delayed enlistment program. Two weeks after graduation from Spencer High, Arthur was in basic training at Lackland Air Base.

During his four-year enlistment, his favorite duty station had been newly-opened Ramstein Air Base in a heavily forested area of Germany near the French border. Ramstein had jets. Lots of jets. Also, Germany was just beginning its economic recovery from World War II, and marks were pegged at four to the dollar. That meant Arthur's pay went a long way on the local economy. German beer was excellent, the food adequate, and plenty of pretty local girls would rather date an airman from Ramstein than a US Army soldier from Kaiserlautern.

Arthur's final duty assignment was one he had dreamed of: Nellis Air Force Base outside Las Vegas. Nellis was part of the Tactical Air Command by the time he arrived. The F-100 series of fighters, the first US jets capable of supersonic speed in level flight, were in the inventory, and the base was earning a reputation as the home of the fighter pilot. Because Nellis had the latest planes, including experimental aircraft, the Air Force needed hot-shot mechanics as well as hot-shot pilots. Arthur, now a Staff Sergeant, was a hot-shot mechanic.

The downside of Nellis was that, unlike Ramstein, Arthur's military pay did not stretch very far in glitzy Las Vegas. However, he had a plan that required a year of working on the latest jets. Just as he had methodically prepared to get away from Spencer, Arthur carefully planned his exit from the US Air Force for a better-paying job. On weekends, while many of his fellow airmen were prowling Glitter Gulch or The Strip, Arthur was at McCarran Airport looking at the big jets, not their pretty paint jobs or the pretty stewardesses coming off the planes, but the engines. Most of them were Pratt & Whitney, and Arthur knew Pratt & Whitney engines inside and out.

When Arthur settled on an airline to work for, he showed up in their offices at McCarran in uniform a month before his enlistment ended. The receptionist at the front desk, used to seeing Air Force pilots, changed her attitude when Arthur said he wanted to fix jets, not fly them. In less than an hour, Arthur was showing his laudatory Airman Performance Reports to a maintenance supervisor, and the supervisor was impressed. When he began to discuss pay levels, Arthur knew he had a job waiting when his enlistment ended.

Arthur started work at McCarran as soon as he was discharged from active duty. The main terminal in those days was on Las Vegas Boulevard, but construction of the all-new facilities on Paradise Road was underway.

At first, Arthur didn't see the opportunity. He was too busy learning his new job and working all the overtime he could. But then, everything moved to Paradise Road, and Las Vegas, which was already booming, went into overdrive. The new hotels and casinos had a nearly insatiable appetite for expensive goods and exotic foods, and they wanted everything immediately. Air cargo at McCarran International exploded. Jewelry, high-end watches, furs, designer-label high-end clothing, lobsters from Maine, all of it came in as air freight.

There was so much cargo arriving every hour; it overwhelmed the storage facilities at the new site. Poorly-fabricated buildings were hastily erected to handle the overflow, but the carriers couldn't put them up fast enough. They began pouring concrete slabs and stretching tents over them. Soon, even that wasn't sufficient, and they pitched tents over wooden platforms to cover the many unlocked storage containers awaiting sorting.

The place was a thief's dreamscape, and Arthur Ransome had airport credentials that allowed access to all of it. No one paid any attention to a guy in mechanics coveralls wandering here and there on his break, a can of 7-Up or Coca Cola in his hand.

Arthur had always been light-fingered, purloining change from his mother's purse and the occasional dollar bill from his father's wallet as a teenager. It was a short step from there to shoplifting. Shirts from the clothing store, 45s from the record shop, and various things from the drugstore. At McCarran, Arthur soon began to steal: expensive watches, jewelry, designer shirts, and sweaters. It was like shoplifting with bottomless pockets. His apartment in Henderson started to look more like a storage room than a place to live.

Arthur Ransome was not the only one feasting at the banquet. Panel trucks, U-Haul trailers, rented trucks, and tractor-trailer rigs came and went at all hours of the day and night. Most were legitimate, but thieves were driving some of them. There was so much traffic; it was hard for the overwhelmed security guards to tell the difference. A gang pilfering in a more organized way became aware of Arthur. One day while he was eyeballing a particularly inviting cargo bay, the leaders approached him.

Arthur feared they were with airport security or law enforcement, so he did an about-face and walked back to the maintenance area where they could not follow without credentials. He figured if they followed him, they were what he feared, but they turned away.

Apprehensive, Arthur stopped stealing but continued to walk. Over the next week, the two crew leaders approached him twice. Both times he left them standing on the tarmac. Both times they did not follow him into the restricted area, so he started to watch for them during his breaks. He soon spotted them coming and going from the air cargo area in a panel van labeled *Red Rock Freight Forwarding* with an address underneath. Arthur searched the Yellow Pages for the company. No such listing. He drove Paradise Road looking for their warehouse at the address painted below the name. There wasn't one. The next time they approached him, he agreed to meet them for coffee at a diner in Boulder City.

Freddie Clemons and Clay Nantz ran a sophisticated operation. They had a twelve-man crew and two cube trucks in addition to the van, but they lacked someone with open access to the airfield to scout for high-value cargo. Arthur negotiated a lucrative deal.

It was a good partnership. Freddie and Clay and their crew gained eyes on the airfield, and Arthur no longer had to steal anything himself. Also, Freddie and Clay were careful to keep Arthur at arm's length, even mailing his share of the proceeds to his post office box. But Arthur's most significant gain was access to a distribution chain that could dispose of just about anything, not just high-value products.

Levis bound for a Las Vegas department store? Before, Arthur would have stolen a pair or two for himself. But Red Rock Freight Forwarding could steal the entire shipment and re-distribute the goods to stores in San Diego that were glad to sell them at a discount and still turn a handsome profit. A consignment of antibiotics? Mom and pop pharmacies all over the bay area would buy them.

And Red Rock's risk, like Arthur's, was low. As Freddie and Clay explained, the air cargo carriers didn't want to report their losses! They were afraid their customers would lose confidence in the rapidly expanding air freight industry. Also, they feared their insurers would raise their premiums. It was easier to make the shippers whole and pass along the losses as price increases to the businesses. So, while the FBI knew something was going on, the crimes were almost impossible to investigate, absent cooperation by the carriers.

Arthur was getting rich, and he thought everything was fine. But Freddie and Clay were greedy. It wasn't long before they pressed Arthur to steal gate keys they would copy. After some time, even that wasn't enough to satisfy their demands. Arthur was soon searching manifests so they could plan heists before the goods even arrived at McCarran.

Arthur never knew what it was that led to his arrest: copying the keys or rifling the manifests. But the criminal mantra, "If you can't do the time, don't do the crime," has a coda: "If you can't do federal time, don't do federal crime."

Stealing air cargo is a federal crime: Theft from Interstate Shipment falls under section 659 of Title 18 of the United States Code. That section prohibits *"the theft or fraudulent acquisition of goods that are part of an interstate or international shipment, whether from the carrier or a holding area, and also the wilful buying, selling, or possession of goods obtained in this way."*

Arthur was guilty of everything described in Section 659. When he was busted, he took the fall. Kept his mouth shut; implicated no one. His refusal to cooperate angered both the politically-ambitious prosecutor, who pressed for the maximum sentence and the judge, who was delighted to drop the hammer. He gave Arthur seven years in a federal penitentiary. While there was no doubt Arthur had to be in a federal lockup, he should never have been sent to a high-security facility. Those are for criminals convicted for violent crimes, and there had been no violence in Arthur's activities. However, judges do whatever judges want, and this one didn't like the tight-lipped Air Force veteran from the hills of West Virginia.

Arthur's attorney visited him in jail to deliver the bad news: Arthur would serve his time in Lewisburg, a high-security prison. Arthur had no idea how terrible life in such places could be. His lawyer did not elaborate.

As mean inside as it looked from the outside, Lewisburg prison squatted on a low rise north of the Pennsylvania town of the same name. An inmate standing in just the right spot could make out the historic home of Bucknell College on the banks of the Susquehanna River through the wire. If the sun were right, it sparkled off the Susquehanna. But it didn't do to wander off into daydreams of walking those distant streets or scoring with a coed; survival at Lewisburg demanded constant vigilance.

Arthur's new home was a two-man eight by ten-foot cell. Everything in it was either steel or concrete. His cellmate was a three hundred pound mean-eyed man in for murder. Arthur was never sure if the judge who sentenced him and made sure he went to Lewisburg had anything to do with his cell assignment, but it wouldn't have surprised him.

A frequent visitor from the United States Attorney's Office for the Middle District of Pennsylvania reinforced Arthur's suspicions. The man always made the same pitch: give up your associates, have your sentence reduced. Refuse to cooperate? Serve the full term with no hope of parole. It was clear to Arthur that the prosecutor from the United States Attorney's Office, Nevada, thought getting information about the air cargo thefts at McCarran would boost his career and saw Arthur as the key to that information.

On the first visit, Arthur's only word was "hello." On subsequent visits, he never spoke at all. But as intended, word of the meetings leaked into the prison, marking Arthur as a possible snitch. There is no lower lifeform in a federal penitentiary than a snitch, and Arthur was in constant fear for his life his first year at Lewisburg, and the fear made him angry. He didn't belong in Lewisburg! He was a thief, not a violent criminal. Nor was he a snitch! He vowed to himself that if he survived his time in prison, he would get even with the prosecutor who sent him there.

In his second year, he caught a break. A new inmate arrived, and Arthur's life changed for the better. The new prisoner was Anthony Provenzano, a Genovese crime family caporegime known as Tony Pro. The Genovese were part of the "five families" comprising the Mafia in New York.

A caporegime, 'capo' for short, is a person of tremendous power and authority. To become a *capo*, a man must first serve as a *soldato,* or soldier, and work his way through the ranks. To take that first step and become a *soldato*, he must be a "made man." Only an Italian or a man of Italian descent can be "made," and only if another made man sponsors him. Once sponsored, the would-be *soldato* has to carry out a contract killing to prove his loyalty. The killing, which cannot be for personal revenge, is known as "making your bones." Only once he has made his bones can the man take the Mafia oath of *omerta,* or silence, and become an *uomo di rispetto*: a man of respect.

Arthur returned to his cell one evening to find two unfamiliar men inside. Two very large men. They stood when Arthur stepped inside. His cellmate was nowhere to be seen.

"Where's Trace?" he asked.

"Wanted to take a walk."

"Who are you?"

"Man wants you."

"What man?"

"Man we represent. Let's go."

They jostled Arthur out of his cell. He found himself sandwiched between them as they moved along the walkway. Arthur felt like a mouse escorted by tomcats. His mind was racing, but he didn't panic. *If they were going to kill me,* he thought, *they would have done it in the cell.*

Because of the locked passing gates at the end of each corridor, it was difficult for inmates to move between cellblocks at Lewisburg. But the two men escorting Arthur passed through the gates with ease. One guard respectfully touched his cap before unlocking a gate.

When the three reached their destination, the two men stepped aside and motioned Arthur into a cell. He saw only one man inside, a big, handsome man with neatly trimmed black hair. The next thing Arthur registered was that there was only one bunk in the cell, and there was a hot plate on a small table. There was also a portable screen in front of the toilet.

Whoa, thought Arthur, *this is some kind of big shot.*

The man gestured toward a padded chair similar to the one he was sitting on behind a small writing desk. More luxury.

"Sit down, Arty," said the man, waving his hand expansively.

Arthur sat.

"I'm Anthony Provenzano. Forgive me if I don't shake your hand, Arty, but I know how difficult good sanitation is in places like this."

Arthur nearly fell off his chair. Anthony Provenzano! The rumor that Tony Pro was coming to Lewisburg had been circulating for weeks. Now Arthur was in the famous gangster's cell! He thought carefully about what he would say. First, he got to his feet.

"Sir, it is an honor to meet you."

Tony smiled. His teeth were a dazzling white.

"Arty, I appreciate the respect. Goes with the good things we've heard about you. Like I said, siddown."

Arthur couldn't believe his ears.

"You've heard of me, sir?" he asked as he sat again.

"Followed your trial out in Nevada."

Arthur once again thought carefully before replying.

"Excuse me, sir, but I'm small-time. Why would you be interested in someone like me?"

"To be honest, kid, not so much in you as in what you were doing. The air cargo stuff. See," continued Tony, "you and me, we was in the same business, just on a different level. We're doing the same thing you was doing in Vegas. We started at JFK, and now we're taking over all the major airports. That's why I had my friends bring you around."

Arthur wasn't sure where this was going, but he didn't want to misstep. He knew the smiling man in front of him could take him off the board with a single word.

"Is there something you would like me to do for you, sir?"

"Yeah. We want you to quit. I brought you here to let you know when you get out of the slam; you're out of the air cargo business."

"Certainly, sir, if that's what you want."

"That's what we want. And thank you for not thinking twice before you agreed to do it."

"My pleasure, sir."

As soon as he said that, Arthur was worried he might be laying it on a little thick. *Oh well, can't be too careful with these Mafia guys.*

"Relax, kid. No need to be nervous."

"Yes, sir. Thank you, sir."

"Like I said, we followed your trial. Saw that prosecutor going for the max. Saw the judge laid it on you heavy."

Arthur permitted himself a bitter smile.

"That he did, sir."

"Yeah, and you a veteran of the United States Armed Forces. Man gave you no consideration at all. And we know why. Prosecutor wanted you to roll over on the guys you worked with. Knew if he could get the gen on the air cargo thefts, make his career. If you had cooperated, coulda got off with a year or two, no priors and a vet and all, but you didn't do it. And we know about the visits you're getting, the offers of parole, and we know you still won't cooperate. You're a stand-up guy, Arty, and we respect that."

"Thank you, sir."

"That's why I wanted to talk to you personal like. So you understand you're done stealing stuff at airports now."

"Message received, sir, five by five."

"Five by …?"

"Sorry, sir. Loud and clear."

Tony smiled his big smile.

"Ah, military talk."

"Yes, sir."

"One more thing and this is the best part for you. We know those visits from the US Attorney give you a bad rap in here. Makes life dangerous for you."

"For sure, sir."

"Well, that's all over now. You're under my protection, Arty. Nobody, and I mean nobody, not inmates, not trustees, not hacks, will mess with you for as long as you're here. Course, you're still going to have to go out max time because you refuse to cooperate. Nothing I can do about that. But is there anything else I can do for you?

"One thing, sir. If you don't mind."

"Go ahead and ask, kid."

"I have no intention of going straight when I get out."

Tony pro smiled.

"That a boy. Why the hell should you, way you been treated?"

Then the smile dropped from Tony's face, and his eyes went hard.

"But no airport stuff, we're clear on that, right?"

"Oh, yes, sir. No doubt at all about that."

The smile returned.

"Then ask away."

"Believe me, sir, I'm not trying to pry into your business, but I'm assuming that when you take over the air cargo in Vegas, you will also take control of the distribution of the contraband."

Tony pro looked at Arthur suspiciously.

"Just in the way of conversation, let's say that's true. What's it got to do with you?"

"I'm going back to Vegas when I get out of here, and I'm going back into the theft business. Not air cargo, of course, but something. I don't know what, and I don't know how, but I want to have a way to get rid of what I steal without hanging around pawnshops if you know what I mean,"

"I do. So, let me get this straight. You want access to the distribution network if you start making some big scores."

"Yes, sir, that's it exactly."

Tony Pro leaned back in his chair and closed his eyes for a while before he replied.

"Arty, normally I'd tell an outsider like you to go peddle his papers, but like I said, I admire a stand-up guy."

Tony pulled open a drawer in the desk in front of him and removed a pen and a small notebook. He wrote something in the notebook and then tore out the page and handed it to Arthur.

"Memorize that name and phone number and give the paper back to me."

Arthur scanned the page and looked away before reviewing it.

He handed the paper back. Tony Pro removed a gold cigarette lighter from his pocket and set it on fire before dropping it in the ashtray on his desk.

"If you get something good, call that number. Tell the guy Tony Pro sent you when you met in Lewisburg. And kid?"

"Yes, sir."

"You make the call: you and only you, Arty. You never, ever give that name and number to nobody else unless the guy gives you permission. *Capiche?*

"Oh, yes, sir."

Tony wagged a thick finger.

"And you never complain about the price you get. Never. In a deal like this, we're going to take a piece of your action, and we decide how big a piece."

"That's fine, sir. Thank you, sir," Arthur said, this time with complete sincerity.

"My pleasure," said Tony with a wink that let Arthur know his earlier false sincerity hadn't conned Tony Pro but was appreciated nonetheless.

"Take this guy back," he yelled.

It was clear the interview was over. Arthur stood and bowed slightly. The two men led him away.

Did I just bow to that guy? Arthur thought as they escorted him back to his cell. *Hell yeah, I did, and I'd do it again. He just saved my life! And maybe my future.*

Tony Pro was true to his word. There was no more violence. No more threats. No more grief from the guards. Arthur soon had a new cellmate and a job in the library instead of the laundry room. The only downside was the years of prison time stretching out before him.

The State wants time to weigh heavily on convicts. Time to think, time to reflect, time to regret the error of their ways, time to resolve to go straight and never return to prison. But that's not what convicts think about. They think first about women and second about what they will do when they're free. Usually, those second thoughts include returning to a life of crime but doing it better. Doing it without getting caught.

Arthur spent a lot of time thinking about making serious money when he got out. Air cargo theft was definitely out, but Tony Pro had granted him access to the mob's supply network. That was a big deal, and Arthur wanted to take advantage of it. There was so much money in Las Vegas there had to be other opportunities, but he just didn't know what they were. Arthur was still turning ideas over in his head when he heard something unusual in the exercise yard one day. Laughter. A lot of laughter.

A federal penitentiary is a cruel and somber place. Laughter is rare unless it's the mean-spirited variety, and this was not. This was fall-on-the-ground-and-roll-around laughter. He looked toward the sound.

A group of cons was gathered around a blond man. Every time he said a few words, the convicts roared. As soon as they stopped, the man spoke again. More belly laughs followed. Curious, Arthur moved closer.

"And then," the man was saying, "fuel tanks on the deuce and a halfs started to explode, and half the damn train caught on fire."

"What," asked one of the cons when he stopped laughing, "made you think you could steal a jeep off a moving train?"

"Well, see," said the blond man, "the train was goin' real slow up this hill in the desert."

More howls of laughter erupted from the group.

An idea took root in Arthur's brain. He wanted to talk to the blond man, but this was not the time. Too many people around. He walked away, thinking about the two things that had caught his attention: the desert and stealing from a moving train. If you had access to a distribution network that would dispose of as much as you could steal, trains loaded with goods seemed like an excellent place to start.

Arthur waited a month before he approached Austin Banner. The man was dumb as a stump, but he had a lot of information. And just because he was dumb didn't mean he might not be onto something. Over the months that followed, Arthur talked to him often and filed everything away. As he did, his excitement grew.

But then Austin was paroled, and Arthur was left in prison with years yet to serve. For all cons, time is a burden to be carried every hour of every day. That burden is heavy, and every convict stacks it a different way. Arthur's way was a cornfield.

The field lay some distance from the prison but close enough to mark the seasons. Year after year for the next six years, Arthur watched as the farmer came and went. Plowing as soon as the ground thawed, pulling a disc harrow and then a cultivator through the field with his Farmall tractor. Putting down a layer of fertilizer and then planting when the warm weather arrived. Spreading netting over the planted area to protect the emerging stalks from birds. Arthur remembered the words he had heard so often from the farmers around Spencer while growing up. "Plant when it's sweaty and hot, and the seed won't rot." "Knee-high by the Fourth of July."

Every year after the farmer applied the first course of herbicides and pesticides, he put up a scarecrow that faced the prison. The crows, of course, were not deterred, and Arthur always thought the farmer put it up for sentimental reasons. In August, the farmer harvested the crop and was not seen in the field again until Arthur's favorite time of year: late autumn.

Something about the cornfield in fall reminded Arthur of the hollows of West Virginia in that season. River birches, their leaves almost completely fallen, leaving their twisted, gnarly bark exposed, groaning in the autumn winds along Spring Creek. Arthur and his friends liked to say the creaking trees were getting ready for Halloween, as were the cattails along the banks, their long, cylindrical flower spikes now brown and ready to be dipped in oil for use as torches during Haloween in the hollows. Trick or treating or flinging shelled corn against the darkened windows of houses where the owners were too cheap to buy candy for children. Good memories.

In early November, the farmer returned with a corn knife, cut the stalks off about a foot above the ground, bundled them into shocks, and stacked them. It was a labor-intensive chore, and Arthur was surprised the farmer didn't hire someone to do it. In mid-November, he came back and hauled away the dried sheaves as silage for the animals on his distant farm and spread manure on the field for the coming year's crop. When the farmer departed, the field lay undisturbed, often under a blanket of snow, until Arthur saw the farmer again the following spring.

In Arthur's fourth year at Lewisburg, the farmer tilled the field in the fall. Arthur knew what that meant, and it saddened him: there would be no corn the following year. The farmer would plant a different crop to rejuvenate the soil. But while he grew barley in the spring, Arthur was pleased to note the farmer put up a scarecrow as if there were corn in the field.

The following two years, the corn was back, and when Arthur left the prison in October of 1972, he walked away from the gate and through the cornfield with its ragged scarecrow and dry cornstalks, thinking about trains. It was almost Halloween.

— **Chapter 4** —

FEBRUARY 1973
Trains

ate one night, a little over three months after Arthur had finished his seven years at Lewisburg Prison, there was a knock at his door. When he opened up, there stood Freddie Clemons and Clay Nantz.

"Come on in. Been expecting you. What took you so long?"

"We've been watching you for a while," said Freddie as he came inside. "Wanted to be sure that prosecutor didn't have a tail on you."

"Does he?"

"Not anymore. Did right after you got that job out at North Las Vegas Air Terminal, but looks like he's lost interest."

"I think that's how he knew I was back in the area. Somebody from Northtown checking up on my record. But who knew a United States Attorney would violate a man's civil rights? I'm so disappointed."

"Yeah, right. By the way, how'd you land that job out there?"

"Being an ex-con and all, you mean?"

"Yeah."

"First aircraft maintenance company I applied to turned me down flat. When I approached the second one, I agreed to work for six weeks for free, so they could check me out, make sure I was reformed and all."

Freddie smiled.

"The lure of easy money. Just as strong for citizens as for thieves."

"Hey, I'm a citizen now."

"You are, Arthur, and God knows you've earned it."

"Yeah, well, we'll see if the company keeps me on. Everything's good now, but word around the place is it will be a reliever airport for McCarran in a couple of years. That means air cargo will come in there. I'm afraid they'll cut me loose when that happens. I'd hate to lose that job. Pays well; enjoy the work."

"That's one of the things we came to tell you. Red Rock Freight Forwarding is out of the air cargo stealing business," said Clay Nantz.

"I know."

"Hear that in prison?"

"From the horse's mouth."

"Huh?"

"Anthony Provenzano."

"You were in the same prison as Tony Pro? You never wrote, so we didn't know where you were doing your time," said Freddie.

"Lewisburg, and I didn't write because they open your outbound and inbound mail there."

"Holy hell, Arthur. That place is for the worst of the worst. How did you wind up there?"

"It'll come to you, Freddie. I'll get us all a beer while you think it over."

When he came back with three bottles of Lowenbrau, Freddie said, "That prosecutor again. Couldn't get you to roll over at the trial, so he tried to squeeze you by putting you in a place full of hard cases."

"Not just that."

"There was more?"

"I got visited in prison, a lot."

"I'm assuming this wasn't your parents."

"Nah, disowned me, but I noticed they didn't return any of the money I'd sent or the Jaeger-LeCoultre Swiss watch I gave my old man. No, my frequent caller was a lawyer from the U.S. Attorney's Office, Middle District of Pennsylvania."

Freddie and Clay absorbed that as they sipped their beer.

"And word got out about the visits. Marked you as a snitch," said Clay.

"It did."

"So the lawyer who dropped you in the hot water has this attorney offer you parole or a reduced sentence if you'll cooperate. But you didn't. You went max time."

"I did."

"It's a wonder you're still alive," said Freddie.

"Had some close calls."

"Man, we knew we owed you for taking the fall on your own," said Clay. "Didn't know 'till now just how much. You musta been tempted, time to time."

"Be lying if I said I wasn't. Had the worst cellmate in the place. Worst job, too."

"Prison laundry?" asked Freddie.

"Yeah."

"Had that one myself, once," he said as he finished his beer.

"Another?" asked Arthur.

"Nah, I'm good."

"So am I," said Clay. "So, back to Tony Pro."

"He sent for me. I had a sit-down with him in his cell."

Freddie laughed.

"I'll bet his was nicer than yours."

"Stardust suite compared to mine."

"I assume he did most of the talking."

"He did."

"What did he say?"

"Three things. First, said he had followed my trial because me and him were in the same business."

"Stealing air cargo?" asked Freddie.

"Right. He told me the mob started at JFK, but they were taking over all the major airports. He wanted me to know I was out of the air cargo business."

"That's the word we got, from a couple 'a big guys looked like they meant business. What else did he say?"

"That I was a stand-up guy."

Freddie let out a low whistle.

"Man, that's a compliment coming from a made man!"

"I thought so."

"Anything else?"

"Yeah, he said my worries were over. Said nobody would bother me the rest of my time in prison. And he was right. No one did."

"What about after prison? Did he say you'd still be under his protection?" asked Clay.

"Yes," Arthur lied, thinking it would be best if these men thought Provenzano was still watching over him.

"But you still had to stack the time," said Freddie.

"Said there was nothing he could do about that."

"It must have been hard."

"Well, you've been inside."

"Did that attorney keep showing up?" asked Clay.

"For a couple of years, then gave it up."

"Arthur," said Freddie, "I gotta thank you again. With my record, if you'd breathed a word, I'da been in jail forever."

"I'd a got a stiff sentence too," said Clay. "Not as bad as Freddie's, but bad enough."

"You're welcome, guys. But, enough about me. Don't tell me you've gone straight since you got pushed out air cargo theft."

"Hardly, but times are tough. I miss those easy pickins at the airport. Most of the old crew quit. It's just Clay and me and four others."

"What are you doing?"

"This and that. Some legit work, but hijacking trucks, mostly."

"Is that hard?"

"Not like working those cargo bays at McCarran, that's for sure. Somma them truckers are tough, especially the independents," said Clay.

"Do you still have access to the distribution network?"

"Not anymore. And that makes everything harder. We gotta get rid of a piece here, a piece there. A real pain in the ass," replied Freddie. "Why, Arthur? You got something in mind?"

"I do, but this may take a while. You're gonna need another beer."

Arthur brought more beer from the kitchen and told a story.

"Once I was sure I wasn't going to get shanked, I started thinking about getting even with the prosecutor who got me sent to Lewisburg."

"Oh, Arthur," Freddie said, "you don't want to think like that. You go after him; you'll be right back in the slam, or maybe even dead."

"Not get even that way," Arthur said. "I mean, get even by getting back what he owes me for putting me in that place and almost getting me killed. I wanted to do something right under his nose and make lots and lots of money."

"Oh, that's better. You had me worried."

"I couldn't figure out how I was going to do it until I met a new fish in the exercise yard. His name was Austin Braxton, and he was from Smoke Tree."

"Jeez, I didn't think there were enough people in that town to spare one for prison," said Clay.

"Two. His brother was in there, too. They destroyed a couple of million dollars worth of railroad and Army property. I guess that's why they got Lewisburg."

"How'd they do that?"

"Trying to steal a jeep off a train."

"That doesn't sound like a couple of million dollars," said Freddie.

"Did I mention the train was moving at the time?"

"You didn't. Christ on a crutch, is that even possible?"

"Turns out it isn't. These two yahoos tried to uncouple the flatcar carrying the jeeps."

"From a moving train? I gotta hear this."

"They had this big wrecker, the kind that can haul a semi. One of the brothers climbs off the wrecker onto the flatcar carrying the jeeps. Hooks on a tow cable. The other one is driving the wrecker on the right of way, keeping up with the train as it climbs a hill."

"Okay."

"They were going to uncouple the car, hold it in place with the wrecker, and then uncouple the other end of the car from the rest of the train, let that part roll back down the hill."

Clay shook his head.

"Man, I can think of a lot of things that could go wrong."

"And they all did. Even though the train was going pretty slow, the brother on the flatcar couldn't get it uncoupled before the train reached the top of the grade."

Freddie smiled.

"And started going faster."

"You got it. The brother on the flatcar jumps off. The other brother is still in the truck."

"Which one were you talking to?"

"The one who was driving the truck. Said he still has bad dreams about that flatcar with the cable attached to it passing the truck. When it did, the cable snapped tight but didn't break. The truck flipped onto its side. He managed to climb to the open window and jump out."

"I still don't see the 'millions of dollars' part."

"Getting to that. The front of this long train is going downhill now and really starting to roll. There's a big pile of railroad ties on the right of way. Truck hits them and gets airborne."

"Okay, so they ruined the truck."

"That's not all. There's a big bottle of oxygen and one of acetylene hooked to the truck with a loose chain."

"For a cutting torch?" asked Clay,

"Yeah. When the truck goes flying, the bottles do too. They hit the ground. Impact snaps the valve off the oxygen tank. Truck hits the ground. Sparks fly. Ignite the oxygen. Fireball is so hot it ignites the acetylene."

"Good God."

"Fuel tank on the truck goes next."

"And some boxcars caught on fire?" asked Freddie.

"Yes. The crew sees the fireball. Engineer slams on the brakes, or whatever it is you do on a train, but train weighs tons and tons. Takes a long time to get one stopped. Meanwhile, the train is still towing the truck. Drags it to a highway crossing. Truck hits the crossing signal and snaps it loose. Train drags the truck, the signal, and the crossing gate across the road. The whole mess hits a big electrical equipment vault on the other side. Rips it off the ground. The fire spreads along the train. There are a bunch of deuce-and-a-halfs on flatbeds with canvas covers. They catch. Fuel in the tanks. Some of it explodes."

"And so, millions of dollars."

"Yep."

"Man," said Clay, "These guys sound too dumb to live."

"You haven't heard the best part yet. I asked the guy what he thought was wrong with their plan. He said they shoulda had a bigger truck!"

Freddie was laughing so hard he couldn't speak.

That got Arthur and Clay laughing, too. When they finally managed to stop, Arthur wiped his eyes.

"Did you ever talk to the guy again?" asked Freddie.

"Yeah. Time or two. Told me one day he worried about his brother surviving prison. When I asked him why he said it was because his brother wasn't as smart as he was."

That made Freddie laugh so hard beer squirted out of his nose.

"Stop, stop," he said as he wiped his face. "I can't take any more of this."

When the laughter died down, Arthur got serious.

"Amazing as that story was, it got me to thinking, and that's why I talked to Austin again. I wondered how they managed to drive that truck fast enough to pull alongside the train. He said those long trains go up the grades really slow in some places on the desert. I asked him if it might be possible to open a boxcar while the train was moving and throw stuff out. He said it would be hard. There are big locks on the door, and when you cut them off, the doors are heavy and hard to slide. He didn't think a guy hanging on the side of a moving car could get one open."

"How does he know all this stuff?" asked Clay.

"Smoke Tree is a railroad town, and his old man's a conductor on freights."

"Lord. I hope he's smarter than his sons."

"I got the impression he wasn't. So, anyway, I figured that means you would have to break into cars when the train was in a railyard, and that's no good. Too many people around. Traincrews, maintenance workers, even railroad detectives."

"Did you ask him if the guys on the train know what's inside the boxcars? At least that way, you'd know which ones were worth trying to get into if the train was going slow enough."

"I did. My first thought was maybe we could get inside information."

"What did he say?"

"Said the conductor has a list of the cars, but it's not specific. Said even the waybills don't have much information about the contents unless they're hazardous. Most of them say "FAK.""

"Which means?" asked Freddie.

"Freight All Kinds."

"Not much help."

"No. I talked to Austin a couple more times, but then him and his brother got paroled."

Arthur laughed a bitter laugh. "Imagine that! Millions of dollars in damage, and they get paroled after three years, and I'm still inside, doing all seven. Anyway, it started me thinking. Not long after I got back, I bought an old pickup truck and started driving around the desert, looking for the kinds of places Austin talked about."

"What did you find?" asked Clay, suddenly much more interested.

"Two that are perfect. The first one is where the brothers tried to steal the jeep. Santa Fe tracks climb a grade from Fenner up to Goffs. I could see why they chose it."

"And?"

"They tried to steal the jeep in '64. Not all that long ago. Probably crews still remember it."

"Be hard to forget."

"Yeah. Legends of stupidity."

"And the other?"

"It's even better. There's this place called Kelso. It's on the Union Pacific between Barstow and Vegas. Big old fancy depot there where trains don't stop anymore. Between the depot and the top of the grade at Cima, freights slow way down. You could walk faster."

"Sounds good," said Freddie.

"It is. Plus, it has a good hiding place. Years ago, the railroad planted a long row of salt cedars west of the depot to keep sand from a bunch of dunes off to the south from drifting across the tracks. We could stage a cube truck there after dark, and no one would see it."

"Where would the guys get on the train?"

"Drop them about halfway up the hill to wait."

"But you'd still have the problem of getting into a boxcar. Those heavy doors," said Clay.

"Thank God for innovation."

"What innovation."

"Pigs."

"You've lost me. We're going to steal pigs?" asked Freddie.

"What the railroad calls TOFCs on the manifest. Trailers On Flat Cars. Crews call them piggybacks, pigs for short. See, they put truck trailers on flatcars. Train takes the flatcars to destinations where the trailers are taken off the cars and hooked to tractor rigs that deliver them. Cheaper and faster than having the trucking companies drive the rigs the whole way."

"How does that help us?"

"Our guys could climb on the flat cars. Cut the locks off the trailers with bolt cutters. Search inside for stuff we could sell. If there's nothing good, just go to the next car. If they find something, they throw it over the side. Guys jump off the train at the top of the grade. After the train's gone, cube truck drives up the right of way, picks up what they tossed out."

Freddie and Clay sat silently for a few minutes, picturing the scenario. Finally, Freddie nodded his head.

"You're onto something, Arthur. It could work. But there must be lots of trains use that line. How do we know which ones are carrying the pigs?"

"That's easy. We have someone in Yermo, where the Union Pacific changes crews for the run to Las Vegas. He watches for the pigs. Trains carrying them are called 'hotshot freights.' Everything in front of them goes on a siding when they come by. When one leaves Yermo, we'll know it's going to be the next train to reach Kelso."

"How's the guy let us know?" asked Clay.

"Phone booths in Baker. Use a different one each time. He calls the number we give him. When the call comes, our cube takes Kelbaker Road to Kelso. Drives up the hill and drops the guys who will climb on the train. Drives back down past Kelso, turns off the headlights, crawls along the right of way to the salt cedars. Hides behind them and waits."

"Wow. You've thought this through. But we still have a problem," said Freddie.

"What's that?"

"How do we get rid of that much stuff? I mean, if we score the amounts I think we might, it'll be harder to get rid of it than it was to steal it."

"I have the solution for that. One more thing Tony Pro did for me: a name and number. We'll have access to the distribution network, less the mob's piece, of course."

"Oh man," said Clay, "that's great."

"But there's a catch," said Arthur.

"What's that" asked Freddie.

Tony said I'm the only one who deals with this guy. And I never tell anybody else the name or the phone number."

"Hey, Tony's contact, Tony's rules. Man, I don't ever want to cross that guy."

"Me either," said Clay. "Good way to wind up in a ditch."

"Then," said Arthur, "welcome to our new line of work. Theft from moving trains."

— Chapter 5 —

FEBRUARY 1973
Chemehuevi Joe

*I**t was a rare morning** on the Mojave. It was raining. Not the late summer monsoonal variety the locals call "gully washers," but rain so gentle it looked like dripping, gauzy curtains hanging in the sky. Although it was but a whispering rain, Joe heard it outside the tack room where he had been sleeping. When he got up and walked outside, the horses in the corral whickered as softly as the rain. They seemed pleased with the uncommon dawn.

Joe went back into the tack room for a tarp. He carried it up the hill and covered the evenly spaced adobe bricks he had set on edge for drying there. Because they were only a few days old, even such a gentle rain might melt their corners. The ones already dry would not have that problem in anything less than a pounding downpour.

Once he had the bricks covered, Joe sat down on a stack of the older ones to watch the light come into the sky. The dawn was colorless, as was the desert in the weak light.

Although the morning was windless, the sweet perfume of wet creosote filled the air around him—the signature smell of rain on the Mojave. Joe's face was turned skyward, his jet black hair plastered flat and gleaming to his head when Horse came up the hill from the house.

"Joe, you're getting wet, and it's cold."

"Been cold. This isn't."

"Where's the coldest place you've ever been?"

"Three-way tie. Minnesota, Maine, Montana."

71

"How about you come down to the house and have coffee with us? I believe Esperanza saved you a piece of that peach pie from last night."

Joe stood.

"Speaking my language."

After coffee and breakfast, Horse went off to work, and Esperanza left to drive the twins to school. Uncomfortable in houses at the best of times, Joe didn't feel right being there alone. He carried a cup of coffee to his seat on the brick pile. The rain was now little more than a drip, and a mist clung to the river bottom below him. Southwest beyond the river, the jagged peaks of the mountains the Mojave called *Huqueamp Avi* and white people called The Needles jutted through the foggy damp.

Joe wondered what woman of the desert moon was doing this morning. By now, she would be back in the shallow mineshaft she called home. It would be bitterly cold at her elevation. Last night, if she had been walking, light snow might have been falling. When he and Horse had been in her crude living quarters, Joe had seen no evidence of heating of any kind.

Why am I worried about her? Joe thought. *She's probably wrapped up in that mummy bag on her cot. She can take care of herself. Tough woman.*

The thought brought a small smile to Joe's face. He admired self-reliance.

He was still sitting on the bricks when Esperanza got home and went into the house below. Not long after, she carried two cups of coffee up the hill.

"Thought you could use one more cup," she said as she sat down beside him.

"No such thing, too much coffee."

They sat quietly for a long time before Esperanza broke the silence.

"This desert can be so beautiful."

"Can," Joe nodded.

"Mist on the river. You can live here for years and not see that."

Esperanza stood and picked up Joe's empty cup.

"Got a chore or two before I leave."

"College?"

"Yes. Class at eleven."

"Careful on 95. Crazy drivers, Monument Pass sometimes."

72

"I will be. I'll leave some sandwiches in the refrigerator for your lunch."

"'Preciate it."

Goodness, she thought as she walked down the gentle slope, *several sentences. Joe must have something on his mind.*

When she looked up the hill before she went into the house, he was working.

The desert was baked into Chemehuevi Joe's bones at a level beyond understanding. He knew the rocks, gravel, and sand, the bajadas stretching away from the mountainsides, the ephemeral streambeds that ran but rarely and then only with floods. Knew the scorpions, tarantulas, millipedes, and solpugids. Knew the hawks, the golden eagles, the ravens, the kestrels, the scrub jays, the shrikes, the quail, the chukar, the phainopepla, and the lowly sparrow. Knew the desert bighorn sheep, the mule deer, the proliferating burros left behind by prospectors, the mountain lion, the secretive bobcat, the coyote, the badger, the cottontail, the jackrabbit, the antelope squirrel, and the packrat. Joe knew the creosote, the cholla, the yucca, the Joshua tree, the catclaw acacia, and the juniper and pinyon pine at the higher elevations.

And Joe knew that high above it all, the turkey vultures circled endlessly, waiting for something to die. Knew that he would die someday but did not fear death. He only hoped that when death came for him, it would find him in some far-flung part of the desert where his body would be consumed by coyotes and vultures and insects and thus returned to the desert before it could be found by humans.

While Joe knew nothing of geology, he was observant. He was well aware the fossilized trilobites on the hillsides of the Marble Mountains near Cadiz, and the fossils of seashells encased in the limestone of the Providence were ancient.

Ocean woman put them here, he thought. *Ocean Woman missed the ocean, and from time to time, she scraped skin from other parts of her body and scattered it about the desert. The dead skin became the shells in the limestone of the Marble Mountains and the Providence.*

Chemehuevi Joe paused mid-stir in his adobe-brick-making. There were hundreds of bricks drying on edge all around him, and he would have to make hundreds more before he could begin building the new house for Horse and Esperanza. But he paused nonetheless. Paused because woman of the desert moon kept drifting in and out of his consciousness, disturbing his concentration.

To the uninitiated, making adobe bricks seems a mindless task requiring no concentration at all. Manual labor at the lowest level. Six shovels of sand, two shovels of clay, a handful of straw, add water, and mix. What could go wrong?

A lot. Each shovelful must be the same as the others, and the straw is more exact than the term 'handful' suggests. But most of all, there is an art to the amount of water in the mix. Not all sand and clay have precisely the same chemical properties and consistency, nor is all straw created equal. Therefore, the adobe maker must adjust the amount of water to achieve an exact critical mass. Too much, and the result is soupy and will not dry correctly. Too little, and the bricks crumble at the edges when removed from the mold. Joe had been making bricks for years and could detect the exact moment the mixture's resistance to the shovel signaled perfection.

Joe was good at many things, but he did one thing at a time. When he was working, he stopped only for lunch; otherwise working methodically, efficiently, and steadily from sunup to sundown, never getting so tired he had to stop; never moving so slowly he wasted daylight. Likewise, when Joe walked the desert, he concentrated on walking: where he put his feet, what was in motion close to him, what was on the distant horizon, and what might lay beyond his vision.

If Joe needed to think deeply about something, he stopped what he was doing, whether it was working or walking, and sat and thought until he understood what was troubling him and why. And so, on this winter morning, he walked away from the trough where he was mixing adobe and sat down on the same stack of dried bricks he had been sitting that morning.

Joe had only talked with woman of the desert moon once. So why keep replaying that brief conversation? Something about the desert? Something about the part of the desert where she had set up camp?

Maybe something about woman of the desert moon herself? People were a mystery to Joe. He wished they were as easy to understand as the desert he walked willingly, with unwavering interest and joy in his heart.

The desert that looked monotonously unchanging to the travelers blasting across it on the interstate looked different to Joe each time he moved through the basins and over the hills. He climbed the crumbling mountains, although he had climbed them many times before, to listen for the whispers of his forebearers. Forebearers who had done for generation upon generation what Joe now did.

Ancestors. Whispers. Wonders. Why did those words come into his head when woman of the desert moon appeared there, unbidden? Perhaps because she had chosen the Providence, home of the caves sacred to Joe's ancestors. Caves turned into a tourist attraction by white people. *See the ancient limestone caverns! For a fee, of course. Always enterprising, these white people. See the stalactites. See the stalagmites. See the columns. See the cave pearls. See the flowstone. And see the paintings made on the walls by ignorant savages long ago!*

The secretive woman of the desert moon had chosen the Providence as her home. Granted, at the opposite end of the range from the sacred caves, but that was because of Cornfield Spring and its trickling waters. But there were other springs in the desert. Piute Spring and its creek. Guitar Spring on the side of Hackberry Mountain. Rock Spring above Watson Wash. Marl Spring along the Old Mojave Road on Cima Dome. Any number of springs in Carrothers Canyon and Fourth of July Canyon. So why the Providence?

Joe rose to his feet. Once again, he had failed to reach a conclusion about the strange woman, and evening was approaching, but he didn't mind. Above all things, Chemehuevi Joe was patient. He was sure he would eventually understand why her distorted face, serene in the moonlight, kept appearing to him. Joe was sure he would talk to her again. He didn't know why and he didn't know when, but he knew where: in the mountains sacred to the Chemehuevi.

But for now, he was behind in his work. He would have to work until dark and then all the next day without stopping for lunch to get back onto a schedule he alone knew. And that thought brought to mind another problem.

Joe liked to work from time to time. He enjoyed construction because he liked the way things fit together at the end of a project. And it was good to be building something for Horse and Esperanza, his good friends.

Joe's problem was that Horse and Esperanza were paying him too much. Too much because Joe didn't want his friends spending all that money, and too much because there were very few things Joe needed. Coffee, ammunition for his guns, simple clothing and boots, and his one luxury: canned peaches in heavy syrup. Everything else, he derived from the desert, and the desert provided at no charge.

Joe had already bought the things he needed money to buy. Had even bought extra canned peaches. So, what would he do with more money? Bury it and then worry about someone stealing it? A waste of time and energy. Open a bank account? Joe had never had a bank account and had no intention of ever getting one.

So, Joe had not been cashing the checks Horse and Esperanza gave him. It wouldn't be long before they noticed. He could say he had lost the checks, but Joe never lied, and even if he did just this once, they would only write new ones.

And there would soon be another problem, maybe two. When Joe finished the Caballo house, Seve Zavala, recently married, would undoubtedly want an adobe house on the property Horse and Esperanza had given him. And what of Johnny Quentin, now engaged? Since he was a white man, Joe thought that perhaps Johnny would want a stick house. But Joe doubted that. Johnny was nearer an Indian than any white man Joe had ever known.

"Going to be a damn Rockerfeller," Joe grumbled aloud.

— Chapter 6 —

FEBRUARY 1973
Trouble at Smoke Tree High

*H*orse was working in his office* when Fred rapped on the door.

"Yes?"

"Someone wants to see you."

"Who?"

"Eletheria Cordier."

"Anything's better than this paperwork. Show her in."

A few moments later, Eletheria was sitting in front of his desk.

"Thank you for seeing me, Captain Caballo."

"Hello, Miss Cordier. Don't tell me you walked out of school again."

"It's lunchtime."

Horse looked at his watch.

"You're right. Paperwork has eaten my morning. The sad thing is, when I'm finished, I have little to show for my time."

"More paperwork."

"Excuse me?"

"You do paperwork. You send the paperwork somewhere, San Bernardino, probably. Somebody there reads it and replies to it. Sends you the reply. You have to reply to the reply. More paperwork."

"You may have hit on something there, Eletheria. And by the way, Eletheria is a pretty long name, and Miss Cordier is very formal. What do your friends call you?"

"Elthie, but I don't like it."

"Why not?"

"My mother and father thought long and hard about a name for me. They chose a good one, and I think the name made me want to be a poet. So, I like people to call me by the name my parents chose."

"Okay, Eletheria it will be. So, why did you drive out here on your lunch hour?"

"Didn't drive. Walked."

"Ah, same as last time. That's a long walk."

"Same distance as last time."

"My point is, by the time we finish our conversation and you walk back to school, you'll be late for class."

"Not a crisis."

"It's not? I heard the last time you left school and walked out here, you earned a three-day suspension."

"I did. But on the other hand, the suspension didn't start until the next week. By then, I had accomplished what I came for."

Horse had to struggle to keep from smiling. *It wouldn't do to encourage this kind of behavior,* he thought, *but damn, this is a smart kid.*

"And would your visit today have anything to do with your visit last fall?"

"It would. But before I begin, I believe Deputy Quentin is on days this week."

"How did you know?"

Eletheria shrugged.

"Your rota is not hard to figure out. One stretch of days, one of swing shifts, one of graveyards. I read about the drug plane that crashed out by Kelso in The Smoke Tree Weekly. It said Deputy Quentin drove you out there, and he must have been on graveyard to drive you out there so early in the morning. That means he's on days this week."

"And you would like him here?"

"Yes, since he was part of this from the beginning."

Horse got up and walked to the door.

"Fred," he called, "is Deputy Quentin involved in something important right now?"

"Just rollin' and patrollin'. "

"Have him come to the station."

"Should I tell him why?"

"Tell him we have a poetic emergency."

"Sir?"

"He'll understand."

Fifteen minutes later, Johnny Quentin was seated beside Eletheria in front of Horse's desk.

"Okay, Eletheria, the gang's all here. Lay it out."

"Captin Caballo, you have a leak in your department. Someone told the father of one of the boys terrorizing those trick-or-treaters on the east side of town that Tony was riding along that night."

"I see."

Horse sat silently for a moment before he continued.

"And the father told the son, and the son told the other boys. None of the boys are happy with Tony, and they are retaliating. Do I have it right?"

"You do. And one in particular."

Which one?"

"Rennie Wrexler."

"Big kid," said Horse. "Played right tackle for the Scorpions."

"Yes."

"I'm sure that's uncomfortable for Tony, but I'm not sure it's a law enforcement problem."

"*Au contraire, mon ami,*" said Eletheria.

"What?"

"French," said Johnny. "Means, 'on the contrary, my friend.'"

Eletheria turned and looked at him.

"That's right, *shérif adjoint,* I find myself very taken with *la langue française* of late."

"And I assume you just called Johnny 'deputy sheriff,'" said Horse.

"I did."

"And you assume we're all friends.".

"We are. We're all in this together. *Les trois mousquetaires,* so to speak."

"The three musketeers?" asked Johnny.

"Just so. Four, actually, counting Tony. It started when I came to see you to stop the problem on the east side."

"Actually, it was Tony Alpino who wanted to stop the problem. You came to ask us to keep Tony from doing something drastic."

"That's right, *Mon Capitaine,* and Johnny talked to Tony and presented him with a better alternative. Tony agreed and rode along that night. The operation was a success."

"I'm with you so far."

"But then, someone in your department with the *grande bouche,* how you say in *Anglais* …,?" she asked in a phony, Hollywood movie accent, looking at Johnny again.

"I am guessing 'zee 'beeg mouth,'" he answered with the same horrible accent.

"Back to why you think we're in this together," interrupted Horse.

"Yes, as I was saying, someone in your department opened his or her big mouth and *laissé le chat sortir du sac.* "

"Let something out of a bag?" asked Johnny.

"*Oui*, the cat."

"So, '*chat'* is 'cat?'

"It is."

"Then it should be '*chat noir.*"

"Black cat?"

"Of course, for Haloween."

You continue to amaze, *shérif adjoint.*"

"Therefore," said Horse, "you think our department is responsible."

"In a good way, yes, but in a way, nonetheless. I know we're talking lightly about this, and that's my fault. I started it with my inadequate French. But let me get serious and state it in American English: that giant bozo is knocking the crap out of Tony at least once a week."

"And this is happening at school?"

"In PE. In the locker room after class. The corner where the lockers come together. The other guys who were there that night make a semi-circle in that corner, so nobody can help Tony."

"I see."

Eletheria suddenly looked like she might cry.

"It's not a fair fight! Tony weighs maybe a hundred and forty pounds. Rennie's at least two hundred and twenty."

"Since this is happening at school, why doesn't Tony go to the principal?"

"He'll never do that."

"But he agreed to accept our help for the trick-or-treaters."

"Exactly. To help innocent children. Not to help himself."

"So, he's self-Reliance."

"Fiercely. Idiotically, in my estimation."

Horse swiveled his chair and looked out the window toward the Dead Mountains in the distance. The wind, so still that morning, had picked up, and a sudden gust bounced sand and small gravel against the glass that rattled in its frame.

Eletheria and Johnny Quentin sat silently while Horse pondered the situation and considered his options. Finally, he swiveled back to face them. All traces of humor were gone from his voice.

"Eletheria, I may have an unofficial solution for this unofficial problem, but you're going to have to step out of the room while I discuss it with Johnny."

Eletheria smiled. It was a huge smile, and it made her beautiful.

"I knew I could count on you. You two are the best."

"Not yet, you can't," he cautioned. "Now, off you go. Turn right outside the door and go down the hallway. You'll find the break room. We'll come for you when we're done."

"Since I'm missing lunch, you think I might find a donut down there?"

Horse wagged his finger.

"Stereotyping, Eletheria. Stereotyping."

"Girl's something, isn't she?" asked Johnny when Eletheria had gone.

"She is. I thought poets were supposed to have their heads in the clouds, but that girl is all nuts and bolts. And, she's got grit."

"Smart, efficient, and very organized. We ought to hire her as a dispatcher. So, boss, what've you got in mind?"

"As far as you know, does Coach Lucas still teach the boys' PE classes?"

"Yes."

"It's a well-known what Coach does if two guys are having a problem on his team. Is it the same in his PE classes?"

"Yes. Has them put on the gloves. Work it out on a gym mat. That is if they agree to do it. Sometimes one of them doesn't want to, and that's the end of it. But let's just say Coach strongly encourages that solution."

"It's pretty obvious he doesn't know this thing with Tony and Rennie is going on."

"Sounds like."

"Do you think Tony and Rennie would agree to settle their differences that way?"

It was Johnny's turn to think for a minute.

"I think Tony would. Kid's fearless. But I don't think Rennie would go for it."

"Really? Why not? I'd think it'd be the other way around."

"Tony's dad was a semi-pro boxer at one time. Pretty good light-heavyweight. He taught Tony a thing or two. I hear the kid is good with his fists."

"Ah, I see where you're going with this."

"Yeah. Put them on the mat with boxing gloves and boxing rules; Tony would make Rennie look like a fool. He might not hurt Rennie, but he'd hit him whenever he wanted to."

"And Rennie would be lucky to lay a glove on Tony. So he'd look stupid chasing him around the ring."

"Yes. Lots of big, strong guys aren't bullies, but Rennie is. Uses his bulk. Crowds the smaller guy. Gets hold of him. Gets him on the ground. Pin and punch, or choke the guy out, maybe."

"So, if Rennie won't box, and Tony has no chance if they don't...."

"Then something in between."

"What about leather work gloves, perhaps?"

"So Tony can punch, and Rennie can grab."

"Yeah. Think Rennie would go for that?"

"In a New York minute."

"Okay. Here are the rules for the fight: no gouging, no biting. Anything else goes. Do you think Tony would go for that?"

"Like I said, fearless."

"But likely to get squashed like a bug if Rennie gets hold of him."
Johnny smiled.

"Unless two guys we know could teach Tony about dealing with a guy who grabs him."

"Yes."

"In a sandpit?"

"That would be a good place to learn."

Johnny's smile grew.

"Any idea where we might find one?"

"Yes, but Johnny, this is strictly voluntary. It would be on our own time."

"And therefore, an unofficial solution to an unofficial problem."

"Exactly."

"Count me in!"

"How long do you think it would take us to teach Tony enough to keep him out of trouble?"

Johnny thought for a moment.

"Well, it's not like we're starting from scratch. His dad has taught him boxing. So, say the end of April?"

"Seems about right. Okay. We'll tell Eletheria what we've got in mind. I'll talk to Coach Lucas. You talk to Tony."

"Sounds good."

"Now, after we talk to Eletheria, you drive her back to school. Park on the street in front of the administration building. Wait for classes to change, then get out and escort her to the office. Walk slow, so lots of students see you."

"Okay."

"Then, have them pull Tony out of class. Walk him out to your car. Lean against your cruiser and explain the whole thing to him."

"You're a step ahead of me here. Why do that?"

"So Rennie and his friends think Eletheria has gone to the sheriff's department about her friend getting knocked around and think that the department is going to protect Tony."

"Which isn't true."

"Right. But it doesn't hurt to have these guys think that for now. They might taunt him, but they won't touch him, at least not for a while."

"Which will give you time to talk to Coach and set this up."

"Yes. And when the fight is set, no reason to bother Tony because the boys will think Tony's going to get his head handed to him."

"Which he is not."

"Exactly. Let's go talk to Eletherei."

Eletheria loved the plan, and she was sure Tony would too. And she loved the part about Johnny driving her back to school.

"I really don't want to get suspended again. Not good for a girl who's likely to be valedictorian of her class."

"Gosh," laughed Johnny, "who could have guessed?"

"What are you going to do after you graduate, Eletheria?" asked Horse.

"Got an academic scholarship."

"And after that?"

"Oh, you mean real life, not college? New York City. Live in the village. Hang around with degenerates. Drink cheap wine. Write poetry."

"Not to change the subject, "said Horse, "but I'm hungry. Johnny, let's treat this young lady to lunch at the Bluebird before you take her back to school."

"That will make me late," said Eletheria.

"It will," Horse said. "On the other hand, you'll have a note for the principal from the head of local law enforcement."

Ten minutes later, they were in Horse's usual booth. Robyn brought them menus.

"Hello, Eletheria. Who are these handsome men aiding and abetting truancy?"

"Hi, Robyn. These are my heroes. The older one is Captain Carlos Caballo, and the younger is Deputy Johnny Quentin."

"Oh, now I recognize them. In fact, I'm going to marry one of them."

Eletheria smiled that great smile again.

"So, I've heard. But which one?"

— Chapter 7 —

NO STOP SHOPPING
February 1973

Monday night, February fifth, Arthur, Freddie and Clay huddled at Arthur's apartment to plan a reconnaissance run. They agreed to send one of the four remaining gang members to Barstow to call them when an intermodal freight loaded with piggybacks passed through. Arthur provided the number of a phonebooth in Baker where Freddie, Clay, and the other three gang members would wait.

When they wrapped up the arrangements, Arthur decided there should be no further meetings at his apartment. While he had seen no evidence the district attorney was still interested in him, why take chances? Especially since he was about to get involved in criminal activity again. Las Vegas, Henderson, and Boulder City were not good options. Arthur told his co-conspirators he would find an out-of-the-way place for their post-operation meeting.

After work on Tuesday, Arthur went searching for a location. He took the freeway thirty miles south to Jean, thinking it would be far enough from Las Vegas to provide them anonymity. But when he got off the freeway, he saw a sign for a place called Goodsprings on State Route fifty-three. Intrigued, he headed that direction.

The road began to climb toward distant foothills, and it was relatively straight. Halfway to Goodsprings, Arthur pulled to the shoulder and watched for headlights behind him. There were none. He waited fifteen minutes. The only thing that came up the road was an ancient Chevrolet pickup. Satisfied no one from the D.A.s office was following him, he drove on. Yucca and a few Joshua Trees flashed in his headlights at the higher elevation.

In town, he drove a couple of the dirt roads. There were very few lights on in what looked like deserted mining shacks from the turn of the century. Most were desiccated wood or stacked stone, and the roofs were corrugated metal or tarpaper.

Arthur drove back to the highway and parked in front of the Pioneer Saloon. He noted the telephone pole sections laid end to end in front of a wooden boardwalk covered by a tin-roof portico. Arthur assumed the poles were there to keep drunks from driving over the walkway and hitting the building. Spoke to a hard-drinking crowd.

Inside, he bellied up to an old cherrywood bar with an actual brass footrail. A rounded mirror fitted into more cherrywood reflected the backs of liquor bottles. It also reflected his fellow patrons. After curious glances, they returned to their conversations.

Arthur ordered a draft Olympia. As he sipped, he surveyed the room. The interior walls were hammered tin, as was the ceiling. A potbellied stove radiated heat below a black ceiling fan. Next to the stove was a table with oak captains' chairs. It was far enough from the bar that men talking quietly at the table would not be overheard.

Better and better, Arthur thought.

When the woman who had brought his first beer left the conversation at the other end of the bar to ask Arthur if he wanted another, he gestured toward a doorway.

"Restrooms back there?"

"Honey, the restrooms are out back, where they've been for fifty years. That over there is the Carol Lombard room."

"Carol Lombard?"

"Clark Gable's wife."

"Oh, yeah. She used to come here?"

"Just once. In 1942, her plane flew into the side of a mountain not far from here. Clark Gable sat at this bar, right where you are, for three days while they searched for the wreckage. Those cigarette burns are from when he fell asleep with his head down on the bar."

Arthur looked at the burn marks and was going to ask the woman how she knew Clark Gable had made those particular marks but checked himself.

"Wow, that's something. And yes, I believe I'll have one more."

The woman smiled. She seemed to be missing a tooth or two.

"It'll be right here waiting when you get back from the little boys' room."

Arthur noticed she neither asked his name nor offered hers.

Perfect, he thought.

Later that same night, Freddie drove the cube truck from Las Vegas to Baker. Clay rode in the cab with him; the three crew members were inside the cube. He parked next to a phone booth on Baker Road. It was after midnight when the phone rang. A hotshot freight carrying piggybacks had just passed through Barstow.

Freddie took Kelbaker Road out of town and drove to Kelso. There, he turned northeast toward Cima. Halfway up the deserted road, he stopped. Clay climbed out and pulled open the back door of the cube. The three crew members climbed out, each carrying bolt cutters, a flashlight, and a canvas tarp. They followed Clay as he crunched through the gravel wash and went under a low trestle to the other side of the tracks. Freddie made a K turn and returned to Kelso, where he took the right of way west to a spot behind the salt cedars.

The waxing sliver of the three-day-old moon had set not long after sundown, and Clay and the crew settled down to wait beneath a moonless sky filled with stars stretched from horizon to horizon.

When the slow-moving freight reached their positions, each of the four waiting men tossed their tarps and tools onto separate flatcars before climbing on. Since this was only a recon, none of them attempted to break into a trailer. They did, however, note what kind of locks were on the trailers. Calculating the length of time it would take to remove the shipping seals, cut the locks, search inside and remove items, the men then tossed their tarps off the flatcars. Before the lead diesel crested Cima grade, they jumped from the train and melted into the desert. Long after the train had passed his position, Freddie emerged from behind the salt cedars and took the right-of-way road to where the men were waiting.

Wednesday afternoon, Arthur hurried home from work for the six o'clock call from Freddie. When it came, he told them to wait half an hour to give him a head start and then drive to Jean, get off the freeway, and drive toward Goodsprings. He explained why he would be waiting for them alongside the road.

When Freddie and Clay pulled off the road next to his car, Arthur said, "Nobody behind you. But let's give it a couple of minutes."

"Nervous, aren't you?" asked Clay.

"Yeah, well, seven years in federal prison will do that to a man."

Arthur gestured toward the table next to the potbellied stove when they walked into the saloon.

"Be right there," he said.

He ordered a pitcher.

"Back again?" asked the woman who had waited on him the previous evening.

"Couldn't stay away."

She brought the pitcher and three mugs.

"What's the charm?"

"The old West."

The woman smiled her gap-toothed smile, rang up the sale on the ancient cash register in front of the mirror, and returned with his change. None of the locals at the bar spoke to Arthur.

The woman leaned forward.

"Less than two hundred people live here, and they don't like questions if you get my drift."

"I do."

"And I'll bet you don't like questions either."

Arthur smiled wider and touched his index finger to an imaginary cap. He picked up the pitcher and the mugs and headed for Freddie and Clay.

The locals, who had fallen silent, returned to their noisy discussion.

"What did you learn?" Arthur asked without preamble when he sat down at the table.

"First, there was enough starlight to see to climb on the train," said Clay in a soft voice.

"What about the locks?"

"Seals and locks on the doors of the trailers. Nothing we can't get off with bolt cutters."

"What kind of locks?"

"Yales, mostly. Long shank."

"We'll need to buy a bunch of those."

"Why?"

"I don't want the train to stop for a crew change in Vegas and have someone notice a bunch of the piggybacks are missing locks. I know there's not much chance of that, but the longer we do this, the more chances we'll be taking. So, let's start right. Get what we want; take the cut locks with us. Put on new ones."

"Good idea. That way, the railroad might not discover the problem until the trailer gets to where it's going, and they can't open the lock. Make it hard for them to figure out where this is happening."

"Any problem getting the tarps on the flatcars?"

"They're awkward. Floppy and heavy; took a few tries to get them on. Fold them tighter next time."

"They're important. After our guys throw stuff over the side, jump down and cover everything. Anyone in the caboose looks the window, stuff blends in with the desert."

"Yeah. We'll work it out."

"And, I forgot to ask, I'm assuming there was no one standing on the rear platform peering into the night when the caboose went by."

"Nope," said Clay.

"Freddie, any problem with driving the truck up the right-of-way?"

"No. There was a UP pickup near the depot, but nobody around. We need to scout around a bit more, though. We shouldn't press our luck driving back down the way we got there. Need to find a place farther east to get off the right-of-way."

"Okay. I'll call in sick in the morning. Drive out there and find a place. Anything else?"

"I'll go to some different hardware stores tomorrow. Buy a bunch of locks."

"Okay. And be sure to remind the guys to take the locks they cut off. I'll call you tomorrow night with the place to get off the right of way between Cima and Nipton. Moon will set about ten o'clock on Thursday night. That should be our first show. Agreed?

"Let's do it. Next stop, the gravy train."

— Chapter 8 —

GETTING HITCHED IN SMOKE TREE

Robyn Danforth was not a dreamer. Far from it. As she grew up, her mother, Sloan Danforth, had systematically destroyed Robyn's dreams. In railroad towns like Smoke Tree in the 1940s and 1950s, mothers raised the children almost singlehanded, so Robyn was at the mercy of her mother. Her father, Weaver Danforth, had very little input. Even when railroad fathers were home, they were hardly there because they needed their rest.

Fathers needed their rest because railroading was a tough job. A shift could last sixteen hours, and railroad regulations mandated only eight hours of rest between trips. The rest period began when the train hit the switch at a crew-change destination, either back home in Smoke Tree, Seligman eastbound, or Barstow westbound. And although the rest period officially started when the train hit the switch, the trainman wasn't off duty yet. He still had to fill out his time slip and have his "block" put in the honeycomb of slots covering the glass wall in the crew dispatcher's office.

In those eight hours before the crew dispatcher called the trainman back to work, he had to eat, shower and sleep. So, in reality, he usually got only four or five hours of sleep before his "block" worked its way to the top of the extra board, and he was called.

If the trainman was in Barstow, he slept at the Harvey House in a room with three other railroaders. In Seligman, where the Harvey House was nicknamed the "Broken Knuckle," he had the luxury of sleeping alone in a room with a bed, a chair, and a bowl and pitcher to use as a washbasin.

So, when Weaver was getting his rest in Smoke Tree, the rule was "Don't Bother Your Father," and when he was at work, Sloan had Robyn all to herself. It was not a good situation. Robyn's mother was jealous of Robyn's beauty. She nodded and smiled at the ooohs and aahs from other mothers in public.

"Isn't she beautiful?" Sloan would ask with her pasted-in-place smile.

But when she got Robyn home, Sloan turned her anger loose. She didn't strike her daughter, although she often wanted to, because she was afraid if she started, she wouldn't be able to stop. So, limited to verbal abuse, Sloan laid on a steady barrage of soul-deadening criticism.

As beautiful children often are, and intelligent children with kind temperaments, in particular, Robyn was popular with her teachers and classmates in school. In response, Robyn loved school. The hours she got to spend away from her mother's suffocating hatred were the best parts of her life. Robyn was brilliant and a hard worker, and she had an appetite for learning and eagerly absorbed knowledge. Of course, her good grades further incensed Sloan Danforth, and while she could do nothing about Robyn's intelligence, she could poison Robyn's perception of every success.

"It's just because you're pretty," Sloan would hiss. And when Robyn reached high school, Sloan added, "most of your teachers are men, and they're just ogling your boobs and your rear end. They know you're stupid, but they give you good grades anyway, and don't you ever forget that, Miss Slutty Body."

When Robyn told her mother that her teachers were encouraging her to go to college, Sloan's response was, "College professors aren't going to fawn over you like the perverts in this hick town high school, Miss Prissy Panties. You'd flunk out first semester, so there's no point in wasting money."

On those occasions when Weaver's schedule allowed a family dinner, the tension had Robyn's stomach in knots because she knew "the speech" was coming. The windup for its delivery always started the same way. Sloan would prepare a wonderful meal, but she would not eat. Instead, she would pick up a small forkful of food from her plate and lift it almost to her mouth before putting it down at the last instant. Then, she would put down her silverware and stare straight ahead, tight-lipped.

Robyn would always think, *don't say anything, daddy,* but Weaver Danforth, a man who wanted peace in his house more than anything else in his life, would always speak.

"Sloan, this is delicious," he would say.

"I'm glad to you think so, Weaver," Sloan would reply, "but frankly, I am too upset to eat a single bite. It's because of your daughter, Weaver. She's on her best behavior right now, but as soon as you've gone to work, she will say vile things to me."

Please don't ask what kind of things, Robyn would silently scream.

But Weaver always asked.

"What kinds of things, Sloan?"

"I refuse to repeat them. They are disgusting, crude, and hateful."

"But Sloan," her father would say, "I've never heard our little girl say things like that."

And then, the explosion.

"Weaver Danforth, you never believe me. You always, always, always take her side."

Sloan would rise from the table, pick up her plate, hurry to the kitchen, dump the food in the sink, and turn on the garbage disposal. If she were in rare form, she would smash her plate to bits in the sink.

Then, she would return to the table, latch on to the back of her chair, squeeze so hard her knuckles turned white, and deliver "the speech."

"Someday, Weaver Danforth, you will come home, and Robyn and I won't be here. You'll be all alone in this dumpy house with its dumpy furniture and your dumpy life in this dumpy town, and you'll never see us again."

Please, please, please don't say anything, Daddy. But if you have to say something, ask her why she would take the daughter who says vile, hateful, disgusting things to her with her when she leaves. Ask Mother to leave me here! ran Robyn's silent prayer.

But Robyn's prayer always went unanswered.

"Now, Sloan," her father would plead. "You've gotten yourself all worked up over nothing. Please, dear, sit down with us."

"I will do no such thing. I have a terrible headache, and it's all your fault. I'm going to go lie down." And her mother would rush, sobbing, down the hall, go into her bedroom and slam the door, leaving father and daughter alone at the table.

Weaver would look at Robyn and spread his hands, palms up as if saying, "what can I do?"

When Robyn was a senior in high school, she finally managed to work up enough nerve to ask her father why he put up with it.

He replied, "Because I love her, Robyn. I love her, and I have to protect her."

"Protect her from what, Daddy?"

A look so sad it broke Robyn's heart came over her father's face.

"From herself, Robyn. From herself," he answered softly.

What about me? Robyn wanted to ask. But she didn't. Robyn loved her father but knew he had no chance of coping with Sloan as long as his daughter was with them. And at that moment, she resolved to get out of the Danforth house on Judea Street as soon as she graduated from high school.

The boys in Robyn's class had always pursued her, and Trent Reubens was the most determined. He had all but begged her to go to the Homecoming dance with him. She was not interested in dating Trent, but she had accepted because it seemed to mean so much to him. And since Trent was a tackle and co-captain on the football team and Robyn was a cheerleader, they were elected Homecoming King and Queen. Trent enjoyed the evening much more than Robyn; she was sure she didn't want to date him again.

But once Robyn decided to get out of her family home, she zeroed in on Trent as the way out. When Trent asked her to senior prom, she accepted. And two months later, when he asked her to marry him, she said "yes."

At the wedding, Sloan played her 'mother of the bride' role to the hilt, fawning over Trent's parents and exclaiming to anyone who would listen about how beautiful Robyn was in her wedding dress. Weaver was skeptical. He had a pretty good idea why Robyn wanted to get married, but he kept it to himself and walked her down the aisle.

Because Trent's father worked for the Santa Fe Railroad, Trent had no problem getting hired right out of high school. He worked the switch job in the Smoke Tree yard while he and Robyn set up housekeeping. He was working the Parker and Blythe locals out of Barstow by September. With nothing to do but work and rest, he should have been saving money, but Trent developed a weakness for tonk, an addictive card game, and spent most of his off-duty time blowing his expense money and most of his paychecks in the game that ran twenty-four hours a day in the trainmen's card room at the Harvey House.

Back in Smoke Tree, Robyn didn't understand why she had to beg money for rent and food. Their marriage was not getting off to a good start. In a year, Trent had enough seniority to bid onto an extra board job working the main line out of Smoke Tree. That meant more pay, but it didn't mean more money. Trent continued to blow his paycheck in card games.

When Robyn pointed out that while there was often not enough money for food, there was always enough for a refrigerator full of beer, Trent knocked her across the room and kicked her when she fell to the floor. He never had a chance to hurt her again because she wasn't home when he returned to Smoke Tree after his next westbound job. Nor would she ever be home again.

Robyn borrowed enough money from her father to rent a dilapidated old house on Las Cruces Street and file for divorce on the grounds of physical cruelty. The lawyer she hired took a beautiful picture of her black eye and took possession of the x-ray showing her cracked ribs. An embarrassed Trent Reubens did not contest the filing.

Robyn got a job as a waitress at the Bluebird Café. Two people never came in during all the years she worked there: Trent Reubens and Weaver Danforth. Trent, because he was bitter, and Weaver because he knew if he were seen at the Bluebird, the Smoke Tree wireless would report his visit to Sloan. Her father did visit her at the little house on Las Cruces Street from time to time, but only after dark. Still, they developed a relationship they had never had over the years while Robyn was growing up in the family home. The connection kept Robyn in Smoke Tree.

In the years after her divorce, many men asked Robyn out when she worked at the Bluebird: most were single, but more than a few were married. While she was unfailingly kind and welcoming to customers, she was never flirtatious, and she turned away every advance. Men tried to flirt with her, but it was a waste of time. And if a man tried to push his luck and made an off-color remark or patted her fanny, he stood an excellent chance of getting a pitcher of ice water dumped on his head.

The first time she did that, Robyn thought the owner would fire her, but he knew many local men who could go elsewhere came in because of Robyn. And because of Robyn, over time, the Bluebird became the informal social center of Smoke Tree.

Outside of work, she had no social life. In her off-hours, she read library books and watched television. On her days off, Robyn either walked in the desert close to town or fished for trout in the Colorado. On those occasions, mindful of some of the crude advances rebuffed at the Bluebird and never forgetting the beating Trent Reubens had delivered to her, she carried a gun. In the desert, she kept it in the daypack slung over her shoulder: at the river, she stored it in her tackle box.

When her twenty-ninth birthday rolled around, she celebrated alone in her little house. When she blew out the candles on the cake she had baked for herself, Robyn accepted that these would be the parameters of her life, but she was not bitter about her circumstances. She was so used to living alone; she wasn't sure she could ever live with anyone.

When Robyn turned thirty, she realized she had been renting a two-bedroom house because she had unconsciously thought she might marry again. She moved into a smaller house on Ophir Street and purged those thoughts from her mind. Statistically, the odds of marrying again would plummet with each passing year, but more importantly, she just wasn't interested. Not interested, that is, until Johnny Quentin stepped into her life.

Johnny was three years younger than Robyn, but she remembered his days at Smoke Tree High. Who could ever forget Johnny Quarterback? Especially what he did his senior year. On the days after the Scorpions weekly games, he was all anyone wanted to talk about. But then the Scorpions' undefeated streak ended with a loss in the C.I.F. semi-finals. Not long after that, Johnny Quentin was gone without finishing high school. He had joined the Army on the buddy system with Charlie Merriman, a classmate of Robyn's.

Because Robyn heard about almost everything happening in Smoke Tree, she knew Johnny had returned to Smoke Tree in 1969. But she didn't see him until 1970 when he showed up at the Bluebird with the man everyone in town called Horse. Robyn hadn't seen them come in together, but when she realized Horse and another man were in his usual booth, she headed that way, dangling two ceramic mugs in one hand and carrying a pot of coffee in the other.

When Horse said, "Morning, Robyn, remember this guy?" she looked at the man sitting across from Horse.

"Johnny Quentin!"

"Hello, Robyn, you're looking well."

She had been surprised Johnny had remembered her. After all, he had been a freshman when she was a senior. But he did remember.

"You too, Johnny," she replied. "Handsome and fit as ever," and then blushed when she realized she was flirting! Her! Robyn Danforth! The waitress who never flirted with anyone!

She covered it up by adding, "Last I heard, you were in the Army."

"Back now."

"For how long?"

"Hard to say, Robyn. Might be for a while."

Oh, I hope so, she had thought.

That was the first of many times the two men met for coffee and conversation at the Bluebird. It didn't take Robyn long to see that Horse was contriving to get her and Johnny together. She was puzzled because Horse didn't seem like the kind of guy who would play matchmaker. But as time went on, she found herself more and more attracted to Johnny. She began to think about what she would say if Johnny ever asked her out and realized her answer would be yes.

But Johnny hesitated. Even though he now came in alone sometimes, he just couldn't seem to bring himself to ask her out. And Robyn thought she understood why he didn't. Years before, she had read in the Smoke Tree Weekly of Charlie Merriman's death in Vietnam and his posthumous silver star. And sometimes, when she glanced at Johnny while he was looking away, she realized there was a deep sadness in his eyes. And there was something else. Robyn thought perhaps it was guilt. Guilt because Johnny was alive and Charlie wasn't. Guilt because Chalie's little boys no longer had a father, yet Johnny Quentin still lived. When she heard how much time Johnny was spending with Charlie's twin sons, she realized Johnny was trying to fill a void.

Johnny was haggard. Worn. Grim. Exhausted. He had the look of someone who never got enough sleep. Perhaps it was terrible nightmares that left Johnny so drained.

Still, Robyn thought he was edging closer to asking her out. But then came the event that would forever be known in Smoke Tree as The Great Train Platform Massacre. Three trainmen confronted Johnny on the platform. They taunted him about his friendship with Mary Merriman and called him squaw man, and he just stared at them. They questioned his service in Vietnam and got no reaction. They tried mocking his supposed martial arts expertise, and Johnny only smiled. But then, they made a fatal error: they desecrated the memory of Charlie Merriman. Johnny dropped his kit bag and motioned them forward.

The first of the three to go down had been Jimmy Sexton. The second was Trent, her ex-husband. But the instigator of the conflict, Craddock Newell, got the worst of it. Witnesses to the fight said that if four bystanders and Trainmaster Mike Langford hadn't combined to pull Johnny off of Craddock, Johnny would have killed him.

The trainmaster suspended the combatants for forty-five days, and Johnny Quentin descended into alcohol-induced madness. Robyn would see him dragging past the Bluebird's plate glass window every morning on his way to Cuz's Liquors and then returning with a bottle in a brown paper bag. A bottle he was drinking from before he reached home.

One day, as he went by, he turned his face toward the window and saw Robyn looking at him. The shame in his eyes made her want to weep; from that day on, Johnny kept to the other side of Broadway.

When the forty-five-day suspension ended, Robyn heard Johnny had quit the railroad. She still saw him walking down Broadway on his way to buy liquor, but then a few months later came bizarre stories of Johnny wandering the desert. Hunters, ranchers, and rock-hounds saw him from the Piutes to the Providence, The New Yorks to the Mid Hills, the Granites to the Old Woman Range, pulling all his possessions in a wheeled travois that looked like a combination rickshaw and child's bicycle.

Then came the strangest story of all.

Johnny Quentin had encountered two men near Cima burying a woman they had killed. The two had murdered several others in the Redlands area and one local man, Chaco Hermosillo. Johnny attacked the two men. Overwhelmed them and hog-tied them. Shot them both in the back of the knee with a .22 in case they got loose and tried to leave. Then, he walked off of Cima Dome down to Kelso and called Horse.

Three days before Christmas in 1971, Horse came in for lunch. He asked Robyn if she would come with him and the Merriman twins to meet up with Johnny near the Blind Hills the next day.

"Does he know I'm coming?"

Horse smiled.

"He doesn't even know I'm coming. He thinks he's meeting up with Mary Merriman for a re-supply."

"Then why will we be there instead?"

"Because, Robyn, it's time for Johnny Quentin to come home. He's not drinking now, hasn't been for some time, but he's still wandering around alone out there."

"How do you know?"

"Chemehuevi Joe."

"Who?"

"Someone you may meet someday. Anyway, Joe says he sees Johnny out there from time to time. Says Johnny is almost his old self."

"Does that mean the Johnny from before Vietnam?"

Horse shook his head.

"Regretfully, I don't think we'll ever see that Johnny again. But he may be the best version of himself he's been since he came home."

"I'm glad to hear that, but why do you want me to come?"

"Two reasons. First, I'm going to try to talk Johnny into going to work for the sheriff's department, and I need something more than the promise of a job to coax him out of the wilderness."

"And you think I'm that something?"

"I do."

"And the second reason?"

"The second reason is that I think you'd like to see Johnny again."

Robyn realized Horse was right, as usual.

"If you think it will help, I'll come along."

"Thank you, Robyn."

As she and Horse and the Merriman boys had approached the point where the two-track from the Blind Hills intersected Black Canyon Road, Robyn saw Johnny. The strange device she had heard about was on the ground beside him.

When Horse stopped the Landcruiser, the Merriman boys bolted from the door. Johnny dropped to one knee, and the boys nearly knocked him down.

"Whoa, easy there, tigers."

"Papa," said Donny.

"Papa," echoed Danny.

Johnny smiled. It was the biggest smile Robyn had ever seen on his face.

"Yes, boys, I think I may be the papa again,"

He was hugging the boys when Robyn approached.

"Hello, Johnny," she said.

He was still smiling when he replied.

"Hello, yourself, Robyn; it's good to see you."

She matched his smile with one of her own and was amazed by what she said next.

"Lord, Johnny. Give a girl a hug."

Johnny stood, and she stepped into his arms.

Horse was standing behind them.

"All right, all right, Enough of that. This is more than a social call."

"Some kind of law enforcement business?" asked Johnny.

After Horse explained he wanted Johnny to join the department and the procedure for doing that, Johnny said to Robyn, "I want to ask you something I was going to ask you before a whole lot of things went sideways."

Robyn smiled. She couldn't seem to stop smiling.

"Of course," she said.

"Pardon?" asked Johnny.

"Of course, I'll go out with you. Why else would I be standing out here, a hundred miles from nowhere, the day before Christmas Eve?"

She and Johnny spent New year's Day together, watching the Rose Parade. Robyn said she would watch the game with him, too, but Johnny said he'd rather go for a walk.

I knew he was my kind of guy, she thought.

Johnny went off to the Sheriff's Academy. When he got back to Smoke Tree, he began courting her. It was an oddly formal courtship for two people their age. For one thing, they never spent the night together. Johnny said he was just old-fashioned, but Robyn knew in her heart it was because of Johnny's nightmares.

And now, less than fifteen months after meeting up with Johnny near the Blind Hills, Robyn was getting ready to do something she had thought she would never do again: get married. The planning for the wedding, scheduled for May, was underway.

Robyn had never cared for the term "getting hitched." To her way of thinking, it smacked of servitude: a mare put into harness. Not appealing. She was more of a "kick over the traces" kind of woman herself. Fortunately, that was one of the reasons Johnny Quentin loved her. Still, she was curious, so she asked Jedidiah Shanks, who was going to perform the ceremony at the Church of the Highway, where the phrase came from.

"From scripture," Jedidiah explained. "Jesus said to his disciples, 'Take my yoke upon you, and you will find rest for your souls. For my yoke is easy and my burden is light.'"

Robyn was glad to learn the derivation, but she still didn't like the phrase. While she and Johnny weren't religious, they both liked the idea of getting married in a church. It seemed to them it implied more commitment than doing it in Las Vegas. And besides, Johnny and Jedidiah were good friends.

Robyn had a matron of honor for the wedding, Esperanza Caballo, and three bridesmaids; Mary Merriman, Connie Zavala, and the newest waitress at the Bluebird, Randi Clauge. There were also not one but two ring bearers: Donny and Danny Merriman and a flower girl, Elena

Caballo. Johnny had a best man, Captain Carlos Caballo, and three groomsmen, Seve Zavala, Andy Chesney, and Danny Dubois. But who would give the bride away? She had asked her father, but he wouldn't do it.

"Sloan would never forgive me," her father said. Robyn was disappointed, but she had long ago accepted that her father would never put his daughter ahead of his wife.

And despite the fact Horse had set this all in motion, he couldn't give her away. He was the best man.

Nor could Jedidiah, since he was performing the ceremony.

Johnny said he had someone in mind but wouldn't tell her the name.

"Just tell me it's not one of your high school buddies," Robyn said. "I refuse to be given away by someone younger than I am."

"My only real friend in high school was Aeden Snow, and he's gone. No, this is someone else, and I haven't asked him yet."

— Chapter 9 —

SHOP 'TIL YOU'RE STOPPED

he first train robbery was productive. Small appliances like blenders, food-processors, even some microwave ovens. Electronics like cassette recorders, component stereos, pocket-sized transistor radios, and Smith-Corona electric typewriters.

They hauled it all to the Red Rock Warehouse, where they made an inventory. They took the list to Arthur when they met again in Goodsprings. Arthur called the number he had memorized from a phone booth on Freemont Street. When a man answered, Arthur greeted him by name and delivered the message from Tony Pro."

"Yeah, Tony said you'd be calling someday."

"I've got a lot of stuff to move. Got a list."

"Don't need no list. Where is this stuff?"

"Arthur gave him an address in North Las Vegas."

"Oh, those guys. I heard we had a little talk with them about the air cargo business."

"That's what they told me."

"And that's not where this stuff came from?"

"Oh, no. Tony told me I was out of that business, and I am, forever, and so are they."

"Don't suppose you want to tell me where you got it?"

"No, I don't."

The man laughed.

"Hey, Arty, can't blame a guy for trying, right?"

"No, sir, no hard feelings."

"Okay, you tell your friends they're going to put a new lock on that warehouse door."

"Okay."

"Call me when they've done it, and we'll set up a meeting for you to deliver the key. Every time you get something, you put it in there and call me. We'll go pick it up at night. When it's gone, call me again, and I'll tell you what we're paying and how we'll get you the money. And by the way, this guy you'll meet with? He's from our office, but he ain't me. You'll never meet me."

"Got it. Call you back tomorrow about getting you that key."

"And one more thing."

"Yes?"

"If you ever complain about our price, we'll never do business with you again."

"Understood."

Arthur delivered the key to a nondescript man outside a coffee shop. The entire shipment disappeared from the warehouse that night. Arthur called the number the next day. The same voice stated a price and the meeting place where Arthur would get the money. Arthur went there and was paid in cash. The man who delivered the money was not the same man who had picked up the key.

Freddie, Clay, and the crew went back to work. They scored men's and women's clothing and shoes. The trip after that, they emptied a trailer filled with musical instruments imported from Japan: Arai classical guitars, Jackson and Fressen electric guitars, and some of the Elk clear-acrylic coated electric guitars that were gaining popularity with American rock and roll bands.

Although Arthur thought they had been stiffed on the Japanese guitars, he didn't complain. There was no denying that access to the distribution network controlled by the mob was essential to moving all the stuff they were stealing. Nobody else could handle that much volume. The products slipped seamlessly into the stream of stolen goods, and Arthur, Freddie, and Clay were soon making close to what they had made stealing air cargo.

After each cash transaction with the mob, Arthur met with his partners at the Pioneer Saloon in Goodsprings and handed over their share. The three became regulars in the saloon, and no one, not even the bikers who sometimes rumbled in from Vegas, paid any particular attention to them.

However, a familiar pattern soon emerged. Even though their greed had ruined their sweet air cargo gig and dumped Arthur in prison, Freddie and Clay were getting greedy again. Arthur had no intention of ending up there again. He managed to keep his partners in check for a while, but he knew it wouldn't be long before he could no longer control them. They were stealing more and more and adding new crew members.

"These new guys, are you making sure they're careful about locks and seals?" he asked them.

"Oh yeah. Don't worry yourself, "said Clay.

Arthur did worry. And when Arthur worried, he began to plan. He still had money from the air cargo thefts buried in various locations in the desert, and he began planting more in other places. If things got hot, Arthur wanted to be ready to leave. Freddie and Clay were the only members of the team who knew Arthur was involved, and Arthur thought he had convinced them he was still under the protection of Anthony Provenzano. Arthur wanted them to fear for their lives if they were arrested and thought about giving Arthur up to get a lighter sentence. Freddie and Clay knew a lighter sentence was no good if you don't live to get out someday.

Besides, Arthur was weary of the desert. In his estimation, a few good days in the fall and spring did not make up for the searing heat of summer and the awful winds of winter, and studying the cornfield outside Lewisburg prison for six years had made him nostalgic about the hollows of West Virginia. He now had a mail subscription to the Roane County Reporter. When he read of plans to dam Charles Fork Creek to create Charles Fork Lake for flood control and recreation, he recalled the rolling Appalachian hills around the creek.

Arthur took a few days off and flew to West Virginia. He scouted the hills around the proposed lake and found a two-acre parcel that would give him an excellent view. Under an assumed name, Arthur paid cash for the property and returned to Henderson to bide his time.

Shortly after Arthur returned, Freddie, Clay, and the crew made their best score: IBM Selectric typewriters. An entire piggybacked trailer of them. As soon as one of the crew found the typewriters, Clay hopped from flatcar to flatcar, telling the other members of the gang to stop what they were doing and come with him. Two of the newer members left cut locks and seals dangling from the trailers they had been looting.

They unloaded crate after crate of typewriters as the train approached the top of the hill, then jumped down to cover the haul with tarps in case someone looked out the window of the caboose. Clay was the last one off the flatcar. When he closed the trailer's door, he snapped a new lock in place. He retrieved the original padlock and seals but had no way of knowing the damage had already been done.

When the train pulled into Las Vegas yard, a member of the wheel crew noticed one of the dangling locks. He called his supervisor. His supervisor called the railroad detectives. The detectives bagged the locks and noted that the seals were missing.

In 1973, the latest IBM Selectrics retailed for seven hundred dollars. The crew had stolen thousands of them. Like many of the largest railroads, the Union Pacific was self-insured, carrying reinsurance only to cover catastrophic losses. A loss of two hundred thousand dollars didn't trip the reinsurance. The railroad ate the loss. Since it was self-insured, the railroad was not a member of the insurance crime bureau, and the theft went unreported.

The Selectrics were a substantial haul, and Arthur thought they might be overdoing the Kelso to Cima route. When he met with Freddie and Clay to pass on their share of the money, plus the money to pay the crew, he convinced them to try a westbound freight. After all, there was a substantial grade between Nipton and Cima.

That led to Arthur's final association with his partners because in late March, on their second robbery of a westbound piggyback, they stole something even a self-insured railroad could not ignore.

— Chapter 10 —

FEBRUARY 1973
Triple A

*A*ntonio Alyoisius Alpino was indeed handy with his fists. With his hands and feet, too. He progressed quickly with taekwondo strikes and kicks and jiujitsu throws. He was slower to get comfortable with being thrown. Still, he was making progress, and Horse told him once he got better at falling, he would be ready to learn the Aikido self-sacrifice throws so essential to dealing with the much bigger opponent who would be trying to overwhelm him.

Tony was eager to learn, which was good, but he lacked conditioning and physical endurance, which could be disastrous. So, Johnny put him on a training program. Every morning Tony got up at first light and ran up and down the gullies behind the pizza parlor. Not satisfied with that, he was soon running the streets of Smoke Tree at night after he got off work.

He showed up to work out in the sandpit with Horse and Johnny every Saturday and Sunday.

"This is a crash course," Johnny Quentin had explained. "For every hour you spend in the pit with Horse and me, you should practice at least four hours on your own." He handed Tony a duffel bag.

"Fill this with sand. Hang it from that chinaberry tree in your back hard. Punch it and kick it as if your life depended on it. Your life won't, but that handsome Italian face might."

"We're going to cram a lot into a short time, so you're going to get just the basics," added Horse. "Still, with the running, the workouts, and the practice on your own, I don't know how you're going to find time to do your homework."

"I'm a senior," said Tony, "and we're on the downhill glide to graduation."

"Do they still call that 'senioritis?'" Johnny asked.

"Still do."

"What do you want to do after high school, Tony?" asked Horse.

Tony hesitated.

"You'd laugh."

"No, we won't," said Johnny.

Tony shrugged. "Maybe when I know you better, I'll tell you."

After each workout session, Tony joined Johnny and the Caballo family for a meal because Esperanza said all the physical activity was reducing Tony to skin and bones.

"Eat, eat," she would say, putting rich food on his plate, "you're burning it faster than you can shovel it down. And cram a couple of those pizzas down your throat at work. Do you like anchovies?"

"Sure."

"Pile them on. They're full of protein. Build muscles. Good for your heart. Good for your bones. Good for your skin, too. Keep you from getting those teenage pimples, not that you have any, lucky boy. But you never know," Eseprazna said, wagging her finger, "you might pop a big one for the prom."

"Not going," said Tony.

"Why not?" asked Esperanza.

"Don't have a date."

"What about Eletheria?" asked Horse.

"We're just friends."

"And what's wrong with friends going to prom together?"

Tony ducked his head and mumbled something.

"Didn't catch that," said Johnny with a smile.

"I said, 'nothin,' I guess.'"

"Well then, hop to it, lad. You could do worse than show up with the smartest girl in your class."

"That's just it," Tony replied. "She's so darned smart—ten times smarter than me. Sometimes when I'm with her, I can't think of anything to say."

Horse, Johnny, and Esperanza exchanged knowing glances. Esperanza tried hard not to smile.

"Tony, there's only one thing you have to remember about taking Eletheria to the prom," she said.

Here it comes, thought Tony, *some kind of lecture about dating.*

"What's that, Mrs. Caballo?"

"Listen carefully because I'm about to reveal a deep secret.

She paused.

"When you pin the corsage on her, don't stick her with the pin. Girls just hate that."

Tony laughed.

This is one nice lady! he thought. *Reminds me of mom.*

— Chapter 11 —

MARCH 1973
The team scores and loses!

Guns! *An entire trailer full of guns!* AR-15s manufactured on the east coast by Colt Arms shipped to retailers on the west coast. Crates and crates of them. Freddie, Clay, and their crew stole them all. They got so excited they forgot to put a new lock on the trailer, but no one noticed the unlocked trailer until it reached the intermodal facility in Los Angeles.

While most shippers might be content with being made financially whole after the theft of one of their shipments, that is not true of firearms manufacturers. Every AR-15 coming out of the Colt factory had a serial number, and Colt was not about to let those stolen guns go into circulation without notifying the FBI and the ATF.

The Union Pacific also reported the loss to the authorities, and a memo went out to all terminals between Chicago and Los Angeles. In February, a railroad detective in Las Vegas remembered missing locks on some piggybacked vans and pushed that information up the chain. Railroad brass passed the information on to the ATF and the FBI.

Freddie and Clay were ecstatic. Arthur was furious, but he kept that to himself. He called the secret number. The crates of guns disappeared from the Red Rock warehouse that night. When he reached the number again, the mystery man quoted him an astronomical figure.

"And Arty?"

"Yes, sir."

"Boss says more of those. Take all you can get."

"I've got something to do somewhere else. I may not be here next time we get something that good. Can I have my second in command call you if that happens?"

Mystery man did not reply immediately, but when he did, he said, "Sure kid, sure. Like I said, the boss wants more shipments like this one."

When Arthur paid off Freddie and Clay at the Pioneer Saloon, they were so excited he had to remind them to keep their voices down.

"Man," said Freddie, "this is the berries!"

"Sure is, brother," said Clay.

Arthur feigned similar enthusiasm. No reason for them to know they would never see him again.

"Guys," he said, "I've got to make a little trip. Family matter. But our fence says I can give you his number in case you get something special while I'm gone."

"Say, Arthur, you've never told us where you're from," Freddie said.

"Minnesota, Twin Cities area."

The following morning, Arthur drove to the aircraft maintenance company. He told his boss he had to go home. He explained that his mother was in the hospital, and the doctors said they didn't know how long she had to live. He said he didn't know when he would be back.

"Where's home?" asked his boss.

"Oregon," replied Arthur.

He spent the rest of the day rattling around the desert in his pickup truck, digging up his stashes. By evening, he had it all. He loaded the money into the trunk of his car and the few items he wanted from his apartment into the back seat. Ten o'clock found him on the freeway, headed northeast toward Utah. Once he reached Beaver, he planned to take back highways to West Virginia, where he would rent a small house in Charleston and live quietly until the heat from the theft of the AR-15s died down.

When enough time had passed, he planned to hire a contractor to build a home on his property. Then, he would look for a job. Although he had plenty of money, it would be better if he had some visible means of support. Parkersburg was less than an hour from where he would have his home built. It had a nice regional airport, primarily general aviation but some commercial stuff. There were no jets there, but Arthur had nothing against piston engines. It was time to slow down and get out of the fast lane. Re-set his clock to West Virginia time.

— Chapter 12 —

MARCH 1973
A voice from the past

Fred rapped on Horse's door. Years before, Horse had convinced the dispatcher it was healthier to walk to his door and announce non-emergency calls than to notify him on the intercom. Now, if he could just convince the man to lay off the donuts and four sugars in his coffee. As if that was ever going to happen!

"Call for you, boss. Line two."

"Who is it?"

"He won't say, but the voice sounds familiar."

"Familiar good or familiar bad?"

"Good, I think, but the name won't come to me."

"Okay, thanks, Fred."

Horse punched up line two.

"Horse speaking."

"You will be visited by three ghosts," whispered a voice.

"Who is this?"

"The first is from Treasury past, the second is from Treasury present, and the third is a snarky ghost from the Fibbies," continued the voice.

"Agent D'Arnauld."

"The very same, Captain Caballo,"

"What's this about ghosts?"

"First, to the ghost of Treasury past. When I was out to see you in '64, we were part of the IRS. They called us the Alcohol and Tobacco Tax Division. And so I am the ghost of Treasury past."

"Makes sense."

"In 1968, we became the Alcohol, Tobacco, and Firearms, but we were still part of the IRS."

"Okay."

"Late last year, the ATF became an independent Bureau in the Treasury Department, which makes me also the ghost of Treasury present."

"So, you're really, no kidding, honest to goodness coming back to Smoke Tree?"

"That good fortune is mine."

"Great! I'll have my mother air out her guest bedroom."

"Alas, my friend, this is a quick turnaround. I'll be in Smoke Tree tomorrow, but I have to return to fly out of Vegas tomorrow evening."

"Sorry to hear that."

"I wish I could stay longer, but I can't."

"Okay, Darnold, so you're the two treasury ghosts. What about the FBI?"

"Oh, Horse, how I wish it was summer. I would love to see the Fibbie in Smoke Tree in his suit and tie when it's a hundred and twenty."

"You're bringing the FBI guy with you?"

"No. We'll arrive separately. I'm flying to Vegas in the morning. I'll pick up a car from the inter-agency pool. Should be in Smoke Tree around noon."

"And the FBI guy?"

"He'll be there at two o'clock. He's a high mucky-muck—assistant special agent in charge in Vegas. And by the way, he's not a bad guy. His name is Jules Johns. He's a little uptight, but all those Fibbies are. Anyway, I want to meet with you before he and I officially brief you at two."

"Okay. I'll take you to the Bluebird for lunch when you get here."

"Hey, that pretty girl who waited on us back in '64, she still work there?"

"Yeah, Robyn's still there. She's engaged to one of my deputies."

"Too bad."

"Darnold, don't tell me you're still single."

"Unfortunately. The hectic life of a super-agent doesn't allow much time for a social life. Also, I have higher standards than I used to."

"Oh?"

"Yeah. Ever since I met your Esperanza. Smart, kind, loving, beautiful. You hit the jackpot."

"I did. She's the best, and I'm blessed."

Horse and Darnold headed for Horse's usual booth at the Bluebird.

"Catch-up time," Horse said as the two men sat down. "Are you still in San Francisco?"

"Yeah, but not for long."

"Why not?"

"You know, Horse, I owe you a lot. That episode in Searchlight made my career. I went from rising star to shooting star."

"Well, keeping automatic weapons out of the hands of the Chicago Syndicate has to carry bonus points, but according to Pete Hardesty, who is Undersheriff Hardesty now, by the way, you were already on the way up."

"Maybe so, but not this fast. My problem is the San Francisco office is highly coveted. I'm second in the command there, but it will be years before I'm the head honcho."

"And so?"

"I've been offered the top spot in Denver or Phoenix."

"I thought you couldn't live without the ocean."

Darnold smiled.

"I guess my desire to be top dog has surpassed my fondness for saltwater. But I gotta tell you; I'm going to miss that good Italian food in North Beach."

"Which job are you going to take?"

"I don't know yet. I'm trying to decide which office is going to grow the fastest. What do you think?"

"They're both about the same size now, right?"

"Yeah. Around half a million."

"Then take Phoenix. It's going to grow faster. All those people trying to escape the cold of the northeast and the upper midwest. I think there will be a million people there in twenty years, and I don't think Denver will grow that fast. Besides, Phoenix is closer to Smoke Tree. You can come and visit us."

"All right, that settles it. Phoenix, it will be!"

The two friends were smiling when Robyn came by.

"Afternoon, Horse, What can I get for you two?"

"Robyn," said Horse, "this is Dave D'Arnauld. He was here with me once before, back during Desert Strike."

"Call me Darnold. Everyone does."

Robyn studied the agent.

"I remember the name."

"But not the face. You see, Horse, that's how it always plays out. Women forget me as soon as I'm out of sight."

When Robyn left with their orders, Horse said, "So, what brings a famous ATF agent to my little corner of the desert?"

Darnold laughed. "'My little corner,' I like that, Horse. You could put San Francisco County and all the counties near it inside your area of responsibility and have room left over.

But on to what brings me down your way. About a week ago, some guys broke into a trailer being piggybacked on a westbound Union Pacific freight. The trailer contained a shipment of Colt AR-15s bound for west coast gunshops, and the thieves stole them all."

"We're talking about the civilian version of the M-16, right?"

"Yes. Colt reported the loss to us. Gave us the serial numbers. We really want to catch these guys."

"And you think I can help?"

"I'm not sure, yet. That's why I wanted to talk to you before Jules shows up for our official joint briefing at two."

"When you say 'official'...."

"ATF and FBI have cleared this through your boss in San Bernardino."

"Go on."

"Well, my office is in it because of the guns. Specifically, how will the guys who stole them get rid of them? You can't exactly have a yard sale to shift hundreds and hundreds of semi-automatic weapons."

"And the FBI?"

"The theft itself is their remit. Theft from interstate shipment falls under Classification 15 of the FBI's central records system. And like us, the Fibbies wonder how these guys are fencing all the cargo they're stealing because these guns are not their first theft. There's only one organization big enough to handle that much volume."

"The mob."

"You've got it. ATF is working on what happened to the guns, and the FBI has the laboring oar because of the theft. And even though the investigations are running on parallel tracks and we're sharing information, we're both trying to get there first."

"Do I detect inter-agency rivalry?"

"We prefer to call it acronymic animosity. So much more dignified. Anyway, I wanted to meet with you early because a little background is in order, so you'll be aware of the undercurrents."

"Go ahead."

"J. Edgar Hoover never cared much for the Treasury Department."

"Why not?"

"Hoover had a hell of a publicity operation going. It was so good; he convinced the American public the FBI took on the mob during prohibition."

"Eliot Ness and all that."

"Yeah. But Ness wasn't FBI. He was part of the Bureau of Prohibition, part of Treasury. Hoover was so jealous of Ness that when Prohibition ended, and FDR told Hoover to integrate the Prohibition Bureau into the FBI, J. Edgar saw to it that Ness didn't get a supervisory position. He ended up chasing moonshiners in Kentucky."

"How'd Hoover get away with that?"

"Because he had files on half the people in Congress. Everyone was afraid of him."

"I see."

"And that wasn't the end of it. Hoover hated 'The Untouchables.'"

"The television show?"

"Right. The one where Robert Stack played Ness. Word is he reached out to the producers to complain because the show portrayed Ness and his crew capturing the Ma Barker gang, which was actually an FBI operation."

"Hoover cared about a TV show?"

"A lot! He made the producers sign an agreement to have a voice-over disclaimer about the operation during any re-broadcasts of that episode."

"Touchy fellow."

"What's the new guy think about the ATF?"

"L. Patrick Gray? Nobody knows for sure, but he might not be happy about Treasury taking the criminal gun stuff away from the FBI. Plus, he's got another problem."

"Which is?"

"Hoover thought the next big thing was going to be drugs. He wanted to absorb the Bureau of Narcotics and Dangerous Drugs and the Office of Drug Abuse and Law Enforcement into the FBI."

"What was stopping him?"

"Nixon was thinking about creating a completely independent agency. Word is it will be called the DEA."

"Another acronym. What's it stand for?"

"The Drug Enforcement Administration."

"And that hasn't happened yet."

"It didn't while Hoover was alive. It turned out he had leverage."

"What leverage?"

"Nobody knows, and again nobody knows what the new guy will do. Maybe he's friendly to Nixon since Nixon appointed him, or maybe J. Edgar gave him whatever he had on Nixon."

"Good grief. You federal guys must have to carry a scorecard and wear a decoder ring to keep up with all this. I'm glad I'm just a simple sheriff's deputy."

Darnold smiled.

"Don't try to run that shuck on me, Horse. You are anything but simple. You may be the best investigator I've ever met."

"Oh, come on."

"Let me remind you about '1964. You talked to an Air Force Colonel during Desert Strike. He mentioned a touch-and-go landing by a C-123 on a temporary landing strip to kick pallets of M-16s out the back door to replace M-14s carried by a unit participating in Desert Strike. Later, some kid you know told you about watching through binoculars when a man driving an Army jeep demonstrated some kind of wicked fully automatic weapon to a couple of guys driving a black Chrysler 300. The weapon was so small he had it concealed under an overcoat."

"Nothing extraordinary about any of that."

"Not so far. But then you dredged up a memory of a couple of gumbahs in your town three years before driving the same kind of car. A car you traced to the Serengeti Casino. You connected the M-14A1s that were about to be replaced to someone who had modified one of them and wanted to steal the surplus guns and sell them to the mob."

"Lucky guess."

"Nothing lucky about it, my friend. It was an extraordinary intuitive leap. I would never have connected those dots."

Robyn interrupted the discussion by bringing their lunch. Neither man ate much before pushing his plate aside to continue the conversation.

"So," said Darnold, "more background for you on the FBI sub-text. And this time, it's closer to home. The Union Pacific reported the stolen guns to us and the theft itself to the FBI, and that's standard protocol."

"Go on."

"This is where more background information if necessary. See, the FBI has been itching to get into cargo theft for years, but they couldn't get their foot in the door."

"Why not?"

"Shippers don't like to report the thefts. They're afraid it will spook their customers. The railroads are so big, and the business is so lucrative, they pay off the shippers for what's been stolen and absorb the losses."

"The Santa Fe does that. It's self-insured, so the Union Pacific must be too. About the only things the Santa Fe reports to my office are stolen shipments of alcohol. I guess they have to report those."

"They do. Anything with an alcohol tax seal. And guns, too."

"Which is why the ATF knows about the AR-15s, but I still don't see what it has to do with my office. You say the guns came from Colt. Their factory is on the east coast. The guns could have been stolen anywhere between here and there, right?"

"We've managed to narrow it down. The FBI has information the shipment was intact when the TOFC transferred to the Union Pacific in Chicago, so they began contacting the crew change points between there and Los Angeles."

"Okay."

"That's how Las Vegas came into the picture. It seems what the railroad calls a 'wheel crew' was inspecting an eastbound hotshot freight a while back and noticed the locks had been cut off a couple of the piggybacked trailers. Called the dispatcher. The dispatcher called the railroad detectives. Detectives investigated. Found the trailers had been looted. Checked the locks for fingerprints, but there weren't any. None on the trailer doors, either. Apparently, the thieves were wearing gloves."

"And the cinder dicks reported the theft to the company?"

"They did. With the usual effect. The company made the shippers whole for the stolen goods, and the whole thing would have died there."

"Plus," said Horse, "the hotshot with the guns rolled into Vegas westbound, not eastbound like the ones with the locks cut off. The trailer with the guns could have been looted anywhere between LA and Vegas."

"That's right."

"Okay, let me think this thing through."

Horse fell silent. Darnold pushed some cold French fries through the catsup on his plate. Robyn came by and refilled their coffee. Horse drank half of his before he spoke again.

"Here's the way I see it. The eastbound theft could have happened in the freight yard in Los Angeles. But the stolen guns were westbound, and the FBI knows the shipment was intact when it left Chicago. Now that they have the information from the railroad detectives in Las Vegas about the cut locks on the eastbound freight, they're thinking the piggybacks moving both directions are being looted somewhere between LA and Vegas."

"That's the way they see it."

"Well, it wouldn't be in Yermo, eastbound or westbound. Trains only stop there for a few minutes for a crew change. That leaves one other option: a slow-moving train. Thieves are climbing onto slow-moving trains, stealing cargo, throwing it off, and picking it up later."

"You've got it!" said Darnold. "And you're familiar with an attempt to steal something from a slow-moving train."

"The Banner boys. On the grade between Fenner and Goffs, during Desert Strike."

"Right. Those boys out of prison yet?"

"Yeah, but Darnold, they were drunk when they tried to steal that Army jeep. We can talk to them, but I don't like them for this."

"I don't either. Not from what you told me about their intelligence."

"So, somewhere between Vegas and LA, some guys stole an entire shipment of guns from a moving train. Which means the train had to be going slow enough for them to climb on, break into the trailer, and throw the guns off the train."

"Yes."

"Not in Yermo, and that's the last stop before LA. And not while moving through the Cajon Pass, because a westbound train would be going downhill too fast."

"That was the conclusion of the Union Pacific."

"So, Cima grade," Horse said.

"Exactly, and that was in the report forwarded to my office by the FBI. When I saw the name "Cima," I almost fell out of my chair because I spent a dusty afternoon there with you back in '64 watching those pallets of M-16s sliding out the back of a rolling C-123!"

"Small world."

Darnold nodded.

"Sometimes."

"So, you told your boss, who told the FBI, that you were familiar with that place."

"I did. And I told them if they wanted more information, Captain Carlos Caballo, commander of the Smoke Tree Substation of the San Bernardino County Sheriff's Department, was the man they should talk to."

"And so, the briefing at two o'clock."

"Yes, and I wanted to you to know about the inter-agency competition between the ATF and the FBI, and how badly the FBI wants to bust open this cargo theft stuff. Forewarned is forearmed."

"Thank you, Darnold. I appreciate it."

"You're welcome. And I have a request."

"Name it."

"After the briefing, I'd like you to take me out to your place. I want to say hello to Esperanza, and your kids if they're home from school yet."

"We'll do that, for sure. But if we hurry, we can talk to the Banner boys before we meet with the FBI."

"Why talk to them if you don't think they're involved?"

"Checking all the boxes."

"And something else?"

"A possibility. I'll know more after we talk to them."

Fifteen minutes later, Horse introduced Dave D'Arnauld to Austin and Braxton Banner in the office at Zack's wrecking yard.

"Austin, where did you and Braxton do your time?" asked Horse.

"Lewisburg."

Darnold let out a low whistle.

"That's a terrible place," he said. "Nothing but hard cases there. Did you guys shoot somebody while you were trying to steal that jeep?"

"Nossir. They sent us there because of all the damage we did."

"Austin, we're talking to you and your brother today because there have been some thefts from moving trains in the area."

"Santa Fe?" asked Austin.

"No. Union Pacific."

Both Banner boys were already shaking their heads."

"Horse, we was drunk; otherwise, never woulda tried to steal that jeep. And we'll never do anything like that again. Scouts' honor," said Austin.

"I believe you, I really do," said Horse. "But the question might come up."

"I cross my heart and hope to die promise you we didn't do it," said Braxton. "We never want to go to prison again. It was terrible."

"One more question, guys. When you were in Lewisburg, did you tell anyone about what you'd done?"

"Heck, yeah," said Braxton. "They laughed at us. Said we was stupid to try such a thing. Made us feel real bad. Don't no one like to be called stupid!"

"That's right," said Austin. "But there was one guy who didn't laugh."

"Go on," said Horse.

"He asked me a lot of questions about what we done."

"Questions like what?"

"Like where we done it. How slow the train was going? Why was it going so slow? Was it easy to jump on? Stuff like that."

"Do you remember the prisoner's name?"

Austin thought for a moment.

"Nossir. I'm not sure I ever knowed it. And even if I did, I'm no damn good with names."

"If you saw a picture of the guy, would you recognize him?"

"Sure."

"Okay. I might need to talk to you again."

When Horse and Darnold left the office, Darnold pointed toward Smoke Tree in the distance.

"What's all that construction?"

Horse shook his head.

"That, Agent Darnold, is a gut punch to my hometown."

"How so?"

"The only remaining piece of old highway 66 in California runs through Smoke Tree, right down Broadway. The construction you're looking at will connect the section of Interstate 40 that runs from Smoke Tree to Topock to the piece they've completed from Ludlow through the Bristol Mountains and over South Pass. When it's finished, Smoke Tree will no longer be the heart of the east/west highway. Interstate 40 will cut the town in half and replace Highway 66 with three off-ramps."

"And you think that will make a big difference to the town?"

"For sure. Almost all the motels will die, along with most of the restaurants and service stations. There go a lot of jobs. Smoke Tree will never be the same."

"Something tells me you put up a fight about this."

"I did. Wrote letters to the Department of Transportation. Told them the time would come when people would want to commemorate Highway 66 as a big part of the country's history. 'Grapes of Wrath' and all that. And what better way to honor the Mother Road than to preserve the final California piece in Smoke Tree? Dump the traffic off Interstate 40 into town. Paint a big "Historic 66" on the street in the middle of every block. Put the traffic back on the interstate on the south end of town. Save the town and Highway 66 and save the millions of dollars it's going to cost to build this final section."

"Get any replies?"

"Buncha form letters."

Horse and Darnold were sitting in the conference room waiting for the FBI agent at the substation.

"Those last questions you asked the Banners. You're onto something. That Horse intuition again?"

"More like the Horse WAG method."

"WAG meaning?"

"Wild Ass Guess."

"Come on, Horse, spill it."

"Well, what if somebody at Lewisburg got the idea of stealing cargo off of a moving train from Austin Banner? I mean, it seems strange someone would have such specific questions about what a couple of dumb guys did, don't you think?"

"It could be."

Fred came into the room.

"Guy from the FBI to see you, boss."

"Send him down."

A moment later, a ramrod-straight man wearing a suit, tie, and highly-polished black shoes walked into the room.

Be damned, thought Horse, *must have used his hanky to wipe off the parking lot dust.*

"Jules Johns, Assistant Special Agent in charge of the Las Vegas office, Captain Caballo."

Lord, thought Horse, *that was a mouthful. Surprised he didn't tell me his rank in his class at the academy.*

"Pleasure to meet you, agent Johns. Everyone calls me Horse."

"So I've heard from Agent D'Arnauld, but I prefer Captain Caballo."

"Okay. Well, welcome to Smoke Tree. Come in and pull up a chair."

Agent Johns nodded to Darnold as he sat down.

"Agent D'Arnauld."

"Jules, I've been trying for ten years to get you to call me Darnold."

"I know, but I…."

"But you prefer Agent D'Arnauld. Okay, Jules, but say, isn't your hair getting a little long on the sides?"

Agent Johns touched his hair.

"You think?"

Darnold laughed.

"Get you every time with that one, Jules."

"Yeah, and it's getting old."

"But you always smile. That gives me hope that a human heart beats beneath that starched white shirt."

Agent Johns tried hard not to smile but gave up and grinned before he waved his hand and began the briefing.

"Captain Caballo, your boss has been made aware of today's briefing."

"Okay."

"I'll let Agent D'Arnauld go first."

"I got here before you, Jules. I've already told Horse about the guns."

"Darn it, Agent D'Arnauld, that's just like you. We were supposed to conduct this briefing together."

"I've known Horse for a long time. We were catching up before you got here."

"I like the nickname though, Agent Johns," interrupted Horse.

"What nickname?"

"Darnit Darnold. Has a certain ring to it."

"Gentlemen, let's get back to the business at hand. If Agent D'Arnauld has told you about the ATF's role in this, let me bring you up to speed on the FBI participation."

Horse listened politely as Jules Johns went through the same information Darnold had shared with him at the Bluebird, trying very hard to look like it was the first time he had heard it.

Jules wrapped up his summary with the supposition about Cima grade.

"Let me be sure I understand everything that's happened so far," Horse said. "The FBI was investigating a theft from an interstate shipment and discovered that the shipment had been intact leaving Chicago. The FBI coordinated with the Union Pacific to check on crew change locations between Chicago and Los Angeles."

"That's right, Captain Caballo. Although, I think they overlooked another possibility."

"Which is?"

"The guns could have been stolen when the train was on a siding to let a passenger train to go by."

"I don't think that's at all likely."

"Why not?"

"Since Amtrak took over passenger service on the major lines, TOFCs have priority. It's the passenger trains that get shunted onto sidings to let them pass."

"And you know this because?"

"Because, as you might have noticed when you drove past the depot, this is a railroad town. It is common knowledge here that hotshot freights take priority over passenger trains now that Amtrak is handling passenger rail."

"Oh, that's good to know. Simplifies things."

"It does," said Horse. "So, to continue, when the FBI learned about the report made by railroad detectives in Las Vegas, that dropped the case in your lap, right?"

"Exactly."

"And when you shared the report from the Union Pacific with the ATF, Darnold recognized the name Cima."

"Yes," said Agent Johns, "and he suggested we talk to you."

"Okay, but I still don't see what role you want my substation to play in this investigation,"

"Agent D'Arnauld tells me you know just about everybody in that area."

"Well, a lot of them. There aren't that many folks out there."

"Then maybe you know someone who might have seen something between Kelso and Cima eastbound or Nipton and Cima westbound."

"Did the Union Pacific ask the train crews if they had seen anything suspicious in that area?"

"They did. The crews said they hadn't."

"Therefore, you think this is happening under cover of darkness, and more specifically, on moonless nights or before moonrise?"

"That's our current supposition."

"Agent Johns, Kelso, and Nipton are tiny places, and there's little else out that way besides a couple of desert ranches that are a good distance from the rail line. I'll ask around, but it doesn't seem promising. You have any other ideas?"

"My boss would like to get somebody on the train crews. He thinks the crews aren't very observant at night and might be overlooking something."

"That could be," said Horse.

"But, he thinks the thieves may have a connection within the Union Pacific, so he's afraid he'll be alerting the criminals that we're investigating. Besides, we don't have anyone who understands train crew work."

"I might have a solution to that problem. Give me a minute."

Horse walked from the conference room to the dispatcher's nook.

"Fred, Johnny Quentin's on swing shift this week, right?"

"Yessir. Due in at four."

Horse went into his office and called Johnny's apartment.

"Quentin."

"Johnny, this is Horse. What would you think about doing some undercover work on the railroad?"

"That might be hard to pull off since I used to work there, and I've known most of those guys since I was a kid."

"This would be on the Union Pacific, not the Santa Fe."

"Where?"

"Between Yermo and Vegas."

Johnny was silent for a moment.

"That could work. The Union Pacific doesn't change crews in Barstow, and their line curves away from ours near Yermo. Santa Fe and Union Pacific crews don't mix. I don't know any of those guys."

"Okay. This undercover job is voluntary, Johnny. You don't have to do it."

Johnny laughed.

"Voluntary like training Tony Alpino?"

"Not informal like that. You'd be working with the FBI."

"Sounds interesting. Sure, I'll do it."

"Can you come to the station right now?"

"On my way."

When he returned to the conference room, Horse told Agent Johns about Johnny Quentin's background as a brakeman on the Santa Fe.

"Would what he did with the Santa Fe be any different than what he'd be doing on the UP?" the agent asked.

"Might be slightly different, but not much. Hanging on the side of a boxcar is probably pretty much the same anywhere. Someone at the Union Pacific can brief him about any minor differences."

Agent Johns steepled his fingers and looked down at the conference table as he thought through what Horse was proposing.

When he looked up again, he said, "I'm sure we could get him hired and assigned to that run, but like I said, we're worried about a possible connection between the thieves and someone inside the Union Pacific. Your deputy's cover might be compromised."

"If you're worried about the local station agent or the trainmaster, go a little higher. It's doubtful the District Superintendent would be involved."

"That could work."

"Okay," said Horse, "but while we're waiting for Johnny to get here, how common does the FBI think this railroad theft stuff is?"

"We think it's something new." Agent Johns hesitated. "Let me qualify that. There have always been railroad thefts. Think Jesse James and Butch Cassidy and the Sundance Kid, but those guys were after cash or gold. We think cargo theft is a new wrinkle. At least from railroads."

"It's more common somewhere else?"

"Well, there have always been truck hijackings."

"I've seen my share of those on 66. What else?"

"Air cargo. It's an increasing problem, especially since organized crime got involved. They started in New York. Very brazen. We knew it was happening, but we had a hard time investigating."

"Why?"

"Even more than the railroads, air freight carriers don't want to spook the customers. Most of what they handle is high value, and they're making lots of money. Don't want to strangle the golden goose by raising the alarm."

"When you say they started in New York...."

"Specifically, at JFK. Over ten billion dollars worth of air cargo goes through there every year, and millions of dollars worth is stolen by organized crime."

"I noticed you were worried about a possible inside connection between the thieves and the Union Pacific. Is that because you think airport officials are involved in the thefts at JFK?"

"We don't. The mafia is so powerful there; they don't need corruption. Not only that, they have a chain of distribution that can dispose of anything they steal."

"And that's why you're so concerned about all those guns? You think they'll disappear into this supply chain?" Horse asked Darnold.

"You've got it," said Darnold.

Darnold turned to Agent Johns.

"Why Jules, I believe I just detected a change in attitude at your organization."

"What change?"

"You guys never used to mention the Mafia."

Agent Johns smiled for the first time.

"You're quick, Agent D'Arnauld. You're also right."

"You two have lost me," said Horse.

"J. Edgar Hoover refused to believe in the existence of any such entity as the Mafia. He said so in a Senate hearing., and that was official FBI policy," Agent Johns explained.

"And the new guy doesn't have that blind spot?" asked Darnold.

"He does not, and it unties our hands."

"Glad to hear it."

"So is everyone in the field."

"Okay, I'm caught up. So, Agent Johns, you say the Mafia has moved into other airports?"

"Yes. Every major airport in the country."

"Including Las Vegas?"

"Yes. Moved in and muscled out the independents."

"Wait a minute. The FBI thinks there was organized air cargo theft going on at McCarran before the Mafia arrived?"

"We know it. We worked with the United States Attorney's Office for the District of Nevada on a case when I first arrived in Las Vegas as an agent."

"How did it go?"

"Not well. We identified an inside man and arrested him, but that's all we got."

"Why?"

"Guy clammed up. He refused to cooperate. Would not identify any of his accomplices."

"Did he have some kind of high-powered attorney?"

"Nope. Public defender. Wouldn't talk to him either, we heard through the grapevine. A very stubborn man."

"What happened to him?"

"The judge got mad and gave him the max."

"Which was?"

Agent Johns thought for a moment.

"Seven years, I think."

"Do you know where he served it?"

"I don't."

"Could you find out for me?"

"I could, but why do you want to know?"

"Just thinking about something."

"Care to share?"

"Not yet. Not fully formed."

"Okay."

"And one more request?"

"Go ahead."

"Do you think you could get me a picture of the guy?"

"I'm sure I could. You want to show it to someone?"

"Like I say, Agent Johns, the idea's not fully formed yet."

"Okay."

Agent Johns was discussing the possible involvement of the Teamsters with the Mafia at the airports when Johnny Quentin arrived. Horse made the introductions, and Johnny shook hands with Darnold and Jules Johns before taking a seat next to Horse at the center of the table.

"Darnold, Agent Johns, I'd like each of you to tell Johnny what you know about the case we've been discussing."

"I'll go first," Darnold said and went on to describe the stolen shipment to Johnny."

"So," he concluded, "we're very concerned about so many semi-automatic weapons falling into the hands of criminals."

Horse turned to Agent Johns.

"Your turn."

"Captain Caballo, unlike the ATF, the FBI, only briefs individuals on a need-to-know basis."

"And you don't think a man we're asking to go undercover needs to know everything you have on this situation?"

"That would be my judgment."

"Then you can get in your FBI car and go back to your FBI office in Las Vegas."

Agent Johns seemed to re-assess the man sitting across from him.

"You are aware, Captain Caballo, that any refusal to offer your fullest cooperation could reflect badly on your future career prospects."

"Nice try, Jules," interrupted Darnold, "but you might want to re-think that approach. This man has a file full of letters of commendation."

"That may well be, but I'm assuming he'd like to be more than a Captain someday."

Darnold laughed.

"Jules, when you get it wrong, you really get it wrong."

Horse got to his feet.

"And that concludes this meeting."

Color rose in Agent Johns' face. He held out his hands, palms forward.

"Let's not be hasty. Let me call my superior in Las Vegas and request permission to fully brief Deputy Quentin."

Horse started for the door.

"Please, Captain Caballo."

Horse stopped.

"Go ahead. You can use my office. But if your boss doesn't give you permission, don't bother coming back in here."

Agent Johns got up and went out the door.

"Congratulations, Horse," said Darnold when the agent was gone, "that's the first time I've ever heard that man say 'please.' I'm curious to see what he comes up with."

Horse began pacing the room.

"Agent D'Arnauld," Johnny began...

"Please, Deputy Quentin, call me Darnold."

Johnny smiled.

"Then I get to be Johnny."

"Agreed."

"Darnold, I'm assuming you know as well as me that any gunsmith worth his salt can convert an AR-15 to fully automatic."

"I see you're familiar with the gun."

"Familiar with its military counterpart."

"You a veteran?"

Johnny nodded.

Horse stopped pacing and sat down.

"Johnny was an Army Ranger. Three tours in Vietnam. One as an advisor before the war got hot, and two consecutive tours doing long-range reconnaissance."

"That's elite stuff! I take it Johnny won't be afraid of the bad guys."

Horse smiled.

"No, but the bad guys should be very afraid of him."

Agent Johns came back into the room.

"I have been cleared to brief Deputy Quentin," he said as he sat down, "but I have a question, Captain Caballo."

"Yes?"

"You could have told Deputy Quentin everything I told you after I left. Why didn't you just do that?"

"Two reasons. First, I was afraid I might leave something out. Johnny deserves to know everything you've got before he does this."

"And second?"

"And second, that's not the way I do things."

"Agent Johns," said Darnold, "you've heard of the term 'straight-shooter?'"

"Certainly."

"It's my firm belief the term was created to describe Carlos Caballo."

Not long after the briefing ended, Horse and Donald climbed out of Horse's patrol car at what Esperanza liked to call "Rancho Caballo."

Esperanza was out the door before the dust had settled.

"Agent Darnold! So good to see you."

"Likewise, Esperanza."

"Come on in; I've got flan and hot coffee."

Darnold's smile got even bigger.

"It's a good thing I don't live around here. I'd probably weigh three hundred pounds."

When the three of them went into the house, Alejandro and Elena were doing their homework at the dining room table.

"*Niños,*" asked Esperanza, "do you remember Agent Darnold?"

"Of course," said Alejandro. "We were little when he was here, but we took him on his first horseback ride."

Elena smiled.

"He was so funny! He kept talking about how far it was to the ground if he fell off. But he did good," she added.

"Did well," corrected Esperanza.

"You're too kind, Elena," said Darnold. "It's a wonder I didn't choke that poor horse; I held onto its neck so hard."

After coffee and flan and conversation, Horse said, "There've been some changes since you were here, Darnold. Got time to take a walk?"

"Sure, as long as you don't try to get me in the saddle again."

Outside, the two men walked past the corral. The horses nickered, hoping for a treat.

"Three horses," noted Darnold. "Last time I was here, you had two."

"The new one is Pepper. He was left to the twins by a dear friend when he died."

They started up the incline above the corral.

"What's that guy doing up there?" asked Darnold.

"Making adobe bricks for our new house."

"You paid off the land contract you told me about?"

"We did. Own the twenty acres above the corral now. Our new place will take the bottom ten."

"I remember you said you were hoping your brother and sister would come back to Smoke Tree."

"I tried to talk them into it, but they're happy where they are. Johnny Quentin and another deputy, Seve Zavala, each have five acres of the top ten. They're going to build here."

"So, since your brother and sister aren't coming back, you sold your deputies the extra parcels?"

"No, Esperanza and I gave them the land."

Darnold stopped walking.

"You know, Horse, they don't make people like you and Esperanza anymore."

Horse motioned him forward.

"Come on; I want you to meet the guy who's going to build our house."

They continued up the hill to where Joe was working.

"Joe," said Horse. "I'd like you to meet someone."

Joe shoveled the last of the adobe from the trough into the mould at his feet. He scraped off the excess, propped his shovel against the trough, and turned to the two men."

"This is Darnold."

Darnold extended his hand.

"Please to meet you, Joe."

Joe nodded and touched Darnold's hand briefly before returning to his work.

Horse and Donald walked on.

"Doesn't say much, does he?"

"No, but I'm curious. What's your first impression of Joe?"

Darnold thought for a while before replying.

"Quiet. Not very big. Looks as tough as an old piece of rawhide. Black hair, no gray. No lines on his face. I have no idea how old he might be. One more thing. I don't know quite how to put this, but there's a kind of intensity to the man. A fierceness, I guess I'd call it."

"Impressive, Darnold. You've got a good eye. Remember during Desert Strike when I told you I had a civilian infiltrate that Army camp out by Macedonia Spring?"

"That was Joe?"

"It was."

"The guy you said could be in the desert right in front of me, and I wouldn't know he was there?"

"Yes."

"Darnold turned to look at the man working in the distance.

"Now that I've met him, I can believe it."

— Chapter 13 —

TRACKS

he next day before dawn, Horse, Joe, and Johnny were at the substation. Two topographic maps containing the Union Pacific tracks from Kelso to Nipton were on easels in the conference room.

"Joe and I will take my cruiser. Johnny, you drive the Landcruiser." Horse began pointing out locations on the topos.

"We'll leave the cruiser just off Cima Road under the powerlines north of Cima. That way, none of the Union Pacific train crews will see it. Joe and I will get in the Toyota with you, Johnny, and we'll drive Joe east down the right of way to Brant siding and leave him there. Joe has a better eye than either of us, so he'll cover the tracks from there to Cima. You and I will drive back to Macedonia Canyon Road and leave the Toyota. You take one side of the tracks, and I'll take the other, and we'll head for Cima. We'll walk up Cima Road and get the cruiser when we get there. Come back and pick up Joe. That'll give us each about ten miles to walk."

"What're we looking for?" asked Joe.

"Railroad shipment seals, mainly. Are you familiar with those?"

"Am."

"And anything that looks out of place: locks that have been cut, tools, that kind of thing. There are plastic bags and gloves in the Landcruiser. Bag up anything you find, and we'll give it to the FBI. Maybe they can pull some prints."

"Okay."

"I figure we better do this. I can't imagine Agent Johns getting his shiny shoes dusty, and I don't think anyone from his office will get their feet on the ground out there either."

Horse closed the conference room door and sat down next to Joe and Johnny at the table before speaking in a voice just above a whisper.

"I didn't tell Darnold or Agent Johns about the person Joe calls woman of the desert moon. We promised her we wouldn't give away her secret. I will honor that promise, but I think we should ask her if she's seen anything."

"Do you think she'll talk to you?" asked Johnny.

"Might shoot us, that big gun," said Joe with what might have been a smile.

"She might, at that," said Horse, "but we have to take the chance. She's the most likely to have seen what's going on out there at night. But first, let's go for a walk."

"Always good," said Joe.

Late that afternoon, Horse surveyed the plastic bags spread out on the conference table.

"No locks, but a lot of railroad seals. It looks like there have been more thefts out there than the Union Pacific is letting on," Horse said. "That squares with what the federal agents told me."

"More on our side of the hill than on Joe's. I'm guessing they started there first and then got worried about working the same stretch for too long," added Johnny.

"Could be." And the tarp Joe found explains why the train crews aren't seeing anything. The thieves work on moonless nights, cover up what they throw over the sides, and the tarps blend into the desert."

"Tire tracks, too. Dual wheels. Not like UP trucks," said Joe.

"So," asked Johnny, "what's next?"

"I'm going to take all this stuff to Las Vegas early tomorrow morning. Give it to Agent Johns. Then, I want him to take me to meet the guy who prosecuted the brains behind the air cargo thefts at McCarren seven or eight years ago. Get some more details on that case, and get a picture of the guy he put in jail."

"You think he might be involved in this?"

"There's a remote possibility the guy served time with the Banner boys. The timeline fits, anyway. I'll know by tomorrow afternoon. The morning after that, we'll go out and talk to woman of the desert moon."

Mid-afternoon the next day, Horse, Esperanza, Johnny Quentin, and Joe were gathered around the Caballo's kitchen table, dipping Esperanza's freshly-made churros in chocolate sauce and drinking coffee.

"We're meeting here," said Horse, "because Eletheria told Johnny and I someone in our department has a big mouth. I didn't want what I'm going to tell you to go beyond us."

"Better coffee, too," said Joe.

"Not to mention Esperanza's excellent churros," said Horse.

"Now, the simple stuff first," Horse began. "Agent Johns is doubtful any useful prints can be lifted from the things we picked up along the railroad tracks. But my visit was productive.

Before you got to the station the other day, Johnny, Agent Johns told Darnold and I about an air cargo theft case he remembered from his early days in Las Vegas in the nineteen sixties. I asked Agent Johns to take me to the office of United States Attorney for the District of Nevada, so I could follow up on a hunch. We went over there, and Agent Johns had an ADA pull the file with the details.

The perpetrator was a guy named Arthur Ransome. He was an Air Force veteran; jet engine mechanic. Last tour was at Nellis. Went to work for the airlines when he got out. He was at McCarren when it first opened. Vegas was booming. High-end air cargo all over the place, a lot of it unsecured. This Ransome guy starts stealing. Expensive stuff, but small. Targets of opportunity."

"And they caught him?" asked Johnny.

"Might never have, if he'd stuck to that, but he wasn't the only one doing this. Whole gangs were involved, stealing stuff by the truckload. The District Attorney's office investigator thought one of the gangs had noticed Ransome. Noticed he had credentials that got him anywhere on the airfield. The gang recruited him as their inside man."

"Got greedy," said Joe as he refilled his coffee cup.

"What makes you think that?"

Joe shrugged. "Humans."

"You're probably right," continued Horse. "The file I reviewed didn't explain how Ransome came to the attention of the D.A.s office. Anyway, he got arrested. Eager young assistant DA prosecuted the case. Tried to get Ransome to roll over on his accomplices. Ransome wouldn't do it."

"Sounds pretty routine, so far," said Johnny.

"It was, but this ADA apparently had higher ambitions. Saw making a bigger case as a career booster, but Ransome wouldn't cooperate. ADA gets a conviction, talks the judge into giving Arthur Ransome the max."

"Which was?"

"Seven years. Hard fall for a first offender, especially one with a good military record. But that's not all. ADA asked the judge to intervene after passing sentence. Judge did. Ransome was sent to Lewisburg prison in Pennsylvania."

"Is that a bad place?"

"One of the worst. Federal penitentiary. Most guys there for really major crime or violent stuff."

"And Arthur Ransome didn't fit that definition."

"No, but the judge justified it because theft of air cargo is a federal crime. And this ADAs ambitions didn't end there. He talks the District Attorney's office in Pennsylvania into sending an ADA to visit Ransome in prison about once a month with a message: 'give up your associates, and we'll recommend parole. Stonewall us, and you'll serve all seven years.'"

"Did Ransome do it?" asked Johnny.

"Nope. But the ADA just kept going back."

Horse stopped talking to let Johnny think about what he'd heard.

"Oh, hell," said Johnny. "I get it. Because he keeps visiting, word gets out. Ransome gets a reputation as a snitch."

"Exactly."

"And still the guy didn't crack?"

"He did not."

"I wonder how he survived?"

"I do, too, and I have to admit, as I read through the file the ADA brought us, I got angry. Because of his ambition, that prosecutor could have cost a man his life. I don't like criminals, but I like law enforcement

142

people who game the system even less. This Ransome was a thief, and he certainly deserved prison time. But purposely putting him in a position where he could have been killed? That's over the top."

"And no parole?"

"Not even a hearing. Arthur Ransome went out max time."

"Which means no parole officer. He's free and clear. An ex-con, but Joe citizen. So, what became of him? Was it in the file?"

"He came back to Las Vegas!" said Horse.

"What? That's just crazy!"

"It is, and I think he came back for some kind of weird revenge. Maybe rub this ADAs nose in it? Like saying, 'I'm out, and there's nothing you can do about it?'"

"But you think he might be involved in this train stuff?" asked Johnny.

"It's a possibility."

"Why would he switch to trains?"

"Because the mob had muscled the little guys off of the airport before Ransome got out of prison. And by the way, Ransome got his revenge," Horse said.

"How?"

"As soon as the ADA learned Ransome was back in Vegas, and working at an airport, no less, he wanted surveillance on him. His boss turned down the request. The ADA went behind the District Attorney's back. Had Ransome tailed for weeks. The surveillance turned up nothing, but his boss found out about it and fired the ADA for ignoring his order!"

"So, if Ransome's not stealing air cargo, what's he doing?"

"After we looked at the file, Agent Johns and I went out to North Las Vegas Air Terminal. That's where Ransome was working as a jet engine mechanic."

"Wait a minute. An ex-con who was convicted for stealing air cargo manages to get a job at an airport? How?"

"Partly because no air cargo comes into that field, but mostly because he worked for free for six weeks!"

"Did you get to talk to him?" asked Johnny.

"We didn't. Arthur Ransome is in the wind. He quit his job right after the guns were stolen. Told his boss his mother was dying, and he didn't know when he'd be back."

"Likely story!"

"Yeah, especially because Ransome told his boss his mother lives in Oregon."

"And?" asked Johnny.

"Ransome is from Spencer, West Virginia. When we went back to his office, Agent Johns called his home. Ransome's mother is alive and well, and she hasn't seen Arthur since he went to prison. Johns told me he's not going to take her word for it. He'll have an agent sit on the house for a while. He'd really like to find Ransome."

"That's quite a story."

"There's more. The two boys from Smoke Tree who tried to steal a jeep off a moving train were in Lewisburg, too, and their sentences overlapped with Ransome's."

Johnn laughed. "The legendary Banner boys. Man, guys on the Santa Fe still laugh about that."

"And here's the punch line: Austin remembers a prisoner at Lewisburg asking him about what they did. And not just once. Wanted all the details."

"Arthur Ransome?"

"Austin couldn't remember the guy's name. When I got back to town today, I took a picture of Ransome to Austin. He said that was the guy with the questions. I passed that information on to Darnold and Agent Johns."

"A Smoke Tree connection! How weird," said Johnny.

"Yeah," said Horse. "I sometimes think half of the country has passed through here at one time or another."

"Okay. So, what's the next step on our end?"

"Tomorrow morning, we go visit woman of the desert moon. There's a good chance she's seen something along the tracks at night. She certainly saw the drug plane."

"Go early, won't be asleep yet," Joe said.

"Good idea," said Horse. "Might keep her from getting mad enough to shoot us."

Before first light, they had crossed the wash below the corral and were climbing the embankment.

"Not as cold," said Chemehuevi Joe.

"I didn't come all the way up with you last time," said Johnny, "but it was cold enough down below that morning."

These guys are breathing easy enough to talk, thought Horse, *and it's all I can do to keep up. Johnny, I can understand, but Joe's older than I am.*

The sun was still below the eastern horizon when Horse stood to the side of woman of the desert moon's door and rapped on it with the butt of his revolver.

"Ma'am, Captain Carlos Caballo, San Bernardino County Sheriff's Department."

"Yes?"

"We'd like to talk to you. It'd be easier if you let us in."

"This about the railroad?"

"Yes, ma'am, it is."

"Is Tracker Man with you?"

"Yes, and one more. The deputy we told you about last time."

"Give me a minute. Don't come in until I tell you to."

"Okay."

The three men could hear the two iron bars sliding across the angle iron attached to the inside of the door. It was another minute before woman of the desert moon spoke again.

"You can come in."

Woman of the desert moon was sitting where they had first seen her, wearing the same full-face, high-gloss-black motorcycle helmet and field jacket. As before, multiple candles flickered from the rock faces, and one of the oil lamps was burning.

"Ma'am," began Horse when he and Joe and Johnny were side by side in front of her.

Woman of the desert moon interrupted. "Don't be rude, Sheriff Man, introduce the new guy."

"Sorry, this is Deputy Johnny Quentin."

"Thank you for letting me in your...," Johnny hesitated because 'home' didn't seem quite the right word..., "place," he finished.

Woman of the desert moon studied Johnny's face for a moment without speaking. *I know him. I've seen his face by firelight. Tracker Man isn't the only person who can see people without being seen.*

"You're welcome, Deputy Man," she said. "You can ask your questions now, Sheriff Man."

"From what you said when I knocked, I guess you've seen something unusual down on the Union Pacific line."

"Yes. One night, I saw headlights on the right-of-way after the train had gone by. Since the train hadn't stopped, I didn't think it was a Union Pacific truck."

"Uphill or down?"

"Me?"

"Sorry. The train. Was it climbing the grade or coming down the hill?"

"Climbing."

"Did you see what the truck was doing?"

"I was only halfway down aqueduct road when I saw it moving. By the time I got down there, it was gone."

"Did you ever see it again?"

"Two nights later. I was closer to the tracks, so I got a good look. It was one of those cube trucks. Painted black. The box, the truck, everything. All black."

"What was it doing?"

"Driving along. Stopping. Whenever it stopped, guys came out of the desert and loaded stuff inside."

"Any other times after that one?"

"Yes."

"Is there some kind of a pattern?"

"Moonless nights. Always moonless nights. Either new moon, or after the first quarter has set, or before third quarter rises."

"Have you ever been close enough to see people on the train? Other than the train crew, I mean."

"Oh, yes. There are twelve of them. They break into those trailers on the flatcars. Throw stuff into the desert, then jump off and cover it with tarps."

"And how many in the truck?"

146

"Two."

"Any idea where the truck comes from before it drives the right of way?"

"Salt cedars west of the depot."

"You're very observant."

"Sheriff Man, some people watch movies, some watch television, but I watch anything unusual that happens out here at night. So tell me, what will happen now?"

Horse was silent as he tried to decide how much to tell her.

"Come on, Sheriff Man, I helped you. Don't stonewall me."

"Okay. You deserve to know, and you're not likely to tell anyone what I'm about to say. Deputy Quentin is going to go undercover on the Union Pacific. He'll be on some of those trains going up the grade, either from Kelso or Nipton, trying to catch the bad guys in the act."

"And if he does?"

"He'll arrest them."

"All of them?"

"No. We only need one or two. If we get a couple, they'll give up the others."

"You say 'we.'"

"FBI is involved. ATF, too."

"What's an ATF?"

"Alcohol, Tobacco and Firearms."

Woman of the desert moon didn't speak for a moment.

"So, these guys also stole cigarettes, or alcohol, or…or even guns? That could make things dangerous for Deputy Man."

"I'll be fine," Johnny said.

"Speaking of danger," said Horse, "I'd appreciate it if you stayed away far away from the tracks from now on. Don't want you getting hurt."

"How about you, Tracker Man? You haven't said a word. Don't you have anything to say?"

"Thanks," said Joe.

"Thanks for what?"

"Not shooting us."

"You're welcome. Now, if you men will go on your way, I'd like to get some sleep."

Horse, Joe, and Johnny could hear the iron bars sliding back into place as they walked away from the cave.

But Daryn did not go to sleep. Instead, she sat behind her makeshift table and reviewed everything the three men had said. Because she spoke to other people so infrequently, she always took in every word, gesture, and nuance and replayed and parsed everything later.

Her first conclusion was that the man who had once pulled an odd device all over the desert looked different than the last time she had seen him. He wasn't as gaunt, but it was more than that. She thought again about his face, changing aspect in the flickering light from his fires, and decided he didn't look as haunted. As tortured. As grim. Something had improved his outlook. She had no idea how he had gone from being a refugee from something unseen to being a sheriff's deputy. Perhaps she would never know.

As for Sheriff Man, he was the same. Competent. Confident, but not in a cocky way. In control of himself and the situation. A leader who treated others as equals.

And Tracker Man. Also unchanged. Enigmatic and mysterious. Self-contained. A man entirely comfortable in his own skin. She felt an odd kinship with the mysterious man for reasons she could not determine.

He walks out here at night, at times. I wonder if he hears the voices?

After turning the words, intonations, and body language this way and that for over an hour, she reached a decision. Despite what Sheriff Man had said about staying away from the railroad, she planned on being there every moonless night. After all, what Deputy Man was going to do would put him in harm's way. She would look out for him. Somebody had to. She didn't want him to survive whatever had driven him into the desert just to be killed by a bunch of thugs.

Back at the substation, Horse picked up a message slip and returned a call to Agent Johns. When the call ended, he and Joe and Johnny returned to the Caballo's hillside home and gathered around the kitchen table again after Horse made coffee.

"Johnny, Agent Johns said you are now officially a Union Pacific employee. You also have a new identity, complete with social security number so you can be on the payroll if anyone ever checks."

"What's my name?"

"Don Quest. You explain that your friends call you Donny. That way, neither name is too far from your own, so you won't just keep walking when you hear it."

"Okay."

"They've arranged an apartment for you in Las Vegas. The lease is signed and first and last and two months paid in advance. Agent Johns has the key. You're to pick it up from him at his office."

"What's my cover story?"

"The district superintendent on the Union Pacific did a little research. Nobody on the crews working out of Las Vegas or Yermo has ever worked for the Kansas City Southern Railway, so that's officially where you hired on from."

"That works pretty well. I know the area they service from when I was stationed in Louisiana."

"Good. Now, I want you to take two days off before you go up there. You'll be working without laying off for as long as this takes."

"I don't need time off. I can start right now."

"Apparently, Deputy Quentin, you have forgotten an important fact."

"What's that?"

"You're getting married in May. You'd better take a couple days to help Robyn with the planning unless you want to start your marriage under a cloud."

"Good point. By the way, what can I tell Robyn about all this?"

"Tell her what you'll be doing, but tell her she can't say anything about it to anyone else."

"I appreciate that."

"Oh, and tell her 'welcome to law enforcement.' Anything else you want to ask me?"

"Can I borrow your truck?"

"Sure."

"Couple of Vegas cops know my 'Vette. Rather not be seen in it up there. And one other thing."

"What's that?"

"You're going to train Tony Alpino on your own?"

"Not a problem."

"Donny," said Joe.

Johnny hesitated a beat.

"What?"

Joe smiled.

"Have to be quicker. Be careful out there."

"That's right," said Horse. "I know you've had much tougher assignments, but don't get careless just because you're not in a combat zone."

— Chapter 14 —

WOMAN OF THE DESERT MOON
Her Origins

*I*n *1812, the San Juan Capistrano earthquake* destroyed the bell tower at Mission San Gabriel Arcángel. The Franciscans, determined to replace it with an even more elaborate structure, pushed the Tongva Indians they had enslaved hard to complete the project. A group of them fled into the Mojave Desert to escape the brutal forced labor.

The Spaniards also needed the Indians they called *Gabrieleños* to tend the mission's vineyards, orchards, and fields. The authorities vividly remembered the Tongva revolt of 1785, led by Tongva medicine woman Toypurina, the neophyte Nicolás José and their co-conspirators Temejasquichi and Aligivit. They recalled there had been no further uprisings after they publicly flogged the three men and exiled Toypurina from the San Gabriel Mission. Therefore, they were determined to capture, return, and publicly whip the 1812 runaways as a warning to others.

A mounted patrol set off after the *Gabrieleños.* FatherJosé Maria de Zalvidea joined the group, hoping to proselytize the desert Indians to the east of the San Gabriel Mountains. The patrol followed the Old Spanish Trail to the place they called The Fork of the Road. There, they turned northeast onto the Mojave Trail. Near present-day Hesperia, they encountered a band of Mojaves. Father Zalvidea stayed behind to attempt the conversion of the Mojaves to Christianity while the mounted patrol continued north along the west bank of the Mojave River.

When the river disappeared beneath the sand, the soldiers considered abandoning the pursuit. However, it had been a wet winter, even in the desert, and they thought they could find sufficient water and feed for the horses. At Afton Canyon, the river re-surfaced, and the patrol found signs of a campsite that might have belonged to the Tongva.

Two days later, the patrol came upon surface water again. Soda Lake, usually dry, had been filled to a depth of three or four inches by the winter rains. In the distance, they saw a human figure near the center of the lake. At first, they thought it might be a mirage but gave chase when the figure began to run. When they caught up, they were surprised it was a woman. They surrounded her on horseback, and she began to shriek at them in a language they had never heard before.

If Father Zalvidea had been with them, perhaps what occurred next would not have happened, but Spanish soldiers often had intentions far less spiritual than those of Spanish priests. Several of them raped the woman in the shallow waters. She staggered to her feet and set off to the north when they had finished. The Sergeant in charge of the patrol looked toward the distant desert mountains and decided that if the Tongva were indeed ahead of them, there would be no way to find where they had exited the lake.

The patrol turned homeward.

The assaulted woman's name was Piyüw. She was Chemehuevi. She was also woman of the desert moon's great-great-great-great grandmother. Recently orphaned, Piyüw had attached herself to a three-family unit typical of the nomadic Chemehuevi. Sick the day before, she had awakened, trembling, feverish, and disoriented in the night and wandered away from the sleeping group. When the sun rose behind her, she saw the water covering Soda Lake stretching away to the west. Still disoriented, she set out across the shallows, occasionally stopping to lave water over her feverish face. Her fever was beginning to subside when she saw men on horseback in the distance. Fearful, Piyüw turned and ran.

After the rape, she stumbled northeast. When she looked back, the men were riding away. It took Piyüw the better part of a day to find her party. When she did, she said nothing about what had happened.

When her pregnancy became apparent later that year, the women in the families she had been traveling with assumed she had slept with one of their men and drove Piyüw away.

Twenty years later, 'Paa, born of the rape of Piyüw, and woman of the desert moon's great-great-great-grandmother, lived with a different wandering group near the Turtle Mountains. A Chemehuevi from a passing group took 'Paa as his wife. Two years later, woman of the desert moon's great-great-grandmother, Ta'va, was born near Cornfield Spring in the Providence Mountains. Ta'va was taken to wife at fifteen and eventually brought forth Mi'ja, woman of the desert moon's great-grandmother.

In 1865, Mi'ja and another Chemehuevi group were selling firewood gathered in the Colorado Riverbottom as fuel for passing steamboats loaded with supplies for the mines upriver in Eldorado Canyon Nevada. Arivs Henkle, an engineer on the *General Jessup,* saw Mi'ja and was enchanted by her beauty. In 1866, Arivs married Daryn's great-grandmother in Ehrenberg, Arizona, near present-day Parker.

The territorial census of 1867 shows the couple living in Ehrenberg, but the column for their address is blank. That may mean they were living in a tent. The census lists their ages: Arvis thirty-two; Mi'ja twenty-five. Under the race column, "white" is specified for Arvis and "mixed" for Mi'ja. Perhaps Mi'ja did not appear to be completely Chemehuevi.

To add additional confusion, the census also shows a daughter, Kestrel, and describes her race as "white." When Mi'ja died of smallpox two years later, Arvis decided Kestrel should never know her mother was Chemehuevi. Why saddle the daughter he so loved with the disparaging epithet 'half-breed' and limit her marriage prospects? And so, the Chemenuevi heritage of woman of the desert moon's grandmother faded into the hazy mists of time.

Resolute Craddock, woman of the desert moon's grandfather, was descended from a Welsh family that emigrated to New England long before the American Revolution. Resolute's ancestors had left Wales in search of religious freedom after the Church of England labeled the

Welsh variant of Christianity non-conformist and dissident. A secondary factor in the family's relocation was the persistent Welsh legend that a Welshman, Prince Modoc, had sailed to the American continent with three ships in 1170 and left behind Welsh-speaking Indians the Craddocks hoped to encounter.

As westering as his forebears, Resolute sought a new life in distant and little-known lands. In 1885, in keeping with his mining heritage, he was scouring the Lower Colorado River Basin for valuable minerals or hard metals when he met Kestrel Henkle. They married, and Kestrel began to accompany him as he continued to prospect in the area.

Although Resolute occasionally discovered "float" in desert washes, he never found any outcroppings of ore, and in1896, he gave up prospecting. He was laboring in the turquoise mines in the Crescent Mountains to secure a more reliable income for Kestrel and himself when he heard that John Swickard was buying mining claims in an area twenty miles to the east.

Resolute's prospecting dreams of wealth re-awakened, and he began secretly following Swickard, staking claims near those the man was buying. Among the claims Swickard bought were those that would someday form the Quartette, the most successful gold mine in the colorful history of Searchlight, Nevada. Resolute staked out three claims nearby, marking the boundaries by the traditional method of written descriptions in tobacco cans nailed to juniper posts supported by rock cairns.

A group of men, including John Swickard, formed the Searchlight Mining District in 1898. The story goes that the district took its name from a remark made by Swickard made while grinding low-grade material by primitive methods: "There is ore here all right, but it would take a searchlight to find it."

Unfortunately for Swickard, that same year, he sold his share of the Quartette to Benjamin Macready and C.C. Fisher for eleven hundred dollars and a team of mules. Macready bought out Fisher and worked the Quartette for a year without success. In 1899, he sold it to Colonel Hopkins, a Bostonian investor. Macready became the superintendent of the mine: Colonel Hopkins became a multi-millionaire.

Hopkins invested heavily in the Quartette, sinking the shaft three hundred feet deeper than any other mine in the Searchlight District, but the effort yielded no high-grade ore. The Colonel was on the cusp of abandoning the project in 1900. Superintendent Macready, fearful the mine would close, and leave him unemployed, ordered his foreman to change the angle of the shaft. The miners struck a bonanza, and the boomtown of Searchlight, Nevada, surged to life.

Not far from the Quartette, Resolute Craddock worked the mine he had named the Esmeralda. Based on Colonel Hopkin's experience with the Quartette, it was plain that any high-grade ore in the district lay more than two hundred feet below ground. Resolute lacked the financial resources for the expensive equipment required to take the shaft of the Esmeralda to that depth. Spurred by the discovery in the nearby Quartette, he took on an east-coast investor, purchased the necessary equipment, and hired workers.

Resolute's crew struck a promising vein at the three-hundred-foot level. The Esmeralda was soon shipping ore by freight wagon to Manvel, the terminus of the Nevada Southern Railway twenty-three bone-jarring miles south. The Nevada Southern carried the ore to Goffs for transshipment via the Atchison, Topeka, and Santa Fe to a stamping mill on the Colorado River. Slowly, the Esmeralda began to turn a profit, but it was not fast enough for Resolute's impatient investor. Resolute bought the man out in 1901 for cash and a demand note for a large sum due in 1904. It was a gamble, but prospectors and hard rock miners are gamblers by nature.

In 1902, the mines just south of the Nevada state line in California that the Nevada Southern had been built to service began to play out. The short-line railroad went bankrupt but quickly re-organized as the California Eastern. It was common knowledge among mine owners in Searchlight that the real power behind the re-named line was the Santa Fe, which meant the Santa Fe was considering an extension into Searchlight. Things were looking up.

That same year, Resolute and Kestrel were living in a tent near the entrance to the mine when Kestrel gave birth to a son they named Reliance. Resolute handed out cigars and whiskey to his crew and told them to get back to work. He knew if he didn't produce results quickly, his investor would claim the Esmeralda in 1904 and sell it to someone else.

The miner's strike of 1903 nearly ended Resolute's dream. The Western Federation of Miners had organized the workers at the Quartette, by far the largest mine in Searchlight. When the Nevada Legislature passed a law in February of 1903 that limited the workday for miners to eight hours, the WFM went on strike to enforce the eight-hour day and improve working conditions.

In retaliation, the Quartette created the Desert Mine Operators Association. The Duplex, Good Hope, New Era, Cyrus Noble, Southern Nevada, and Ranioler mines signed on. Fearful that if the strike lasted he would be unable to pay the note due in 1904, Resolute joined the Association. The hard-rock miner who had once labored in the turquoise mines in the Crescent Mountains for minimal pay became an anti-unionist overnight.

At first, the town's newspaper, *The Searchlight,* supported the miners. However, the local businesses that were *The Searchlight's* advertisers soon began to feel the pinch of the work stoppage. By October, the newspaper had reversed its position. It now claimed the miners no longer had the community's support: a strange assertion since the town's roughly one thousand inhabitants consisted almost entirely of the men who worked in the mines.

Strike-breakers arrived from as far away as Colorado and Missouri. They went to work under the same rules that had been in effect before the strike. No longer able to support their families, many strikers returned to work. Those who did had to sign cards promising not to involve themselves in union activities. The strike ended.

If Resolute Craddock had any misgivings about turning on the men he had once worked with, he consoled himself with the increasing value of the ore now coming out of the Esmeralda. Before 1903 ended, it was clear he would have no problem meeting his note in the coming year.

In 1906, the Santa Fe publicly "leased" the California Eastern and began extending the rail line to Searchlight. The track reached the town in 1907. Because by then the Quartette was Nevada's most productive gold mine, most of the ore in the cars departing Searchlight came from its mineshaft, now over nine hundred feet deep. The Quartette was operating twenty-four hours a day. It had its own electrical plant to power its mining equipment, and there were telephones on the surface and throughout the mine.

But while Resolute's Esmeralda was a distant second to the Quartette in production, it was still highly profitable, and Resolute and Kestrel were rich. They could have afforded opulent quarters, but rather than building an impressive house that would befit their status, they ordered a sawed and fitted knockdown summer cottage from the Aladdin Company of Bay City, Michigan.

The kit cost two hundred and ninety-eight dollars, plus shipping, and arrived in a boxcar. Resolute assembled the pre-cut and numbered pieces. When he and Kestrel and their son moved in, Kestrel remarked it was the first place she had lived without canvas or sky for a ceiling.

The home stood on a hill near the entrance to the Esmeralda. People in town thought Resolute had built the cottage there to watch his mine. But the Esmeralda wasn't all that Resolute was keeping an eye on.

In 1907, Searchlight, Nevada, was at its peak. It had a railroad, electricity, telephones, hotels, saloons, schools, grocery and mercantile stores, rooming houses, and restaurants. There were three doctor's offices, a small hospital, five lawyers, a justice of the peace, baseball teams, and even a tennis court.

But like the desert mountains surrounding it, Searchlight's success began to erode the moment it reached its highest point, and by the middle of the year, the town began its long decline. The quality of the ore in all forty-four Searchlight Mining District mines decreased in parallel with the increased cost of bringing it to the surface. There was no relief via the price of gold, stuck at twenty dollars and change per ounce. That price would not change significantly until 1933, when the government pegged it at thirty-five dollars an ounce.

An additional factor in the town's decline was the Panic of 1907. Second only to the Great Depression as the major American economic catastrophe of the twentieth century, the panic that hastened Searchlight's decline was caused, ironically enough, by the turmoil surrounding a mining company. Two investors had tried to corner the market in copper by acquiring all the stock in United Copper in Butte, Montana. The attempt was unsuccessful. The two men went bankrupt, and the banks that had loaned them money to pursue the scheme failed. The insolvency spread to other New York banks. The largest was the Knickerbocker Trust. When it failed, the Panic of 1907 spread throughout the country. Before it ended, the U.S. Stock Exchange had fallen by fifty percent. Money from the east coast, which had fueled much of Searchight's growth, dried up as quickly as raindrops falling on volcanic rock in August.

While still very profitable, Resolute Craddock's Esmeralda was having the same problem as the rest of the mines in the area. However, Resolute was not as concerned as the others. He was a sole owner and had no eastern investors who suddenly called their loans to meet financial obligations. In addition, by dint of resourcefulness and frugality, Resolute and Kestrel had already amassed a fortune.

Most of the Craddock wealth was in gold, paper money, and negotiable instruments secreted in safe deposit boxes in various California banks. He was especially partial to the Bank of Italy, founded in San Francisco in 1904. None of it was in Searchlight Bank and Trust, the local bank that failed with many others during the Panic. Resolute was a cautious man. He had been poor most of his life and never intended to be poor again.

Even after 1907, there was still money to be made in Searchlight, and mining, though less profitable, continued. The Quartette was driving ever deeper, as was the Esmeralda. And although Colonel Hopkins and his son rarely descended into the Quartette on the few occasions they were in town, Resolute was in the Esmeralda daily. He could often be found in the deepest, hottest part of the mine, inspecting footwall drifts and wandering through the spreading stopes. His workers noticed he sometimes carried a compass and wondered at the practice. Surely the boss didn't think he might get lost in the mine?

But that wasn't why Resolute carried the compass. He also used it outside. Specifically, less than a hundred yards from the bottom of the steep hillside where workers entered the Esmeralda. A spot where he had staked second and third claims next to the one that became the Esmeralda. Resolute often sat on a large rock there, staring at the hillside. Sometimes he spread a large map at his feet. It was a precise map of the interior of the Esmeralda. There were azimuth readings penciled on the map.

Resolute Craddock had a theory: a theory that might be of great importance to the financial future of the Craddocks. A theory he did not intend to test until the Esmeralda and the Quartette both played out, and most of the people now living in Searchlight moved away.

— Chapter 15 —

WOMAN OF THE DESERT MOON AND SEARCHLIGHT'S BEST KEPT SECRET

*T*he American west is rife with tales of hidden mines of incredible value known only to the miners who discovered them. Resolute had often heard the stories and discounted them. Not anymore. If his calculations were correct, he owned one. But his was not in some remote canyon. It was hiding in plain sight less than half a football field from the Esmeralda beneath the smaller claims he had paced off years before and marked with Prince Albert cans.

But those calculations were best kept to himself. Any activity on that claim would attract too many eyes in present-day Searchlight. Besides, he and Kestrel had all the money they would ever need. However, that might not be the case for young Reliance and his potential offspring.

If Searchlight's future unfolded as Resolute suspected it would, by the time Reliance grew up, the town would be but a shadow of its present self. When that day came, Reliance could tap the resources of Resolute's other claims. But it would be best if he knew how to do the work himself. Involving anyone else would not do at all.

When Reliance Craddock began elementary school in 1908, he was one of thirty-six students in grades one through eight. In the years that followed, there would never again be as many. Colonel Hopkins died in 1910, and his son returned to New England to live off his millions.

Operations at the Quartette were winding down. By 1912, there were only eleven students in the small school atop a hill in the middle of town.

By 1912, the Esmeralda was no longer active, and Reliance was usually with his father when he wasn't in school. He and Resolute spent hours exploring the desert around Searchlight. And in the summer, Resolute, Kestrel, and Reliance often camped for weeks near Piute Creek, a spring-fed body of water lined with cottonwoods and willows less than twenty miles south of Searchlight in Piute Gorge.

Young Reliance was a desert boy, through and through. Although he had inherited the blue/green eyes characteristic of many Welsh people from his father, he had his mother's high cheekbones and jet-black hair. Reliance did not sunburn in summer; he simply turned darker beneath the blazing sky.

During one of those camping trips between Reliance's seventh and eighth-grade years, his mother and father told him that he would have to go away for high school because schooling in Searchlight ended after the eighth grade.

Reliance had always assumed the eighth grade would mark the end of his schooling, but his parents explained they had decided Reliance should go to college. Therefore, not just any high school would do.

Resolute and Kestrel had researched private high schools throughout neighboring California and discovered almost all were Catholic: Resolute and Kestrel were not. In addition, since Resolute's ancestors had fled Wales to escape sectarianism within the Anglican church, Resolute was adamant that his son attend a non-sectarian school. Head Royce School in Oakland was the only school with the academic rigor and non-sectarian outlook Resolute desired for his son. Therefore, Reliance would be a freshman at Head Royce School in 1916.

Reliance didn't like Oakland. While he enjoyed his classes at Head Royce and excelled at sports, he detested bay-area weather. Cold, damp, and foggy ill-suited a lad raised on the Mojave. Reliance initially hoped the First World War, which had started in 1914, would save him from the damp, especially when the United States declared war on Germany in April of 1917, his sophomore year. He was soon dreaming of being a pilot in the newly-created Army Air Service, just like young John

Macready, son of Benjamin Macready, former Superintendent of the Quartette mine, but the Great War ended in Reliance's junior year.

When Reliance was home the summer before his last year at Head Royce, Resolute took him for a stroll. Father and son walked down the dusty hill from the little cottage, and Resolute revealed a secret to his son in the wash below. By the time they returned to the hilltop, Reliance knew why he would be attending the Colorado School of Mines in Golden, Colorado, after finishing his secondary education.

In the summer of 1923, college graduate Reliance Craddock returned home. The Union Pacific deposited him in Nipton at dusk on a June evening. The Searchlight he returned to had fewer than a hundred people. The State of Nevada had closed the Quartette Mine for safety reasons in 1922, and mining activity was almost nonexistent.

The morning after his return, Reliance stood with his father at the bottom of the hill below the family home: the same place they had stood before Reliance's senior year at Head Royce School. Just as he had on that morning, Resolute explained his theory. This time, he brought his map.

Reliance, bolstered with the knowledge gained during four years at the Colorado School of Mines, studied the map, the wash, and the hillside.

"Father," he said, smiling, "you might be right."

"Then, let's get to it," Resolute replied with a smile of his own.

They climbed to the top of the hill, unblocked the adit, and then walked southwest and unlocked the gates to the Esmeralda. Father and son descended to the lowest level of the Esmeralda and set to work. They created a blasting pattern on the face of a particular stop-wall drift. Once they had packed the face with explosives, they retreated a safe distance and fired the charges. Seven hundred feet above, inside the Craddock home, the explosion caused a mild rumble followed by a faint "whump."

The Esmeralda was more than a mile "t' other side t' mountain," as local parlance had it, from the Searchlight business district. The sound of the detonations from deep in the mine did not reach what remained of the town. Resolute and Reliance waited for the dust to settle and fresh air to seep in from the mine entrance and adit. Then they went to work, side by side, armed with picks and shovels like two troglodyte hard-rock miners from times long past.

When Resolute and Reliance emerged from the Esmeralda that night, they each had a long soak in a tub of hot water before their evening meal. After dinner, they sat in the small living room and told Kestral about the day's work. That day and the evening that followed established a pattern.

Before sunrise each morning, Resolute and Reliance descended into the mine carrying lunch buckets filled with sandwiches. They worked all day while Kestrel cleaned the little house, washed their clothes from the day before, and cooked the evening meal. After father and son bathed and had dinner, the Craddock family sat in the living room and talked until Resolute began to nod off.

Resolute and Reliance were tunneling southeast at a downward angle, following a meager quartz vein neither of them thought would yield anything of consequence. The vein was merely a guide to something better Resolute was convinced lay beyond its termination.

Three months after they had started work, the quartz vein dwindled to nothing, and that evening in the living room, the Craddocks discussed the pros and cons of going deeper or moving laterally. The work was becoming more demanding the deeper they went because the detritus of each day's blasting had to be hauled uphill in an ore car.

They decided to continue southwest but go no deeper. The decision was fortuitous, and in October, they were rewarded with a magnificent discovery: a relatively small but unbelievably valuable ore pocket.

"Impossible," said Reliance when they found it.

'Why impossible?" asked Resolute.

"Because," said Reliance in a tone of reverent awe as he ran his hand over the rock face, "the geology is all wrong. This is calaverite. It shouldn't be here."

"Where should it be?"

"Calaveras County, the western Sierra. Angel's Camp, specifically. Or Cripple Creek in Colorado. But not in Searchlight. We studied this."

Resolute smiled.

"Did you also study Kalgoorlie?"

"We did."

"Shouldn't have been there, either. But it was."

"That's true."

"How much of the Kalgoorlie story did you study?"

"Just the characteristics of the ore."

"Then you missed the best part."

"Which was?"

"The Australians were prospecting for gold. When they found calaverite, they didn't know what it was."

"Because it shouldn't have been there."

"Precisely."

"What did they think it was?"

"Son, if you were an early hard rock miner, what would you think of a deposit, buttery or brassy colored, that looked like the average citizen's concept of gold."

"That's easy. I'd think it was iron pyrite: fool's gold."

Resolute brushed rock dust out of his hair before he continued.

"And that's what the Australians thought. They used the ore to build houses in Kalgoorlie in 1893. And to patch potholes in the streets. Potholes! It wasn't until years later they realized what they had discovered in 1893. When they did, they tore down the houses, dug up the streets, and processed the ore. It was worth a fortune!"

"And," said Reliance, "It shouldn't have been there," father and son said together, smiling broadly.

"Strange and powerful forces created this world," Resolute said. "I don't think we'll ever understand them."

"And so," said Reliance, "we see what we think we're supposed to see."

"Like fool's gold."

"When did you see clues in the Esmeralda?"

"One day, my foreman tossed me a rock. 'Fool's gold,' he said. I almost threw it away, but I put it in my pocket for some reason. When I got to the surface, I remembered I had it, pulled it out, and studied it in the sunlight."

"And realized it wasn't fool's gold."

"Yes."

"Did you know what it was?"

"I knew about the rich ore they had discovered at Angels Camp in 1893, and I remembered the description. I didn't want it assayed anywhere close to here, so I took it to San Francisco. Figured someone there would have seen Calaverite. Sure enough, they had. Told me my little rock was thirty-four percent gold.

I got out of there quick. Kept looking back over my shoulder. I boarded the train and got off in L.A. I walked around town, checking to see nobody had followed me from San Francisco. Spent the night. Came home the following day and went back down into the mine. Found every tiny fragment of Calaverite I could. There weren't many, and they were all close to that drift. When I had them all, I took them up by the Castle Peaks and threw them away; one at a time and about a mile apart."

"And waited."

"And waited for you to grow up. I needed someone to help me find what I thought might be here. Someone I could trust."

"Father," said Reliance, "you're an unusual man." He waved his hand at the wall of Calaverite. "Weren't you ever tempted by the possibility all this wealth might be down here?"

"No. I told your mother about it, and we agreed we already had more than we needed. But we decided that someday, future Craddocks might need this. And so," Resolute waved his hand at the future embedded in the rock beside him, "we can work this very quietly now that the blasting is done. Our private bank."

"Right," said Reliance. "Break up the ore with hammers. Drop the pieces in hydrochloric acid. The acid will eat away everything but the gold, which will be left behind.

"Just so," replied his father.

"One question?"

"Go ahead."

Reliance paused to collect his thoughts.

"When I was in college, I read a story by a young writer, F.Scott Fitzgerald. The story was, 'The Diamond As Big As The Ritz.'"

"Go on."

"Well, see, in the story, this wealthy family lived on top of a mountain, and the entire mountain was a huge diamond. That's why they were so rich."

Resolute laughed.

"Sounds familiar."

"But the thing was, the family killed anybody who found out about the diamond. Killed them to keep the secret. We're not going to do that, are we, Dad? No matter how valuable this mine is, we're not going to kill anyone who finds out. Right?"

"No, son, we're not; we're just going to try like hell to keep anyone from finding out."

In December of 1928, Reliance was in Boston. It was the last stop of an east coast swing to secrete five-hundred gram gold bars in safe deposit boxes at major banks. He had been making the trips for five years.

Reliance usually made the east coast trips during summer months and those on the west coast in winter, but in 1928 he reversed the geography for the final journey to be in Michigan just before Christmas. There, he would pick up a Ford Model A built at Ford's new Rouge River plant in Dearborn. Resolute had already paid the dealership in Detroit for the car.

Reliance planned to have the car shipped by rail to Goffs. He understood operation the of the transmission in the Model A was very different from the Model T he and his father had driven for years. In addition, roads in the upper Midwest could be treacherous in winter, and Reliance had no intention of driving an unfamiliar car in those conditions.

He was surprised Resolute wanted the newest model. While the Craddocks could afford any car they wanted, Resolute had no desire to call attention to their wealth. They still lived in the kit house Resolute had built years before and drove a used Model T. The "tin lizzie" served them well on the primitive desert roads around Searchlight. Still, Resolute was intrigued with the new Ford.

"If Henry Ford is replacing the 'T' with it," he said, "it must be good."

Resolute himself rarely traveled more than twenty or thirty miles from Searchlight, so it fell to Reliance to go by rail to various banks on both coasts and stash the gold he and his father were surreptitiously mining from the supposedly played-out Esmeralda. The trips made Reliance nervous. There's something about traveling with a reinforced leather, double-locked Gladstone bag packed with fifty, five-hundred-gram gold bars that could make the boldest of men wary. In addition, lugging fifty pounds of gold along with a large suitcase full of clothes was tiring.

Resolute would drive Reliance to Nipton in the flivver. He would park next to the tracks at dusk to await the westbound Union Pacific passenger train or before daylight for the eastbound. Flashing the flivver's headlights signaled that a passenger was waiting to board at the unscheduled stop.

Reliance would allow the conductor or the car attendant to hoist his suitcase into the vestibule but always lifted the Gladstone himself. Nor did he ever at any time allow it out of his sight. In addition, he carried a .38 caliber Smith & Wesson Safety Hammerless with a two-inch barrel in his suit pocket. Anyone trying to separate him from the Gladstone would wind up dead or badly wounded.

Reliance was weary of traveling by the time he arrived in Boston, his final east coast stop. Fortunately, the Gladstone was much lighter than it had been at the beginning of the trip: only five gold bars remained. He walked from the railroad station to the Lenox Hotel, where he had booked his usual end-of-journey suite. After a good meal, Reliance planned to take a leisurely bath and settle down with a good book in front of the corner fireplace. In the morning, he would make his final drop and get back on the train to tend to the matter of the Model A in Detroit.

To save money, Reliance timed the legs of his journey to allow him to sleep in Pullman cars instead of staying in hotels. But on each trip, he indulged himself once. He had ended last year's west coast swing at the newly opened Mark Hopkins in San Francisco. Like the Mark Hopkins, the Lenox was very expensive, but Reliance saw it as a reward for all the travel.

The following morning, refreshed after a quiet evening and a good night's sleep, Reliance paid his bill, left his suitcase at the Lenox for safe-keeping, and stepped out into the cold air of a Back Bay morning carrying the Gladstone containing his final deposit. He walked through Copley Square to the Putnam Massachusetts Bank. Once inside, he signed the register to access the safe-deposit boxes held in his name. He and a respectful bank employee inserted their keys into one of the boxes and pulled it from its slot. The employee then escorted Reliance to a small, private room where he could be alone.

He slid the final five bars inside, waited for a few minutes so it would appear he was examining something, and then signaled for the employee. Reliance carried the box back to its location, and the two men re-inserted their keys and locked it away.

When Reliance came out onto the main floor, he was greeted by Horace Putnam himself. Reliance, already thinking about the next part of his trip, ordinarily would have nodded his head and continued on his way. However, the most beautiful woman he had ever seen was standing with the bank owner.

Reliance stopped.

"A good morning to you, Mr. Putnam," he said.

"Good morning to you, Mr. Craddock. I trust my staff has met your needs."

"Most competently, sir, as usual."

"Good. Mr. Craddock, this is my daughter, Clarice Putnam. Clarice, this is Reliance Craddock from Nevada."

"Ma'am," said Reliance, doffing his hat.

"Mr. Craddock," she said in a melodious voice.

"Clarice is a student at Wellesley College. She'll be graduating in the spring."

With a boldness Reliance had not thought he was capable of, he said, "Miss Putnam, I will be back in Boston early next summer. If your father has no objections, I would like to call on you."

"No objection at all," beamed Horace Putnam, well aware of the size of the account the Craddocks maintained in his bank.

"Since Father has no objection, I can't imagine why I would have one," said Clarice. "I will look forward to your visit. I've always wanted to know someone from the wild west."

"Until then," said Reliance and left the bank.

As he walked back to the Lenox, he thought, *I've just met the woman I'm going to marry.*

When Reliance returned early the following summer, he called on Clarice at the Putnam Mansion, and the courtship began. Clarice was intrigued by this westerner, so serious and so different from the Ivy League boys she knew. When she thought of Nevada, she pictured wild horses galloping through canyons and gleaming white haciendas with red tile roofs staffed by obsequious Mexican servants.

Reliance was besotted. He was so overwhelmed by Clarice's beauty that he could not see past it and so taken with her mellifluous voice that he misinterpreted almost everything she said. He was intimidated by this glamorous young woman. After all, she had graduated from one of the Seven Sisters, while he had only been to the Colorado School of Mines. Reliance had no grasp of how much more intelligent he was than Clarice. Nor did he understand that the content of his character far surpassed that of hers.

Within a week, Reliance had proposed. Within two, Clarice had accepted. Reliance wanted to take her to Nevada to meet his parents, but Clarice held out for one last summer season with her friends at Newport. That should have told Reliance something, but it didn't. Such is the blindness of love. They scheduled their marriage for fall, and Reliance returned home alone.

When the Craddock family traveled east for the wedding, it was the first time Kestrel had been away from the desert. She felt inadequate and out of place among the members of Boston's elite who gathered at Trinity Church on Copley Square for the ceremony. Still, she was by far the most beautiful woman at the ceremony. Her trim body, jet-black hair, and stunning face received many admiring glasses from men, at least until they took in the large, muscular man by her side. Something about Reliance's cold stare made them avert their eyes from his wife.

Clarice's first view of her new home came on the drive from the Union Pacific whistlestop at Nipton to Searchlight. It was a world unlike any she had ever seen and one to which she took an immediate dislike. Legions of what Reliance called Joshua Trees climbed the hills in all directions like battalions of giant crabs with outstretched claws. And as if the strange trees were not bad enough, the town itself was worse. Crumbling shacks, abandoned headframes, and piles of tailings where nothing would grow.

Bleak, thought Clarice.

So good to be home, thought Reliance.

Reliance and Clarice married a little less than a month before Black Thursday, the stock market crash marking the end of the Roaring Twenties and the beginning of the Great Depression. A new Craddock arrived in the middle of that long-lived and cataclysmic event: their daughter, Daryn. But this cygnet born of a socialite swan would grow up a bird of a very different feather: far more akin to her rough and ready grandmother than her delicate mother.

Black Thursday and the Depression that followed did not damage the Craddocks. First, they owned no stock. Second, Resolute had carefully chosen the banks where Reliance had stored the bulk of the family fortune in safe deposit boxes. When the newly-elected President, Franklin Delano Roosevelt, declared a banking holiday on March 6, 1933, Resolute was not concerned.

"They'll re-open," he assured Reliance. His confidence was rewarded when Congress passed the Emergency Banking Act on March 9, 1933, and the banks reopened within a few days.

When FDR signed Executive Order 6192, "forbidding the hoarding of gold coins, gold bullion and gold certificates within the continental United States," Reliance panicked. Resolute did not.

"Son, every speck of our gold is in safe deposit boxes. There is just no way the government is going to go into banks and pry open safe deposit boxes. It's not going to happen."

He was right. The government did not open safe deposit boxes, and the Craddocks kept their gold.

In a way, the Depression benefited the Craddock family. Gold, trading at twenty-six dollars an ounce in the early part of 1933, rose to thirty-five dollars when the President signed Executive Order 6192.

FDR made the Craddocks even richer.

— Chapter 16 —

WOMAN OF THE DESERT MOON
First Sign 1952

*C**larice Craddock*** delivered a second body blow to her daughter Daryn while she was still reeling from the first: the loss of Kestrel Craddock, her grandmother. Daryn had loved the decidedly unladylike woman who had always been willing to scramble over desert hillsides and down desert washes with her. The Craddock family had buried Kestrel in the primitive cemetery in Searchlight only the day before. Clarice hoped her daughter would be less likely to resist what Clarice planned to announce.

She would never have dared to make such a demand when Kestrel was alive. Clarice had been more than a little afraid of her mother-in-law, a woman whose jet black hair, high cheekbones, and slightly Asiatic eyes spoke to a distant ancestor who had crossed the land bridge in the Bering Strait twenty thousand years before.

The only confrontation Clarice had ever risked with Kestrel concerned the construction of Clarice's dream house: a Victorian that harkened back to her youth in the Putnam family mansion in Boston. And even then, Clarice waited until the day after Resolute Craddock had been buried to suggest it.

The grieving widow had offered little resistance. Her only condition had been to leave the kit house she and Resolute had lived in so happily for so many years in place, and though Clarice hated the little house, she acceded. When the Victorian monstrosity was complete, Kestrel had the kit house to herself and lived out the remainder of her life there.

Grief worked for me once, and it will work again, thought Clarice when she and Daryn were seated across from each other in the rarely used parlor, flanked by a baby grand piano no one ever played. Walnut wainscotting extended halfway up the walls of the ornate room. Above that was brocaded silk wallpaper displaying Victorian peacocks against a red, floral background.

The heavy drapes of the brooding building looming above the Esmeralda were drawn against the fierce summer sun Clarice detested. A black ceiling fan turned below the high ceiling but had no perceptible effect on the hot, stale air in the room. It would have been cooler on the porch, but Clarice knew Daryn was more comfortable outside than in, and her goal was to keep her daughter off balance.

How, Clarice had often wondered, had she, the proper daughter of a premiere Boston family, ever brought forth such a wild child? Clarice saw Daryn as two separate versions of a single human being.

The first version was the annoying, boisterous but unintimidating girl who coursed through the Victorian with such boundless energy Clarice feared for her Wedgwood china and fine crystal. That girl scampered up and down the hillsides of Searchlight with the rag-tag children of mining families, ragamuffins who were not allowed in the Victorian but were always welcome in Kestrel's little house for cookies, board games, and radio programs.

It was the second version of Daryn that gave Clarice such pause. The one who would often go silent and squat on the hillside above the Esmeralda for hours on end, staring off at distant mountain ranges where she saw something apparently only she could see. It unnerved Clarice to part the curtains and see Daryn out there, hands on her knees, hour after hour, sphinx-like and utterly self-contained beneath the desert sky.

One such day, Clarice decided to snatch her daughter from her trance-like state. She stepped onto the porch and called Daryn's name. There was no response. Exasperated by what she perceived as disregard or even defiance, Clarice stepped down from the porch and walked toward her daughter, repeatedly calling her name as she strode. Still, no reaction. Irritated, she took two final steps and slapped Daryn on the back of the head.

Daryn rose to her feet in a sinuous motion of such feral rapidity that Clarice could scarcely believe her daughter was face to face with her. Surprise gave way to alarm when the girl dropped into a predatory crouch. At that moment, Clarice thought her daughter might strike her.

"Don't you dare," she had screamed, backing away.

"Don't dare what, mommy?" Daryn asked as she straightened and became the innocent if rambunctious little girl with blue/green eyes. But Clarice was not fooled; she had seen the grisly hidden huntress.

"Never mind," said Clarice over her shoulder as she stumbled back to the safety of the house she saw as an outpost of civilization in a brutal landscape.

Now that she had to summon the courage to confront Daryn again, Clarice knew the day after Kestrel's funeral might be the best chance she would ever get.

Since she wanted to shock her daughter, Clarice told Daryn what she had planned for her when she graduated from high school with no preamble to soften the blow.

"You're sending me east?" her daughter shrieked: the exact reaction Clarice had expected.

Daryn sat back in the ornately carved and upholstered Victorian parlor chair and took a deep breath to regain her composure.

"Why, momma? Why do you want me to send me away?" she asked, struggling to modulate her voice.

"Daryn," Clarice snapped, "how many times do I have to tell you? You are to address me as 'mother,' not 'mommy,' not 'mom,' and certainly not 'momma!'"

Emotion flooded back into Daryn's voice.

"You're turning my life upside down, and you lecture me about proper forms of address?"

"That's part of the reason we're sending you. You have…"

"Wait a minute!"

"Don't interrupt me!"

"Wait a minute! You said 'we.' Has Daddy agreed to this?"

"It's 'father,' not 'daddy.' And yes, Reliance has come around to my way of thinking. Now, don't interrupt me again. That kind of thing

175

is why we're sending you to Miss Perkins' Finishing School. She will smooth your rough edges and provide polish. Make you a lady."

"But, I don't want to be a lady."

"You should. How else are you going to attract the right kind of man from the right kind of family?"

"I already have a boyfriend."

"'Boyfriend,' spat Clarice, "some ruffian from Basic High School in Henderson? Well, let me tell you, Miss Daryn, there's no one there befitting the social status of a Putnam."

"I'm not a Putnam; I'm a Craddock. My Grandfather was a prospector and a hard-rock miner."

"More's the pity, daughter mine. It's a legacy I hope we can shrug off in a generation or two."

"And the money?"

"What of it?"

"Do you want to shrug it off, too?"

"You're talking nonsense! It may not be old money like Putnam money, but it is substantial. It would be foolish in the extreme to turn our backs on such wealth."

"This 'Miss Perkins' place, how long would I have to stay there?"

"Two years. You'll be a day student. You'll live with my sister Margaret. She has an elegant home in the best part of Boston."

"But I'll be home in the summer?"

"Oh, I don't think that would be best, all things considered."

"What things?"

"Daryn, let me put this as delicately as I can. You're a little too, should we say, 'brownish?'"

"Brownish?"

"Yes, brownish. No matter how often I tell you, you refuse to stay out of the sun or even wear a bonnet and a long-sleeved dress. Or any dress at all, for that matter. Bib overalls, that awful t-shirt, and workman's boots, for heaven's sake! By August, you always look positively, positively...."

"Positively what?"

"Well, to refrain from using a less forgiving term, let us say 'Italian.'"

"What's wrong with looking Italian?"

"What's wrong? Italians are swarthy thugs and gangsters. They made their money breaking the law during Prohibition, and now they run Las Vegas. We even have one right here in Searchlight."

"You mean Mr. Martello?"

"'Mister,' my dear Daryn, is reserved for gentlemen, one of which he is most definitely not. He is simply 'Willie.'"

"With his whores."

"Daryn! We do not use that word! The preferred terminology, on those rare occasions when such persons must be spoken of at all, is 'women of ill-repute.'"

"So, I'm not to be allowed to come home in the summer?" asked Daryn as the enormity of what Clarice was saying began to sink in.

"No. Winters in Boston should leach that walnut hue from your skin. Of course, you will spend the summer season at Newport with your Aunt. That's where all the fashionable people go, but I want you to remember to be as covered as you can during daylight hours. A wide-brimmed hat and something with long sleeves should suit, nicely. The addition of a parasol would not be remiss."

"I don't want to go, Momma. Everything I love is here. Father, the desert, Piute Creek, the Castle Mountains, Cottonwood Cove on Lake Mojave."

Clarice noted that Daryn had not included her in the list of things she loved.

"It's 'Mother.'"

"*Mother,* I don't want to live anywhere else. This is my world!"

"That's because you've never been anywhere else."

"Las Vegas."

"Las Vegas! Criminals. Gamblers. Rude tourists. I don't know which are the worst."

"And I've been to Los Angeles."

"Hah! Not even a proper city. A roadside assemblage of buildings sprawled all over."

"All right then, San Francisco."

"Well, I have to admit San Francisco has its points. After all, there are Putnam businesses there."

"There, you see? I have been to other places, but I can never wait to get back home."

"Home? You call this misbegotten, sun-blasted ghost town home?" asked Clarice, irritated by the sweat now coursing down her sides.

"I do."

"Well, I don't. Home is Boston. When I married your father, I thought we would live there. God knows we're rich enough. But no, Reliance had to be here with his father and mother, a pair of penniless nomads who wandered the desert until Resolute struck it rich. Pure luck!"

"And hard work."

"Pure luck! And then Resolute died, and still Reliance would not leave. But now that your Grandmother is gone, there is nothing to hold us here."

"Nothing but me, you mean!"

"And so, I'm hoping we will relocate to the east, to civilization."

Clarice softened her voice.

"But you must go first, Daryn. Learn the social graces. Learn the skills you'll need to attract the right kind of man. Marry him. Make a home. Have children. Our grandchildren. Then perhaps I can pry your father off this hilltop."

Daryn leaned forward, head in her hands, struggling for a coherent argument against her mother and anguished that her father had agreed to this.

Suddenly, she felt a terrible pain behind her right ear, a pain so severe she thought for a moment she had been stung by a wasp. Then, her neck stiffened, as did her right cheek and the area surrounding her right eye. When she tried to blink the discomfort away, her left eye blinked, but her right did not. Alarmed, she tried to close it. It did not respond. It was as if it had disconnected from the rest of her.

In the dim light of the parlor, it looked to Clarice like the right side of Daryn's face was melting.

"What's wrong with you?" she asked.

"I don't know, momma. My face doesn't feel right, and my eye won't close."

"Don't move! I'm going to get your father."

Clarice ran out the door and into the glare of the pitiless sun. She had no doubt where she'd find Reliance; he would be in the old house Resolute had constructed from a kit kicked out of a boxcar when the railroad still came to Searchlight.

Reliance was sitting in Kestrel's favorite chair, face in his hands, almost a parody of the pose Daryn had been in before she was stricken by something unknown.

"Reliance," Clarice shouted. "Come quickly! Something's happened to Daryn."

He was out the door before she was. When they reached the parlor, Daryn was sitting rigidly upright, afraid if she relaxed, whatever had happened to her would get worse.

"Daryn," said Reliance, "what's wrong?"

"I don't know, Daddy. At first, I had this pain behind my ear, and then part of my face went numb. Now my right eye won't close."

Stroke! was Reliance's immediate thought, improbable as that seemed in one as young as Daryn. He knelt on one knee in front of her.

"Sweetheart, I want you to lift both hands over your head at the same time. Can you do that for me?"

She did, with no apparent difficulty.

Reliance turned to look at Clarice, who had collapsed into her chair.

"It's not a stroke. Thank God for that."

He looked at Daryn again.

"You seem to be talking okay."

He turned to Clarice again. "We're going to Las Vegas. Call Dr. Brandt. Tell him we're coming."

"But, it's Saturday," said Clarice, unable to process what was happening.

"Call him at home. Tell him it's an emergency."

Clarice hurried out of the room.

Reliance stood and held out his hands.

"Squeeze my hands, sweetheart. As hard as you can."

She squeezed hard.

That's my girl, thought Reliance, *wiry and tough as ever.*

"Okay," he said, "can you stand up?"

Daryn rose to her feet.

"Keep hold of my hands, and walk with me."

Reliance began to walk backward. Daryn followed.

"I'm going to let go of your hands, okay?

"Okay,"

"Any balance problems at all?"

"None."

"Let me see you walk on your own."

"Walk where?"

"Let's go in the living room and join your mother."

Clarice was on the phone when they got there.

"I don't know, Doctor. It was horrible. Shocking."

"Give me the phone, Clarice," Reliance said, "and take Daryn out to the car."

"But, I'm not dressed for town; I need to touch up my hair and my makeup."

No good in a crisis, thought Reliance, *never has been.*

"Clarice, this is an emergency. Please, take Daryn to the car. I'll be right there."

"But…"

"Now!" commanded Reliance in a tone he had never before used with his wife.

Clarice recoiled as if slapped, but she took Daryn by the arm and steered her toward the door. As mother and daughter walked away, they could hear Reliance talking to Dr. Brandt.

"Not a stroke. No arm weakness. No balance problems. No trouble walking or talking, but one eye won't close, and she says her neck and the side of her face feel stiff. We're on our way. We'll meet you at your office."

When Reliance went outside, his wife and daughter were in the car.

"Clarice," he said as he got in, "trade places with Daryn."

"But I always ride in front."

"Please, Clarice. I need to keep an eye on Daryn."

Clarice got out, and after she and Daryn traded places, Reliance drove their Lincoln Capri down the only cement residential driveway in Searchlight. He turned onto the dirt road leading into town at the bottom of the hill. When they reached Highway 95, he pushed the accelerator to the floor. The V8 roared in response.

Reliance and Clarice watched nervously in Doctor Brandt's office as their family doctor first questioned Daryn and then examined her. When he finished, he turned to them.

"You're right, Reliance; it's not a stroke. Nothing that serious. I have an idea what it might be. We'll know in a moment."

"But Doctor..."Clarice began.

Reliance squeezed her arm.

"Let him work, darling."

The doctor moved to a white cabinet and returned to Daryn holding a cotton swab.

"Daryn, don't be alarmed. I'm going to brush the tip of this swab against your eye, but I'll do it very gently. I promise not to hurt you."

When he touched her eyeball, Daryn did not blink. The doctor turned back to Reliance and Clarice.

"Lack of corneal reflex. That narrows this down considerably. Tell me, did Daryn have rubella as a child?"

"No."

"Flu last winter?"

"No."

"How about mumps?"

"Why yes," said Clarice. "When she was younger."

"That's probably what caused this.

"Caused what?"

"Because of the pain behind her ear, the neck and facial stiffness, and the lack of corneal reflex, I think this is Bell's palsy. Remnants of a virus, probably from the mumps, has lingered in her system all these years. However, with Bell's palsy, in addition to a latent virus, there's usually a triggering event. Some kind of extreme emotional stress."

He turned back to Daryn.

"Did something happen that really, really upset you?"

"We were having..." began Daryn, but before she could finish, Clarice was out of her chair and at her daughter's side. She seized Daryn and hugged her, pressing her daughter's face against her chest. Daryn was so surprised she could not speak: her mother had never hugged her before.

"No, Doctor," said Clarice. "Nothing like that."

"Could it have been the death of her grandmother?" Reliance asked.

"That was last week," said Doctor Brandt. "I'm looking for something more recent."

"We had her graveside service yesterday," said Clarice. "That must have been it."

Daryn tried to pull away, but Clarice hugged her even tighter.

"Well, I suppose that's possible," Doctor Brandt said, "but it would be very unusual. Still, Bell's palsy is a mysterious affliction."

"What's the prognosis?" asked Reliance.

"Good, in most cases. Eighty-five percent of these occurrences resolve with no lingering effects. Generally, time is all that's required."

"How much time, Dr. Brandt, "asked Daryn as she managed to free herself from her mother. "I can't go to school like this!"

"Well, Daryn," said the doctor, that's almost three months away. I think this is a mild episode. You should be fine by then."

— Chapter 17 —

AGAIN

Doctor Brandt was almost **right,** but not one hundred percent. By the time she returned to Basic High School in the fall, minor residual paralysis, nearly undetectable, made Daryn's face just the slightest bit asymmetrical. Oddly enough, that transformed her from merely beautiful to mysteriously stunning.

She discovered that Lenny Vaught, her boyfriend during their sophomore year, had moved away. Lenny's father, a sergeant at Nellis Air Force Base, had been transferred. While Lenny's role as 'boyfriend' had been limited to eating lunch with Daryn and occasionally holding hands, Lenny was a kind boy, and Daryn missed him.

Remembering her mother's inaccurate description of the mild-mannered Lenny as a ruffian, Daryn decided to go all-in on the real deal. She was soon involved with Jason Raucsche, a senior with slicked-back hair who rode a motorcycle and wore a jacket like Marlon Brando's in The Wild One.

Unlike the Triumph 650 twin Brando rode in the movie, Jason's motorcycle was a Harley Davidson 165 cc single-cylinder that developed all of five and a half horsepower. Still, it was a motorcycle, and after a lot of pleading on her part, Jason taught her to drive it. Soon, Daryn was riding desert roads between Henderson and Boulder City, the wind streaming her long, black hair behind her.

Had Clarice known about Jason, she would have been horrified, but Daryn boarded during the week with a Henderson family, the Blakes. Mr. Blake worked for Basic Magnesium Company, whose owners had built Basic High during the war. Since Daryn was always home on time and got good grades, the Blakes had no complaints. They also had no use for her stuck-up mother and might not have reported Daryn's relationship with Jason had they known of it.

But it did not become an issue because Daryn's romance with the louche senior ended before Halloween. One day when they were sitting on a desert hillside, Jason decided that since he let Daryn drive his motorcycle, she should let him reach inside her blouse. Each time he tried, she rebuffed him. Frustrated, he opted for force.

Daryn punched him in the mouth. Cut his lip. He retaliated by slapping her. Hard. When he drew back his hand to hit her again, she snatched the hat pin securing her baseball cap to her long hair and stuck it two inches into his bicep.

Jason screamed and scrambled away.

Daryn lowered her hand and turned it palm up. "Touch me again, and you won't like where I'll stick it."

And that was that.

Daryn worried her confrontation with Jason would bring on another episode of Bell's palsy. As she walked toward town, she stopped and touched her face. No numbness. She blinked her right eye several times, and when it responded without hesitation, she smiled. In a way, she found the whole incident amusing. Especially the look on Jason's face when she stabbed him with the hatpin.

Still, she minutely examined her face in the bathroom mirror when she got home. Nothing had changed, but she wanted reassurance, so she began going to the main library in Las Vegas to read everything she could find about Bell's palsy. She learned it was something that happened to less than thirty out of every one hundred thousand people in the United States. Her reading also confirmed the statistic Dr. Brandt had quoted: Eighty-five percent recover with no lingering issues.

But she also found information he had withheld, probably in hopes of not upsetting her: ten percent of patients suffer partial facial paralysis, and five percent required comprehensive treatment. And, she was horrified to discover, one-half of one-tenth of one percent suffer attacks that affect both sides of their faces, and in one-tenth of one percent of those, both sides of the face remain paralyzed.

Daryn had inherited her father's mathematical abilities, so she knew what a minuscule number that final percentage represented. *Still, she thought, it must happen to someone. The percentage is tiny, but it's not zero.*

Still, her research reassured her sufficiently that she decided she could discuss the Miss Perkins' Finishing School issue with her father without triggering another attack. She went for a long walk with him during Christmas vacation. As they walked the desert they both loved, Reliance assured her that going to Miss Perkins' school did not mean the family would leave Searchlight when she finished.

But Daryn understood her father's relationship with Clarice better than Reliance did himself. After all, she had been watching her parents all her life. She knew Reliance desperately loved Clarice, and she knew Clarice did not love Reliance in equal measure. That disparity made her father subject to manipulation, and there was very little he could refuse Clarice now that Daryn's grandmother and grandfather were gone. Plus, Daryn had no doubt her mother would work on her father during the two years Daryn was gone. She had no doubt Clarice would grind him down.

The question was, what could Daryn do about the situation? *Oh well,* she thought, *I've got a year and a half to think about it. Maybe I can come up with something.*

— **Chapter 18** —

BAD TO WORSE
1953/1954

nsurprisingly for a boomtown that began life as a mining camp on the American frontier, prostitution had a long history in Searchlight. But while the number of ladies of the night had declined with the town's fortunes, that number resurged during construction of the dam that created Lake Mohave. And when it was payday at Nellis Air Force Base, there were so many men in town it seemed as if Searchlight's glory days were back.

Since the world's oldest profession was a significant driver of what remained of the town's economy, businesspeople resisted all efforts by Clark County law enforcement to put an end to it. Officials could not persuade a single resident of Searchlight to file a complaint, and when sheriff's deputies raided a brothel, no prostitutes could be found because the owner had been tipped off. If the deputies posted "closed until further notice" on the door, the notice was torn down as soon as they left town.

The Craddocks lived so far outside town that they were unaffected, and when Clarice arrived and got up on her high horse about the situation, Resolute told her, "It's not our business, so we don't meddle in it." However, like everyone else in Searchlight, Clarice knew where all the bordellos were, and she made sure Daryn never walked near any of them.

But there was no avoiding Willie Martello's El Rey Lodge and Casino on Highway 95 in the center of town. And while Willie was Searchlight's most prominent bordello owner, he did not allow prostitutes, even his own, on the premises. However, all a man had to do was ask a bartender about 'the girls' to get directions to the brothel where they worked.

Daryn was walking past the El Rey the summer before her last year of high school when two drunks came out of the casino headed for the parking lot. One of them let out a wolf-whistle and shouted, "Man, I'd surely like to tap that!"

"Hell yeah," roared his friend," she's a damned sight prettier than any of Willie's whores."

Daryn should have ignored them and kept walking, but her temper got the better of her. She turned toward the men.

"Hey, you ignorant peckerheads," she shouted, "I can hear, you know."

"Come on, little lady," said the one who had whistled. "Don't get your panties in a knot."

"Yeah," said the other, "we were just appreciating the south view while you were going north."

Furious, she stomped toward them. She was going to say, "You're too dumb to live," when she felt that terrible pain behind her right ear, and the words came out, "yah a duh ah wiv." Her neck stiffened, and the right side of her face turned numb. The corner of her mouth turned down. When she tried to close her right eye, it would not cooperate."

"Holy hell," said one of the drunks. "I take it back. Look at that face! You'd have to turn her around and put a bag over her head."

"Yeah," said the other, "and put a bag over your head too, in case hers fell off."

The men laughed and walked away.

Daryn fled for home.

Two hours later, Reliance and Clarice were once again in Doctor Brandt's office, watching as he examined Daryn.

"It's much more serious than the first episode," he said to her when he had finished, "but don't despair. I've read about good results for Bell's palsy with an experimental corticosteroid called prednisone. It seems to return Bell's palsy sufferers to normal much faster. Clinical trials are underway, and I can enroll you in one if your mother and father will permit it."

"Eeeese," Daryn beseeched her parents.

"Anything to help our little girl," Reliance told the doctor.

By the time Daryn started her senior year of high school, the prednisone had eased her symptoms, but only somewhat. Her right eye was now half-mast instead of frozen wide open, but she still had to apply moisturizing drops. Portions of her right cheek were still numb, and there was a pronounced twist to the right corner of her mouth that gave her a look of grimacing disapproval. The Blake family assured Daryn that her symptoms were barely noticeable, but she knew better, and if she temporarily forgot, her classmates were more than willing to remind her.

Some sociologists maintain that the phenomenon known as the American Teenager began during the Great Depression. The median number of years of education achieved by Americans in the Roaring Twenties was eight. Few Americans went on to high school, and "teenagers" were just young workers contributing to their families' economic well-being. Black Friday and the Great Depression changed that. Americans by the millions lost their jobs, the youngest workers first. Suddenly, there were young people in their 'teens, neither employed nor in school.

But the true flowering of the American Teenager began after the Second World War. By the early 1950s, the United States was without equal in the world, militarily and economically. Well-paying jobs were plentiful, and since the maximum tax bracket for millionaires was ninety-eight percent, wealth was more equitably distributed than today. The gap between the upper and middle-classes was much narrower, and middle-class children suddenly had sizeable amounts of disposable income.

The music industry courted them, and Rock 'n Roll was born. The motion picture industry courted them and cranked out movies like Brando's "The Wild One" and James Dean's "Rebel Without a Cause." Youth culture was suddenly a nationwide fixation. Movies like "Blackboard Jungle" helped parents understand their suddenly-sulky adolescents. In that film, Glenn Ford plays the adult who straightens out the miscreants to assure America all would be well. The audience for that movie was middle-aged; teenagers mostly skipped it.

But while teenagers may have rebelled against adults, they conformed like lemmings swarming toward the sea within their own subculture.

Only certain clothes would do. Certain shoes. Certain hairdos. Certain music. Certain movies.

Anyone different was excluded, and Daryn Craddock was suddenly different. Boys who had previously pursued her now looked away when she passed. Girls who had resented her beauty and popularity now got even, whispering and giggling behind her back. Daryn had always been more independent and self-Reliance than other girls at Basic High, but it is a rare teenager who can entirely disregard rejection by peers.

In the second half of her senior year, her symptoms abated further, but strangely enough, Daryn's anxiety increased as her symptoms receded; increased because the time when she would have to leave Searchlight for the east coast was drawing ever nearer. Her trepidation surged when she thought about the possibility of another Bell's palsy episode while she was at Miss Perkins' school. Surely the ridicule from the girls there would be greater than what she had suffered at the hands of students she had known for years.

Her fears came to a head two weeks before graduation. The yearbook staff handed out the 1954 annuals, and seniors gathered during lunch to sign each other's books. A girl who had always resented Daryn took the opportunity to inflict one last wound. Priscilla Gastad wrote, "It's been great knowing you. Best of luck. I hope your face doesn't go all twisted up and ugly again."

Appalled anyone could be so cruel, yet determined not to let Priscilla know how hurt she was, Daryn closed her yearbook and walked silently away. But as she walked, she felt the dreaded first signals of an impending episode. She turned toward the girl's bathroom and picked up her pace. As her face grew numb, she began to run.

Daryn was glad she had the bathroom to herself because she could feel her worst nightmare becoming a reality. She watched in the mirror as her face twisted surrealistically into opposite configurations on each side. Her right eye and the right side of her mouth drooped downward as her left eye and the left side of her mouth twisted upward. And as she watched, drool began leaking from the right corner of her mouth. She tried to maneuver her lips to contain it but could not. It dripped from her mouth onto her blouse, and the spreading stain tipped her over the edge. She began to cry. *I can never, ever let anybody I care about see me drooling all over myself,* she thought.

Daryn moved into one of the stalls and locked the door. *What am I going to do? What did I ever do to deserve to be the one half of one-tenth of one percent?* she thought as she stood there. But Daryn was tough, and the self-pity didn't last long. *Hey! You knew the chances weren't zero. You knew it had to be someone, so snap out of it. Think about what comes next.*

Daryn now understood she had been turning over the possibility that this might happen in the back of her mind for a long time. And yes, she knew what to do, and she would do it. It would be terrible, but she could do terrible! There was no choice else. Convinced the world would recoil from her twisted face, she would act first and absent her face from the world.

She remained locked in the stall until she heard the passing bell. Five minutes later, the tardy bell rang. She waited another ten minutes, then unlocked the door and left. She crossed the campus, throwing her yearbook in the first trash can she saw. She turned her face from every passing car as she walked toward town.

In the Woolworth's five and dime, she picked out a baseball cap, several red handkerchiefs, needles and thread, a package of half-inch elastic fabric, and a pair of scissors. The look on the cashier's face when she paid confirmed the necessity of what she would do next.

Daryn walked to Burkholder Park and sat down with her back against a tree. She cut the handkerchief in half and trimmed two inches off the side. Her hands shook as she stitched the altered piece into the sweatband of the baseball cap and cut two eye holes in the fabric. She fashioned elastic loops, and sewed them to the cloth, then cut another piece of elastic and sewed it together to make a band that fit snugly around her neck.

Daryn clamped the hat firmly on her head, hooked the elastic loops over her ears, and secured the bottom of the handkerchief under the neckband. She stood and began the long walk to the pool hall, where her ex-boyfriend wasted his days before starting his swing shift at Basic Company.

When she got there, Jason's motorcycle was outside. Daryn rolled it into the alley, unscrewed the gas cap, and looked inside. Full. *Well,*

Jason, she thought, *you're not entirely worthless.* Since the Harley operated off a magneto, no ignition key was required. It was awkward wearing a skirt, but she climbed on, stomped the kick-starter, and started it up. She bunched up her skirt, tucked it between her legs, and sat on the excess fabric to keep it from getting caught in the chain.

Daryn drove the little motorcycle to Las Vegas, where she went into the bank where the Craddocks kept their local accounts. When Daryn stepped up to a teller window, the woman was startled.

"Why are you wearing that mask?" she asked. "You're not going to rob me, are you?" She tried to make it sound like a joke, but she looked fearful.

"No. I need to talk to the manager. Tell him Daryn Craddock wants to see him."

"I can't understand what you're saying."

Daryn realized she was slurring her speech. "Can you hand me two pieces of paper and pen?" she asked, speaking very slowly as she pantomimed writing and held up two fingers. When the teller complied, Daryn wrote a note. The woman read it, stepped away from the window, and moved to the rear of the bank. When she returned, Mr. Sleiker was with her.

"Miss Craddock," he said, "can I help you with something?"

Daryn handed him a second note she had written. *Can we go to your office?*

"Certainly, let me get the door for you."

He cleared his throat when he was behind his desk with Daryn seated in front of him.

"Why the mask, Miss Craddock?"

She answered very slowly: "It's not a mask. It's a face covering."

"All righty…care to tell me why you're wearing it."

"No, I don't."

Mr. Sleiker cleared his throat again.

"Miss Craddock, you're slurring your words. Pardon me for asking, but have you been drinking?"

"No. Something wrong with my mouth."

"Ah! Well then, what can I do for you?"

"If you don't understand anything I say, stop me."

"Certainly."

"First, I need five hundred dollars from my account. And second, I need paper, an envelope, and a pen. I'm going to write a note for my father. After I leave, I want you to call him and tell him you have it."

"That's a highly unusual request, Miss Craddock."

"You asked what you could do."

Mr. Sleiker opened his desk drawer and pulled out a legal pad and an envelope. He took a pen from the holder on the desk and handed the items to her.

"Thank you," said Daryn. "I'll write the note while you get my money."

Daryn began writing as the manager walked away.

> *Dear Daddy,*
>
> *I've had another attack. The worst one by far. I look terrible. I don't want anyone to see me. I'm going away, but I will be fine. You know I can take care of myself. You and Grandmother taught me well. I would appreciate it if you would put more money in my account. I will come to the bank to get some now and then.*
>
> *Please, Daddy, don't try to find me! Please! If you do, if I even think you're looking, I'll run far, far away and never come back. And tell Mother she won't have to send me to finishing school now. I'm already finished.*
>
> *I Love you, Daddy*
> *Your Daryn*

When Mr. Sleiker returned with her money, she handed him the sealed envelope with "Reliance Craddock" written on it.

"Mr. Sleiker," she said slowly, "I have told my father that if he thinks you have opened or attempted to open this envelope, he is to move our accounts elsewhere."

The manager looked offended, but he nodded, tight-lipped. When Daryn got up to leave, he asked, "Will I see you again, Miss Craddock?"

"Not if you open that envelope."

Outside, she drove Jason's motorcycle west through the back streets of Las Vegas to the Union Pacific rail line south of town. When she reached the tracks, she turned onto the right-of-way. She wasn't sure exactly where she was going.

Navigating by feel, she thought. *I'll know where I should be when I get there.* That thought brought her to a halt, and she sat on the idling motorcycle. *Then why am I heading south? Why not north toward Mesquite or Caliente? Because something is pulling me south. I have to trust myself. There's nobody else.*

She started off again, frequently stopping to survey the tracks in both directions so she could get off the dirt road if she saw a train coming. She didn't want anyone to see her using the access road as her personal highway.

Two hours later, Daryn reached Nipton. She cut away from the tracks and rode to the little service station.

"Why the hanky over your face?" asked the man who filled her tank and brought her change.

"Allergic to dust," Daryn said. "Allergies make it hard for me to talk right, too."

"Okay. Well, good luck, huh?"

"Thanks."

Daryn waited until he went back into the office before she went through the awkward procedure of starting the Harley and adjusting her skirt.

At the top of the grade, she circled around Cima. It was a spontaneous move, but when she thought about it, she understood she might be nearing her destination and didn't want to be seen by anyone in the area.

The Mojave Desert is vast, making it a perfect place to drop out of sight, but Daryn knew it wouldn't do to enter any of the little towns close to where she might hide. People in out-of-the-way places are curious about strangers, and they ask too many questions, so when Kelso appeared at the bottom of the grade, Daryn left the right of way again. Before she reached Kelbaker Road, she turned again. Crossing two well-established dirt roads, she took the third one because it was partially paved.

The road led her to the deteriorating buildings at the Vulcan Iron Mine. The open-pit mine had made Kelso a World War Two boomtown.

Trains loaded with iron ore had left Kelso every day, bound for the Kaiser Steel Mill in Fontana, California. The steel manufactured there built every U.S. Navy ship launched from the west coast during the war.

But like other desert boomtowns, Kelso had proved as ephemeral as a flash flood. In 1947, the pit at Desert Center went into production, and Vulcan Mine was abandoned. However, the remains of the bunkhouses where most miners had lived were still standing.

Daryn parked the Harley next to a bunkhouse and went looking for water. She walked half a mile to the open pit, and there she found all the water she could ever want. The bottom of the deep crater was an emerald lake. She circled the steep sides until she found the haulage road that spiraled into the pit. The water smelled faintly of sulfur when she reached it, but it was potable.

Daryn walked back to the camp and poked through the abandoned maintenance buildings. She found some rope and a dented Jerrycan. The Jerrycan made her think about fuel requirements. The Harley's 165cc engine could go almost a hundred and fifty miles on two gallons of gas. That was a pretty good range, but it would be best to have more at hand. She carried the can and the rope back to the motorcycle and studied the optimistic metal seat attached to the back fender. Optimistic because the bike was so underpowered it could not carry two people more than five miles an hour. She lashed the Jerrycan to the seat.

Daryn was suddenly exhausted. She was hungry, too, but food could wait until tomorrow. She wheeled the motorcycle into the bunkhouse, tilted it onto the kickstand, and lay down beside it. The room was empty, and it smelled of dust, dried wood, and times long past. Daryn had no blanket, but it was a warm, late-spring night.

She lay, staring at the ceiling, and thought about the strangest day of her life. A day that had started routinely enough but lurched into nightmare. Now, here she was, alone in a place with deserted buildings and sulfurous water. *But I want to be alone. Tomorrow, I'll start looking for a place to hide until I want to be around people again.*

Daryn was still wearing the handcrafted face covering. She took the cap off, set it aside, rolled onto her side, and waited for darkness to descend. She was asleep long before night settled over the abandoned mining camp.

— Chapter 19 —

EXIGENCES AND EXILE

When *Daryn awoke in darkness,* the previous day's events flooded her mind. She sat up. Reviewed everything. Decided she had handled her disappearance well. Felt bad for her father. Thought her mother would be relieved that she was gone.

Time to move. I don't ever want anyone to see me anywhere near here in daylight. Daryn rolled the Harley out of the bunkhouse. The moon, a few nights past third quarter, was angling eastward. Daryn drove out of the camp and turned southeast on a dirt road, the beam of the Harley's inadequate headlight projecting little more than a few feet in front of her.

In less than two miles, the road she was on intersected one that ran due east and west beneath massive metal towers supporting high-voltage lines. Daryn turned east. As the road climbed gradually, darkness began to give way to the first scatterings of morning twilight, and she saw she was in a pass. When she reached the top, she hit the kill button on the motorcycle.

The sun had not yet risen, but precursors of dawn spoked into the sky above the horizon. As Daryn sat there, she heard the crackling of the cooling exhaust pipe and something else: the soft murmur of unintelligible voices. Alarmed, she looked around but could see no one in the dim light.

The top of the sun jutted above the horizon, and the light grew brighter. Still, she saw no one, but as the light increased, the voices diminished. By the time the sun was entirely above the horizon, she could no longer hear them.

Shaken, Daryn sat astride the motorcycle, scanning the surrounding terrain and listening. No people, only rocks, creosote, yuccas, and silence. Daryn sat a while longer, wondering if the unintelligible talk had been her imagination or some horrible new symptom of her Bell's palsy.

She shook her head, re-started the Harley, and drove into the valley below. When the powerline road reached a two-lane blacktop stretching north and south, Daryn crossed it and continued east until she found a dirt road that ran more or less parallel to the paved one.

The road took her to Essex on Route 66. She drove out of the desert and onto the apron of a service station next to the busy highway. A man came out of the office and filled her tank. She handed him a five-dollar bill.

"What's with the mask?" he asked when he brought her change.

"Not a mask," Daryn replied. "It's a face covering. I have bad allergies. Dust makes them act up. Makes my voice weird, too."

"Oh."

"Say, is there a store around here where I could buy some food?"

The man pointed west where 66 climbed a grade.

"Up that way. Chambless General Store. But you're not going to ride that little motorcycle on the highway, are you? Big trucks will blow you right off the road."

"Nope," she said and kicked the Harley to life.

Where'd she come from? the man wondered as he watched her drive into the desert. Then a car came off 66 and pulled under the overhang. He turned away and forgot about the girl with the hanky over her face.

At Chambless General Store, Daryn got sardines, crackers, Vienna sausages, beenie-weenies, a few cans of fruit, a loaf of bread, and a can opener. The old store had clothing, too, but only mens'. She picked up two pairs of the smallest Levi's she could find and two t-shirts.

Daryn answered the usual question about the handkerchief covering her face when she paid for her items. There were gas pumps outside the store, and she had the attendant fill her Jerrycan. *I think this bike can carry another forty pounds; probably wobble all over the place, but I'll just go slow.*

When she paid and answered again the inevitable question with what was now her stock answer, she asked the man if he had a bag of some kind. He held up one finger and went inside to get her change. When he came out with it, he handed her a burlap sack.

"How much do I owe you?" she asked as clearly as she could.

"No charge, miss. And good luck with them allergies. My momma used to suffer something terrible with 'em."

Daryn put her purchases in the sack and tied it in a loose knot. She started the bike, looped the bag over the left handlebar, and wobbled off down a dirt road into the desert. Stopping a few miles from the station, Daryn looked around to be sure she was completely alone. Satisfied, she unknotted the burlap sack and removed a pair of Levi's.

She took off her skirt, tossed it away, and put on the pants. They were stiff and way too big, but at least she wouldn't have to bunch them up between her legs every time she drove. They were too long, so she rolled the cuffs. With both hands, she pulled one knee at a time toward her chest a few times until the fabric felt less like cardboard.

She climbed back on the Harley, wrapped the sack around the handlebars again, and set off, abandoning her skirt.

Later that day, a dust devil spinning across the landscape snatched up the skirt and twisted it high and away into the deep blue sky of a desert spring day. The dust devil dissipated miles from where it had picked up the garment. The skirt fluttered to the ground. There was no one there to see it land.

— Chapter 20 —

THE SEARCH

Daryn *had thousands of square miles* of desert to explore. Because she had decided she never wanted to be seen close to where she slept, she was always well away from the Providence before first light. Also, there were those voices. Whenever she came to the top of the pass between the north and south Providence, she stopped to hear them. Since they faded with the coming of first light, she arrived earlier and earlier to sit and listen. Soon, it was clear the voices were not in the world around her but in her head. She had no idea what they were saying, but she loved to listen because they seemed to forge a connection between her and the mountains.

When she had driven to an area she wanted to explore, she left the Harley beneath a cut bank, next to a stand of catclaw or under a juniper, and set off on foot. In late afternoon, she drove her motorcycle to one of the service stations strung out along the Mother Road between Ludlow on the west and Mountain Pass on the east: Siberia, Bagdad, Amboy, Chambless, Danby, and Essex.

Highway 66 was always busy, and the constant flow of travelers granted Daryn a certain anonymity. She was doing her best to be forgettable despite the face covering. She had cut her hair to within a few inches of her scalp so it did not stick out from under her cap, and her oversized Levi's and baggy t-shirt rendered her sexless. Because she did not draw as many curious stares in poor light, she timed her arrivals for dusk when visibility was worst: daylight fading to purple, but the lights above the pumps not yet on. Adding other stations in out-of-the-way places like Goffs and Rice to the ones on 66 made it easy to avoid going to the same station twice in the same week.

Daryn traversed the open desert on remote two-tracks, always watching for dust that signaled another vehicle. She rarely saw another human being as she visited the Granite Mountains, the Old Woman Mountains, the Clippers, the Bristols, the Old Dads, the Marls, the Turtles, and the Stepladders, and no one ever got close to her.

She returned to Vulcan Mine well after sundown, parked the motorcycle inside the bunkhouse, and fell asleep beside it. Long before the next dawn, she was up and on her way again.

Month after month, she searched for Goldilocks locations: ranges where she might find a spring and profound isolation. She discovered many such places, but none seemed exactly right, so she continued to explore. Daryn wasn't sure exactly what she was looking for, but she was sure she would know it when she found it.

From time to time, Daryn had to replenish her supply of cash and find items she could not buy at gas stations. On those occasions, she drove the Union Pacific right of way to Las Vegas, timing her trip to arrive when the bank opened. The tellers were used to her and would summon Mr. Sleiker. He would escort her to his office, get her the cash she wanted, and give her the latest letter from her father.

Reliance's message was always the same: Please, come home. We miss you. We're worried about you. The responses Daryn left for him were equally repetitive: I'm fine. Don't worry about me. I don't know when I'm coming back.

On one of her visits, she gave Mr. Sleiker the license number of the Harley and asked him to find the name and address of the owner. He had the information for her on her next trip. She had him stamp and address an envelope for her because she was afraid Jason might recognize her writing. She withdrew an extra five hundred dollars from her account and sealed it inside. The amount was more than twice what Jason had paid for the Harley. On her way out of town, she dropped the envelope in a mailbox.

By late October of 1954, Daryn had crisscrossed the Mojave for five months. One morning, she was feverish and decided to stay in the bunkhouse and rest. She was asleep in the late afternoon when she awoke to gunfire. Familiar with guns, she could distinguish between the sounds of rifles, pistols, and shotguns. These were shotguns.

Quail, she thought. *Quail season has opened.*

But when she heard more shots, they were followed by the sound of breaking glass.

Frustrated hunters? Hunted all day with nothing to show for it? Taking it out on a bunch of old buildings? Nobody here to tell them they can't?

More shots. More breaking glass. The sounds were coming closer.

Don't want to be here if they shoot into this building!

She clamped on her hat. Got to her feet and eased the door open. Got the Harley off its kickstand. Started it. Revved it hard. Flew out the door.

There was but one route from the mining camp to the road, and five teenage boys were walking down the middle of it. She drove right at them.

"What the hell?" one yelled as they scattered.

About a mile from where Vulcan Mine Road intersected Kelbaker, Daryn came upon two pickups parked on the shoulder. She stopped. California plates on both trucks.

Probably from Smoke Tree.

'Well, boys," she said aloud, "you like vandalism? Here's some for you."

She let all the air out of the front tires on both trucks, climbed back on the Harley, and cut north across the open desert. She passed the first road she always crossed on her way to the Union Pacific right of way, but at the second, she paused and sat there, engine idling.

Trust your instincts, she thought, and turned southeast on the road. It climbed toward the north end of the Providence range. Partway up the hill, she crossed another powerline access road. Soon after that, she began seeing sections of pipe washed out of the ground by flash floods.

After four miles, Daryn reached a corral. She crossed the wash below, navigating around a series of big rocks. Beyond the wash, the road climbed straight up a steep embankment.

No reason to mess with that. She shut down the Harley and clambered up the embankment. On top, she found a good road. Rabbitbrush bloomed dusty and golden along both sides. The road ended at an above-ground pipeline, and Daryn heard a sound welcome to any desert traveler: running water.

She climbed toward the sound and found ponds formed by water flowing slowly across mossy stones. Desert willow crowded the edges of the pools. A trail between the pipeline and the creek led upward, and Daryn followed it to the water source for the stream. The area around the spring was dense with catclaw and desert willow.

To the east lay a huge canyon Daryn knew she would explore someday, but she decided to turn back down the pipeline trail for now.

Trust your instincts.

Down the hill, and west of the road, she found a short copper tunnel carved into the face of a cliff. She stepped cautiously inside, wary of snakes. When her eyes adjusted to the dim light, she saw the copper-bearing ore had only extended a short distance into the hillside, and the miners who had created the tunnel had abandoned their efforts. She studied the evacuation left behind.

This place could be something.

A single word floated into her mind.

Home!

Daryn relocated to the cave. She now ventured outside only at night and was back in her cave before first light eased into the sky. The remainder of October and most of November, she scrounged materials from the buildings at Vulcan mine and ferried them piece by piece to her new quarters.

Her first creation was a massive wooden door she assembled piece by piece, using wood screws and a hand drill from the maintenance sheds. There was no way to hinge the door into the solid rockface. Still, while Daryn had inherited her grandmother's fierceness, she had also been blessed with engineering and problem-solving skills from her father. She affixed scrounged metal brackets to the inside of the door. Iron bars inside the framework could be drawn behind rocks inside the tunnel to secure the door from within. It was laborious work, and she was exhausted at the end of each night, but she enjoyed the task. Daryn Craddock was creating a sanctuary where she could be safe from prying eyes.

Daryn outfitted the interior of her new home with makeshift tables and chairs. She was well aware of the oncoming winter; she made several trips to Las Vegas to bring back a sleeping bag, a cot, and several pieces of winter clothing from the Army surplus store.

Once her sanctuary was complete, Daryn drove to Las Vegas so infrequently she often had several letters from Reliance when she went to the bank. She always read them in the manager's office so she could write a reply before she left. On one visit, there was also a letter from her mother.

> *Daryn,*
>   *You are a selfish and cruel girl. You have ruined my life. Your father will never leave Searchlight now. Thanks to you, I will live out my existence in this flyspeck excuse for a town. I hope you're happy.*
>
>   *Mother*

Daryn read the letters from her father and responded to each of them, but not to her mother's. Why bother? When she returned to her mountainside, she added her father's letters to the ones he had previously written, then lit an oil lamp and reread them in order. They were filled with love and without recrimination.

She reread the letter from her mother. Then she burned it.

There was so much to explore near Daryn's new home. When the moon was full or nearly full, she hiked the dangerous places: steep canyons and cliffsides with unstable footing where a stumble could end in death.

One such night, she was resting near Cornfield Spring when a mountain lion emerged from the desert willows and stood not far from her, tail twitching, eyes glowing yellow in the moonlight. She and the big cat stared at one another for a long time. Daryn should have been afraid, but she wasn't. After what seemed like hours, the animal turned in one sinuous motion and moved away, muscles rippling beneath its tawny hide.

"Come back," Daryn wanted to say. "Come back, I want to talk to you; there's so much I don't know," but the words stuck in her throat, and the mountain lion faded into the willows as silently as it had appeared.

Under a full moon another night, Daryn entered the canyon to the west of Cornfield Springs, intent on climbing the highest peak in the Providence. She soon found herself boxed in by sheer cliffs thousands of feet high. Clearly, only a skilled mountaineer with good equipment could scale them. Daryn turned back.

Two nights later, she dropped partway down the aqueduct road and hiked eastward until she hit the remains of an old mining road into Globe Canyon. Daryn took the road to Summit Spring and entered Barber Canyon. It was hard going, and the canyon walls soon blocked the moonlight. Afraid she would plunge to her death in the darkness, she turned back, but at least she had found a way to climb Edgar Peak.

Another time, Daryn thought, *when I'm feeling more courageous.*

On moonless nights when the steep hillsides were too dangerous, Daryn often walked down the aqueduct road far beyond the corral to watch the Union Pacific trains thundering down the hill to Kelso or laboring up the grade toward Cima, diesel engines thrumming. She loved to hear them blow for the crossings at Kelbaker and Cedar Canyon roads, especially on cold, winter nights when the sound rolled away across the valley on all sides before being swallowed in solitude.

Sometimes, Daryn hiked east all night to reach Round Valley before daylight. She loved the valley, so much beauty sandwiched between the Pintos and Table Top. Daryn thought it would be a lovely place for a town but was so glad there wasn't one. She didn't go there as often as she liked because she couldn't get there and back before sunrise. That meant she had to find a place to go to ground for the daylight hours, and being outside absent the cover of darkness made her so nervous she couldn't sleep. She was always exhausted when she returned to her cave, two long nights and one sleepless day later.

On one occasion, Daryn was hidden in a narrow declivity between giant boulders in the Mid Hills after hiking all night. As usual, her unease made it impossible to sleep, and as she waited for sundown to return home, she heard the sound of a horse below. Cautiously easing forward, she peered between the boulders and saw a beautiful Asian woman riding the flanks of the Pinto Mountains.

The rider passed not far from her hiding place, and Daryn was amazed by the similarity of the slight woman to her Grandmother, Kestrel. The same jet-black hair. The same high cheekbones. Kestrel's skin had been darker than the rider's, and her eyes not angled upward as much, but the resemblance was uncanny. Intrigued, Daryn risked more trips to Round Valley but never saw the Asian woman again. Once, however, she saw a man riding the same horse. He was older, but Daryn wondered if he were the beautiful woman's husband. Because he had a kind face, it pleased her to think so.

One early-fall morning, not long after Daryn had returned to her cave, she heard the echo of a rifle shot from the box canyon to the east. *Deer hunter! May the wind spoil your aim! May sand file the rifling from your barrel! May the deer disappear into the junipers before you can get off another shot!*

In her early years near Cornfield Spring, that was the only time Daryn ever heard hunters. It was the only time she heard anyone at all. When she zipped herself into her Army surplus sub-zero mummy bag and pulled the drawcord hood tight around her head after a long, cold night outside, she often thought to herself, *Inconvenience and isolation are my shields.*

Some mornings as she lay on the cot, the same coyote pack that had awoken her in the early evening serenaded the canyon as it ended its night hunt. Those mornings, she was satisfied with her life. Other times, she was so lonely she didn't think she could stay another day, but that feeling always passed.

It was the desert that held her. The emptiness stretching away on all sides was its own reward, even if frightening in its immensity. The simultaneously wonderful yet terrible isolation. Mile after countless mile of nothing but creosote, white bursage, and matchweed; drainage upon drainage trending away from brown mountains. The myriad stars on a winter night. Soft light coming into the sky summer mornings; sunsets burning purple, bronze, and gold on summer evenings. The joy of being happy with the little she had. The satisfaction of knowing she could make do with even less. The confidence that came from relying on no one but herself.

As the years slipped by, the nights walking the canyons, hillsides, and arroyos wove a blanket of engulfing solitude for Daryn. And yet, some of those nights, she got the distinct feeling someone was watching her. Daryn wrote it off to her encounter with the mountain lion. The way it had soundlessly appeared and stared silently at her, evaluating her for reasons of its own. She knew she would never have seen the big cat if it hadn't wanted to be seen. Perhaps it watched her still.

She also wondered if the feeling of being observed had anything to do with the voices. The voices she had first heard on the pre-dawn mornings at the top of the pass between the central and south Providence. Those voices had now followed her home, and she heard them every night. She had been hearing them for so long she recognized some of the words, even though she had no idea what they meant: *ope̍mp, paegenau, ju'nakem, iisu, 'paa, inigapic, ni-wa, i-nip, na̍nc, mu'ru, ha'wiv,* and, most often, *nu'nosi.*

— Chapter 21 —

LAST LINK SEVERED

By May 1959, Daryn had been living a life of isolation for five years. It was apparent from Reliance's letters across those years that he had never given up hope that she would return home. Whenever she drove her motorcycle to the bank, Mr. Sleiker had letters for her. Their theme was similar to those of the first few years: I miss you. I love you. Please, dearest Daryn, come home. But in May, Daryn detected a shift. The messages became more urgent, and that worried her. Was his health failing? Did he think was he was running out of time?

Daryn was well aware her father had long lived a life divided. The two people he loved most disliked each other, and he had always been the fulcrum on which their feelings about each other balanced. It was an awkward circumstance.

Clarice thought of herself as a Putnam and had always resented the Craddocks. Regarded them as inferiors. Thought Resolute a tight-fisted old miser and Kestrel the closest thing to a savage. Thought them worthy of neither love nor respect and therefore resented Reliance for loving and respecting them.

And then, Daryn, the Craddock Clarice resented most of all, was born. Such a strange child. Dark skin but blue/green eyes. Wild as a March hare. Fierce as a lynx. Exasperating at her best; frightening at her worst.

Of course, all this was Reliance's fault. If only he hadn't stopped to speak to her father that long-ago morning in Boston! Of course, she had to admit, her father bore some responsibility. He had been so impressed with the balance in the Craddock family's account. He was so eager to marry off his last remaining daughter and be done with the appalling business of marriages and their extravagant expense.

In her darkest moments, Clarice even admitted a certain amount of responsibility. She had misjudged Reliance. He had been so taken with her she was sure she could bend him any way that suited her needs. But she was wrong. He was as strong as his father, that flinty hard-rock miner, and his mother, the steely woman who had intimidated Clarice from the moment they met.

For her part, Daryn neither loved nor hated her mother but understood Clarice no better than Clarice understood her. When Daryn was very young, her mother had tried to shape her into a proper young girl but soon became frustrated and abandoned the effort. At that point, mother and daughter entered into an uneasy truce which entailed keeping one another at arm's length.

Then came the meeting in the parlor the day after Kestrel's burial next to Resolute in the shabby Searchlight cemetery; Clarice's attempt to strike at Daryn when her daughter's resistance would be at its lowest. Daryn's angry reaction, followed by her first bout with Bell's palsy. Clarice always thought Daryn blamed her for the attack, even though Daryn never said so. A second episode followed, worse than the first, and then the worst one of all. Daryn fled into the hidden reaches of the Mojave Desert, leaving Clarice imprisoned in Searchlight, a place she detested, and leaving Reliance more conflicted than ever about where his loyalties lay.

Reliance loved Clarice, but what kind of a father would he be if he didn't try to bring his only child home? He missed Daryn so much he sometimes slept in the little house his father had built because he felt closer to her there; she had loved her grandmother so. The conflict threatened to tear him apart, and he intensified his efforts to reunite his family. It was a delicate balance, trying to pull Daryn toward him without forcing Clarice away.

By mid-summer, Daryn's concern for her father was eroding her determination never to be seen again. But, she was still deterred by an experience in 1957, three years after she had turned her back on the world. Curious to see how she would feel around people again, she traveled to Las Vegas on Halloween. Putting on a mask that covered her face completely, she mingled with the throngs on Freemont Street. It did not go well. Accustomed to solitude, the crowds alarmed her. Used to silence, she found the raucous laugher and screams of the revelers invasive. Attuned to the comforting darkness of desert nights, she found the flashing neon lights jarring and offensive.

Determined to get away, she had forced her way through the throngs. Three drunken young men stopped her. One pulled off her mask, yelling, "Come on, sweetheart, gimme a kiss!" followed by, "Oh my God! Put it back on!" That settled any question about whether she would ever willingly allow others to see her face.

So, the prospect of returning to Searchlight gave her pause. What would life be like there? Maybe she could live in the attic, like that poet lady from New England, only talking to people through the door. If Clarice had her way, Daryn would be relegated to the mine, and Reliance forced to lower her meals in a bucket!

However, Daryn thought there might be a safe way to get together with her father for a conversation. Perhaps they could meet in Mr. Sleiker's office at the bank. That way, Daryn could assess Reliance's health. If indeed it were failing, maybe they could work out agreeable conditions under which Daryn could return home until his health improved. The more she walked and thought about it, the more confident she became about the strategy.

In August, convinced she had a solution to the dilemma, she rode to Las Vegas to pen a note to her father. When she walked into the bank, the teller she approached gave her a look Daryn could not interpret before going for the manager.

It was a distressed Mr. Sleiker who escorted her to his office.

"What?" she asked when the manager did not speak after they were both seated.

"Your mother and father,"…Mr. Sleiker paused, unable to go on.

"Yes?" she prompted.

"They're…gone, Daryn."

"They went back east?"

"No. They died. In a plane crash." Mr. Sleiker struggled to find the right words. He couldn't and settled for 'they're gone," again.

Do not cry, she told herself as she fought to maintain her composure. "An airliner?"

"No. They had their own airplane."

Daryn dug her fingernails into her palms and bit down on her lower lip to keep from losing control.

"I didn't know that."

"Your father didn't want you to know. He was afraid you would think he was searching for you."

That opened the floodgates, and when Daryn started crying, she couldn't stop. She put her hands over the cloth that covered her face and sobbed, shoulders heaving.

Mr. Streiker came around his desk and stood beside her. He lifted his hand as if to rest it on her shoulder but then let it fall. Unsure of what to do, he simply stood next to her until she stopped crying. When she did, he returned to his chair.

"What," she choked out and stopped again. "Please, Mr. Sleiker, tell me everything you know about what happened."

"Well," he began, "as I said, your father owned a plane...."

As the years following Daryn's disappearance rolled by, Clarice Craddock had grown increasingly irrational. The entire concept of loving a child more than oneself was alien to her. It infuriated her that Reliance would not leave Searchlight for more than two or three days because Daryn might need his help. Clarice didn't care if she ever saw her daughter again and secretly wished the girl would just die and free her from her Searchlight purgatory.

In the first years after Daryn's disappearance, Clarice had traveled to Boston alone a few times to visit friends and family. Each trip, the questions about why Reliance was not with her grew more pointed. She briefly considered divorce, but divorce was simply unacceptable among the staunchly Episcopalian members of Boston's Back Bay elite, and since keeping up appearances was almost as important to her as breathing, she stopped visiting.

With divorce and travel to Boston out of the question, Clarice began demanding excursions to expensive vacation spots close to home. Even there, she was somewhat stymied. Three was the maximum number of days Reliance would remain away from Searchlight, and it took most of a day to drive to La Jolla or Corona Del Mar or Santa Barbara. That left only one day at a resort before they had to return home.

Clarice suggested a private airplane. Reliance was amenable. He remembered when John Macready, son of Benjamin Macready, superintendent of the Duplex Mine, had joined the U.S. Army Air Service during the First World War. Reliance had wanted to join and learn to fly, too, but the war ended before he was old enough. Also, Willie Martello, the infamous El Rey Club owner, built an airfield in Searchlight to bring gambling junkets to town, and there was hangar space available. Reliance took flying lessons in Las Vegas and got his pilot's license. He bought a Cessna Skyhawk, and the places Clarice liked to go were now only a few hours away.

On an August morning in 1959, the temperature in Searchlight began to rise. By mid-afternoon, it was unbearable. Clarice called resorts from San Diego to Morro Bay, but the searing heat had spread from the desert to all of Southern California. Everyone wanted to go to the ocean for relief. Every one of Clarice's favorite places was packed. Desperate, she called a lodge in Big Bear. Surely, it would be cooler high in the mountains. There was only one room left, and she booked it.

Early the next morning, Reliance and Clarice flew to the mountain town. The temperature there was a relief after the terrible heat of the desert. However, the following day the heatwave climbed into even the highest elevations of the San Bernardino Mountains. After lunch, Clarice sat fanning herself on the veranda. Capricious as ever, she suddenly proclaimed, "This is nothing like the coast, and now that terrible heat has followed us. If I'm going to be miserable, I might as well be miserable in my own house. Take me home!"

It was ninety degrees by the time they packed and got to the airport. Reliance, who had never taken off from Big Bear before, neglected to take the physics involved into account. Ninety-two degrees at sixty-seven hundred feet creates an air-density altitude equal to ten thousand, three-hundred feet. Lower air density equals less lift beneath the wings, equals longer to get airborne, and slower to climb.

The Cessna used most of the runway taking off, and once in the air, it felt sluggish and unresponsive. They were in danger of not clearing Big Bear Dam. Alarmed, Reliance pulled back too hard on the yoke. The Cessna stalled, rolled to the left, and plunged into the forest. Reliance and Clarice died instantly.

When Mr. Sleiker finished his narrative, Daryn broke down again. The rag covering her face was saturated with her tears, and saliva dripped from beneath it onto her baggy, olive drab t-shirt. Once again, the bank manager waited patiently for her to regain control.

"I'm so sorry, Miss Craddock," he began, but she burst into tears a third time. This time, the sobs subsided more quickly.

"Daryn,… that is, Miss Craddock, there are matters to attend to. Years ago, your father gave the name of an attorney who was to probate his estate if he and your mother…," there was a catch in his voice, and it took him a moment to continue, "if he and your mother were to, were to…perish, at the same time."

Daryn pulled her hands away from her face. Mr. Steiker could see little more than the pupils of her eyes through the off-kilter slits in the wet cloth.

"That can wait," she said.

"I thought you might say that," he nodded, "but there is something that cannot."

Mr. Steiker withdrew an envelope from his desk drawer and pushed it across the blotter on his desk. *Daryn* was written on it in Reliance's hand.

"Your father said to tell you that you must open this envelope before you leave the bank."

Daryn stood, picked up the envelope, and crammed it into the pocket of her Army surplus field trousers.

"No. I'll read it later. '

"Please, Miss Craddock. Your father made me promise. I gave him my word."

She hesitated, then sat down, retrieved the envelope, and opened it. Inside were a key and a letter. She set the key on the desk and unfolded the letter.

> *My dearest Daryn,*
>
> *If you're reading this, your mother and I are both gone. I know this will be hard for you, and you won't want to deal with everything right now. That's to be expected. The probate can wait, but what you must do right now cannot.*
>
> *The key opens my safe deposit box. Mr. Streiker has a notarized letter granting you access. Inside, you will find the original of my will. Also, there is a wooden box. It contains keys and a note. Read the note. It will explain what you are to do next.*
>
> *Daryn, you are the best daughter a man could ask for, but PLEASE, my dearest daughter, honor your father's wishes and DO THIS TODAY!*
>
> *All My Love,*
> *Daddy*

By the time Daryn finished reading the letter, she was crying again. Mr. Streiker gave her more time before he spoke.

"Miss Craddock, I don't know what that letter says. However, your father told me it is imperative you follow his instructions before you leave here today."

Daryn nodded.

"Please, come with me."

In the safe-deposit vault, Dayn and Mr. Sleiker inserted and turned their keys. Mr. Sleiker removed the metal box, handed it to Daryn, and escorted her to a private room.

"Push the button when you're done, Miss Craddock," he said as he left her there.

She saw the wooden box and a bound document titled Last Will and Testament when she lifted the lid. Inside the wooden box were keys, two passbooks, and two folded letters: one had "read first" written on it.

Daryn,

Thank you for doing as I asked. Read this note carefully and follow the instructions.

First, as to the passbooks. They are for the accounts at this bank: one checking and one saving. The savings account contains a very substantial sum. The money is yours to do with as you wish, but you will have to pay estate taxes on the combined amount. More on that later in this note.

The keys in the wooden box open safe deposit boxes in various banks on the east and west coasts. There are twenty-three keys in all. The other paper is a list of the numbers on the keys and the addresses of the banks holding the boxes the keys will open. I have added you as a signatory for each box.

Each box contains gold bars. Someday, it will again be legal for Americans to own gold. Leave the gold where it is until that day arrives. I would also suggest you leave the gold in place for at least one additional year from that date to allow it to attain a price expressing its intrinsic value.

Second, do not tell anybody about the gold! Specifically, do not mention it to the lawyer who probates the estate. Your grandfather and I mined every ounce of that gold from our mine, and there is no reason for you to pay estate taxes on it!

Third, as to the probate, Mr. Sleiker has the name and address of the lawyer who will handle the estate. He has a copy of the will. You now have the original. When you are ready to visit the lawyer, Mr. Sleiker will accompany you. He is a good man and has my trust. He will watch out for your interests.

Last, I have provided Mr. Sleiker sufficient funds to handle our burial arrangements. That task should not fall to you. Your mother's body is to be returned to Boston, where she will be buried in the Putnam family vault. Bury me next to my mother and father in Searchlight so you can visit us from time to time because I know the desert will always be your home.

Daryn, this will be a terrible time for you, but take heart. You are strong, and I know you will persevere.

With All My Love,
Daddy

Daryn put everything back in the metal box. She sat in the private room for a long time, lost in sorrow, before she pushed the button to summon Mr. Sleiker. An anguished Daryn Craddock drove the right-of-way to Kelso that night. When she was back in her cave, she lay on her cot and cried until she was hoarse. "Oh, Daddy," she wailed aloud, "I should have reached out when I first noticed the change in your letters, but I was too wrapped up in myself. Now I've lost you forever."

— Chapter 22 —

ONWARD AND UPWARD

For five months, *a brutal chisel of toxic grief* chipped away at the foundation of Daryn's sanity as she struggled with the death of her father. The appalling finality of it. The undeniable truth that she would never see his smile again. Never see his beautiful blue/green eyes. Never hug him again. Sometimes she screamed in anger at the unfairness of it. Sometimes, coyotes howled in response from the hillsides around her.

Most people dealing with such terrible loss have family or friends to help them cope. Daryn had no one. Self-sufficiency is a remarkable trait, but it has limits. Just when it seemed she might drift into unrecoverable madness, Daryn awoke one cold, windy evening at the end of January, thinking about her failed attempt to climb Edgar Peak. *Perhaps climbing the peak is something I have to do.*

Hopeful for the first time since her father's death, Daryn buttoned the wool liner into her field jacket. She picked up her most prized piece of cold-weather gear, an army surplus World War Two overcoat made of Melton wool, and stepped out into the bitter cold beneath a full moon.

Long after midnight, she reached the point where she had faltered on her first attempt. As before, the steep canyon blocked the moonlight, making the merely treacherous footing completely impossible. But this time, Daryn did not turn back. Instead, she wrapped herself in her overcoat and huddled beneath a pinyon pine to await the dawn. It was the longest night of her life. The temperature dropped to twenty degrees below freezing. The terrible sand-and-grit-filled wind howling out of the north seemed intent on scouring her from the canyon wall.

For a long time, Daryn heard only the wind. But just when she thought she could bear the cold no longer, she detected a sub-text. It was the voices. Voices speaking words she recognized, in a language she could not understand But for the first time, she thought she understood what they were telling her. It was similar to the words her father had written. Shivering, she muttered the words over and over for the rest of the night: *Take heart. You are strong. You will persevere.*

The pale winter sun finally rose through a thin scrim of clouds shredding in the wind. It was the first time Daryn had been outside so close to her cave in daylight. However, she reasoned, she was in a place so treacherously inaccessible there was no chance of anyone seeing her.

Even in daylight, the task before her was daunting. She weighed down her overcoat with rocks and left it beneath the pinyon before beginning the treacherous scramble up the eastern flank of the mountain. Dense thickets of cactus and rugged rock outcroppings often brought her to dead ends. When that happened, she had to retrace her footsteps and seek a different path, and moving downhill was more dangerous than climbing. One misstep in the loose rock could send her cartwheeling into the ravines below.

The climb from where she had clung to the canyon wall overnight to the summit of Edgar Peak was less than two miles, but it involved an altitude gain of two thousand feet. During one challenging section, she heard a noise above and looked up to see a desert bighorn sheep moving so effortlessly across the mountainside it looked like it was floating. She had often seen their scat, but since she was out only at night, this was the first time she had seen one of the magnificent animals.

I wish I could climb like that! It took Daryn four hours to cover the distance, and she was trembling with exhaustion when she reached the top.

But what a reward! The clouds had dissipated. It was freezing but clear, and blessing heaped upon blessing, the wind stopped. Below were Wild Horse Mesa and the turrets and caverns of Hole-in-the-Wall. Beyond there lay the Piutes, and then Avi Kwa'ame in Nevada, sacred to the Mojave.

Farther to the east were the Black Mountains in Arizona. To the north, the New York Mountains, and well beyond them, the snow-covered peak of Mount Charleston outside Las Vegas. Far to the northwest, the hazy outline of Telescope Peak high above Death Valley, and to the west, Mount San Gorgonio in the San Bernardino Mountains and Mount San Jacinto above Palm Springs.

Lines from a poem her high school English teacher had read in class came to her: "Boundless and bare, the lone level sands stretch far away."

Daryn turned circle after circle, taking it all in, acceptance in her heart for the first time since learning of her father's death. *Thank you, father. I have persevered. I am atop my world! You and the voices led me here. Now I know I can go on.*

When a teller summoned Mr. Sleiker from his office, he said, "It's been a long time, Miss Craddock."

"It has."

"Are you ready to visit the lawyer?"

"Yes."

When Daryn and Mr. Sleiker were seated in front of Vester Ernswhile's desk, the lawyer said, "Before we begin our discussion of the probate procedure, I have two questions. First, Miss Craddock, why is your face covered?"

"None of your business."

"Well, that's an inauspicious beginning, but I won't press the issue. The second question is for Mr. Sleiker. Why are you here?"

"I promised Reliance Craddock I would accompany his daughter to this meeting. I have the notarized letter delineating his request if you'd like to see it."

Mr. Sleiker reached for the inside pocket of his suit.

"That won't be necessary," said the attorney. "Are you to be compensated for your assistance?"

"No. This is a favor to a man I admired and respected."

Vester Ernswhile turned his attention to Daryn.

"Miss Craddock, I assume you have the original of your father's will."

"I do," she said and handed him the bound document.

"Give me a moment, please."

Daryn and Mr. Streiker sat silently as the lawyer scanned the will, comparing it to the copy he had on his desk.

"I see no changes or codicils. It matches the copy signed, witnessed, and notarized in this office. The primary assets are three mining claims, two houses, and a substantial sum at the bank where Mr. Streiker is the manager. Does that mirror your understanding of your father's estate, Miss Craddock?"

"Yes."

"All right. Will you be living in either of the houses?"

"No."

"Then I assume you want me to sell them and add the proceeds to the account at the bank?"

"No."

"Pardon me?"

"There are two houses. Board up the little one so it won't be vandalized. Burn the big one."

"Burn it?"

"Burn it. But tear it down, first. I don't want the fire to damage the smaller house."

"I'm afraid I don't understand."

"You don't have to. Just do it."

Vester leaned forward, put his elbows on his desk, and steepled his fingers."

"Since I will have to find a contractor, negotiate a price, and render payment, I would suggest you assign me power of attorney to act on your behalf."

"That's not going to happen," said Mr. Sleiker.

"Then how am I to proceed?"

"Find the contractor. Negotiate a price. Send the contract to my office. I will have Miss Craddock sign it the next time she's in town, and she will arrange two cashier's checks for the costs: Fifty percent payable immediately and fifty percent when the job is done."

"Anything else?"

"Yes," said Daryn. "There is a baby grand piano in the parlor of the big house. Have the contractor haul it to Basic High School and tell them it's an anonymous donation to the music department."

"Anonymous?"

"Yes."

"But you won't get any tax benefit from the donation."

"I don't care."

"What about the remaining contents of the larger house."

"Burn them, too."

"Everything?"

"Everything!"

"Since all this is highly unusual, additional questions may arise during this process. Tell me, where do you live, Miss Craddock, if I need to get in touch with you."

"No."

"Excuse me?"

"No, I won't tell you. You can contact me through Mr. Sleiker."

"I don't think that will be satisfactory."

"I think we're done here," said Mr. Sleiker as he got to his feet. "Give Miss Craddock the original of the will, and we'll be on our way."

"To where?"

"To find another probate attorney. Of course, that means you will miss out on a substantial fee. There's a lot of money in those accounts."

Vester Ernswhile held up his hands, palms outward.

"That won't be necessary. I can do everything Miss Craddock has asked."

"Without knowing where she lives?"

"Of course."

"Without asking any more questions she does not wish to answer?"

"Absolutely."

Mr. Sleiker sat down.

"All right. I have researched your fee structure, and it seems reasonable."

"You shopped me?"

"Certainly. One never knows exactly what to expect when visiting an attorney, and it is best to be prepared."

"One more item," said Ernswhile. "Miss Craddock, Mr. Sleiker, as an attorney, I am an officer of the court, and it is my duty to ask if there other assets of the estate of which I have not been informed?"

"I thought," said Mr. Sleiker, "we agreed there would be no more questions."

Vester Ernswhile looked as though he might object but thought better of it and held up his hands again. "Just so, Mr. Sleiker. Just so."

The meeting ended.

When they returned to the bank, Daryn and Mr. Streiker conferred briefly before she stood and extended her hand.

"Mr. Sleiker, I may have misjudged you all these years. Now I understand why my father wanted you to go with me. His trust was well placed. Thank you."

Mr. Sleiker reached across his desk and shook her hand.

"You are most welcome, Miss Craddock. If there's anything I can help you with in the future, just ask."

The probate was complete by Spring, and Daryn Craddock was a very wealthy woman, even without the gold under lock and key on both coasts. She decided to indulge herself. She drove to Las Vegas and parked the little Harley two blocks from a motorcycle dealership.

It was a slow day. The owner did not seem put off by the woman with a cloth covering her face, and he walked her around the shop, explaining the virtues of various models. Daryn was drawn to a beautiful Triumph TR6 twin with a six hundred and fifty cc engine.

"They call that one the desert sled," said the dealer. "High exhaust pipes and good ground clearance: a real off-road machine."

This one will go up the embankment! I won't have to carry my supplies so far.

"By the way, Got a helmet?" asked the dealer.

"Never owned one."

"Come with me.."

He led Daryn to a shelf holding white helmets.

"This is the latest and the very best: the Bell 500-TX. Steve McQueen wears one."

"Who?"

"You know, the guy from "Dead or Alive?""

"Is that a movie?"

"TV show."

"Oh. Why's he wear a motorcycle helmet?"

"He races motorcycles. On the desert. Rides the one you just looked at."

She picked up a helmet and turned it around in her hands.

Could sew my face cover into the liner. Look like a desert racer. Stares, sure, but maybe not so many.

"Okay. I'll take that TR6 and this helmet. I'll be back with the money. Any discount for cash?"

"Why not?" said the dealer, suddenly sure that when she walked out the door, he'd never see the strange woman again. "How about five percent?"

"Deal," said Daryn. "Total it up. Include license and registration."

He put the numbers together at his desk and handed her the total.

"Be right back," Daryn said and walked out.

Yeah, right, he thought.

Darn drove to the bank and withdrew what she needed. She told Mr. Streiker she was buying a new motorcycle and would use the bank address for the registration. He said he would hold it for her when it came.

She left the little Harley a half-mile from the motorcycle shop.

"Hope you find a good owner," she said aloud as she patted the tank. "You've been a faithful companion."

She glanced back several times as she walked away.

At the dealership, she paid the surprised owner in cash and filled out the paperwork. Out in the shop, he asked her if she knew how to ride. Her response was, "What's the shift pattern?"

"One down, three up."

Daryn climbed on, looped her new helmet over the handlebars, kicked the engine to life, and drove away.

In August 1971, President Nixon took the United States off the gold standard. The price of gold rose to forty-three dollars an ounce, and by the end of 1972, it had climbed to sixty-five. It continued its rise. Daryn, already enormously wealthy, grew richer by the day but didn't know it and wouldn't have cared if she had. She had everything she needed.

Time flowed down the mountainsides and pooled in the valleys below. Life changed there, but up where Daryn lived, it stayed the same. Her life of solitude rolled seamlessly on until a night in early 1973 when a drug plane skidded off the abandoned airstrip near Hayden Siding. That night, she paralleled the pilot as he moved up the aqueduct road to Cornfield Spring and later pounded on her door. He didn't leave until she punched four holes in the door with her .357 magnum.

After sunrise that morning, a Sheriff announced himself. She let him in because he was law enforcement, but she hadn't been happy about it, especially when a slight man came in with him. Tracker Man. Her reaction to what Tracker Man said about seeing her off and on for years had been hostile, and she had irritated him in turn when she accused him of watching her bathe by moonlight.

It was only weeks after the men had gone that Daryn realized she felt an affinity with Tracker Man. She had no idea why, especially since she understood it had not been a mountain lion giving her the feeling she was being watched.

The Sheriff and Tracker Man returned to her cave two months later. A deputy came with them. They asked her for information about something happening on the Union Pacific, and Daryn told them what she knew. When the sheriff said Deputy Man was going undercover on the Union Pacific to catch the thieves she had seen, Daryn resolved to watch out for him. After all, what else did she have to do?

— Chapter 23 —

ON THE (RAIL) ROAD AGAIN

Donny Quest, formerly of the Kansas City Southern Railroad, made two student trips on the Union Pacific: one to Yermo and one back to Las Vegas. The rules and procedures were similar to those on the Santa Fe, and Deputy Johnny Quentin settled smoothly into his undercover role. His apartment was adequate, and it gave him a private place to phone Horse, who was his intermediary with Agent D'Arnauld and Agent Johns.

Agent Johns had initially demanded to be briefed personally by Johnny. Horse knew Johns' intent was to avoid sharing the information he received with Agent D'Arnauld. To keep that from happening, Horse maintained Deputy Quentin needed enough rest between trips that he wouldn't become a zombie and thereby endanger his life. When Johns stubbornly refused to relent, Horse said, "Then get yourself another boy." And that was the end of that.

Johnny didn't want to arouse suspicion on his new job, so he couldn't very well ask the dispatchers to call him for night trips only. He took whatever came up in the regular rotation. By never marking off the extra board, he increased his chances of being on the right train on a moonless night. Another man who never marked off was the conductor Johnny was often paired with. In Yermo and Las Vegas, he and Johnny hit the switch together, timed out together, and were usually called for the next job together.

The conductor was David Westover. Since conductors signed on with their initials, including their middle names, he was D R Westover.

The 'R' was for Richard. And just as on the Santa Fe, conductors' first and middle initials were modified to make nicknames, so D R Westover was "Dirty Rotten Westover."

But D R Westover was neither dirty nor rotten. What he was, though, was observant. After watching Donny Quest for a few trips, he spoke up.

"What is it with you, Donny?"

"What do you mean?"

"Well, first, you never mark off."

"Neither do you."

"Wife wants a new house. I'm saving for the down payment."

"And I want a Chevelle Super Sport."

"Okay, that makes sense, but that's not the only thing that makes me curious about you."

"Oh?"

"I've worked with a lot of guys who take this job seriously, but I've never seen anyone so, so…" he struggled for the right word, "so relentless. Especially at night, sitting up there in the cupola staring into the darkness. Most guys fall asleep up there from time to time, but I don't think you ever do."

"Just doing my job. Watching for hot boxes."

Johnny didn't think the conductor bought that answer. Then came the morning a week later when the two men were walking toward the employee parking lot at the depot in Las Vegas. A Las Vegas Police Department cruiser was rolling by when the brake lights flashed, and the car backed up.

"Hey, Quentin!" called the officer in the passenger seat, "get over here."

"Forgot my name already, officer?" yelled Johnny. "It's 'Quest.'" Turning to Westover, he said, "you got on ahead. I've got to talk to these guys."

It was two officers Johnny had encountered before. The first time was in 1969 when Johnny leveled a casino owner's bodyguard in a parking lot. The second time was the previous year when they tried to roust him when he'd been in Las Vegas ordering Robyn's engagement ring. They had been bitterly disappointed to learn he was a deputy sheriff in Smoke Tree.

"What the hell, Quentin? You working on the railroad now?"

"Like I said, it's Quest," Johnny said loudly as he waited for D R Westover to get out of earshot before he leaned toward the car. "And yeah, I'm working for the railroad."

"Get yourself fired, did you? Never thought you had the stuff to make a decent cop."

"If 'decent' had anything to do with it, you two would've been off the force years ago."

"And what's with this 'Quest' scam?"

"I'm working undercover."

"Yeah, right, a sheriff's deputy from California working undercover in Las Vegas! Give us a break, Quentin."

Johnny leaned in closer.

"It's Quest, Donny Quest, and if you ever talk to me again, which I'm hoping you won't, you'd damn well better use that name. I'm undercover for the FBI."

The officers began laughing.

"Oh, my, what a hoot! Undercover for the FBI!"

"Call Special Agent Jules Johns at the Vegas office."

The officers began laughing again.

"Jules Johns? Is that even a real name?"

"He's the Assistant Special Agent in Charge."

The two men stopped laughing.

"Seriously?"

"Seriously. And if you call, do it from a payphone."

"Why's that?"

"Because if you call from the cop shop, and word gets out and blows my cover, Johns will see to it that you two spend the rest of your careers working the parking detail."

"Agent Jules Johns."

"That's right."

"Don't think we won't make that call, Quentin."

"You damned well better, and for the last time, dumb ass, it's Quest."

On their next westbound job, it didn't take D R Westover long to bring up the incident with the policemen.

"That cop," he said, "called you Quentin."

"Yeah. Not good at names, I guess."

"Why did he recognize you?"

"Little scuffle outside a bar. He and his partner showed up."

"Were you charged with anything?"

"Nah. Maybe if I had been, the guy would've remembered my name, but it was just a minor incident."

D R Westover was silent for a moment.

"I don't believe you."

"You don't believe it was something minor?"

"I don't believe it was anything at all. I don't think you hang around bars, and I think that guy called you by your real name. You're Quentin, not Quest, aren't you?"

Johnny pulled out his wallet, removed his Lousiana driver's license and social security card, and handed them to Westover."

Westover examined them briefly and shrugged.

"This is Las Vegas. Get that kind of stuff on any street corner."

"Good enough to hire on with?"

"I'm still not buying it. There's some reason those guys recognized you, and there's some reason you watch the train more at night than in the daytime."

Johnny, who would be almost as good as Chemeheuevi Joe when it came to staying silent, said nothing.

"I don't think you're a criminal," said D R.

He stared at Johnny a moment longer.

"But you're not a cop, either. Huh-uh. You know way too much about railroad operations."

He snapped his fingers.

"Got it! You're a railroad detective!"

Westover paused again.

"Ah, it's the guns, right? The stolen guns. Everybody's heard about it. Freight trains, you know, are rolling rumor mills. You're watching for the thieves! And the U.P. thinks it might be an inside job. Probably watching the crews, too. Well, I'll be go to hell! I'm riding the rails with a cinder dick! Not going to admit it, though, are you?"

"Some guns were stolen? Must have been before I was hired."

D R Westover smiled.

"Yeah, it was, and now that you mention it, those two things happened awfully close together."

"Well," said Johnny, "I'd better get up top. This train's not going to watch itself."

Three hours later, when Johnny climbed down from the cupola to eat his sandwiches, D R picked up where he had left off.

"I've changed my mind. The Union Pacific wouldn't use a railroad detective, not even one from a different division. Too good a chance someone would recognize you. No, Quest or Quentin or whatever the hell your name is, you're from some government agency."

"Too many trips across the lonely desert, D R. You're losing it," said Johnny.

"No, I'm not. I may not have it all, but I'm closing in on it, and I've got another piece. The government doesn't think the guns were stolen when the train was in the yard. They think someone climbed on the train when it was moving and threw them overboard."

D R leaned back and paused.

"And that's why you stare out into the night. Especially when we're going up the grade to Cima! You think that's where they climb on, and you're looking for anything they might have thrown off. Come on, admit it. Dirty Rotten Westover has figured it out."

"I have no idea what you're talking about."

"Yeah, you do. But don't worry about it; I won't say anything to anybody. But let me think about it some more. When I've got it all, I'll let you know."

Johnny just kept eating. He had no intention of confirming the conductor's suspicions. However, he wasn't perturbed. Johnny had the man pegged as one of the good guys and believed him when he said he wouldn't tell anyone else.

The next night, Johnny and D R Westover caught an eastbound hotshot out of Yermo. D R waited until they had thundered past Kelso before telling Johnny what he had on his mind.

"Quest, or Quentin, or whoever you really are, you're never going to catch those guys looking out the window. You're going to have to move up and down the train after we slow down because that's when they're going to climb on."

Johnny didn't respond, but when the train began to slow, he stepped out onto the rear platform, climbed to the top of the caboose, and disappeared.

He didn't return until just before the laboring diesels reached the top of the grade. When he stepped back inside, D R said, "I guess that's all the confirmation I'm going to get."

"What more do you need?"

"Ah," said D R, "it speaks!"

For weeks, Daryn Craddock had spent every moonless night near the rail line. She had seen the thieves three times, but never Johnny Quentin. And then, one night, there he was! He moved like quicksilver over the flatcars, and she felt lucky to have spotted him.

Saw you again! Saw you, but you didn't see me. I'm as good as Tracker Man! Well, maybe not that good, but pretty darn good!

— Chapter 24 —

PLANS AND REVISIONS

*O**n a Sunday his third week undercover,*** Johnny made two phone calls. The first was to Horse at his home. Horse, still disturbed that someone at the substation suffered from loose lips syndrome, had decided no one there should know what Johnny was really doing. The official story was that Deputy Quentin had been sent to the FBI's new facility at Quantico for special training. The only people in Smoke Tree who knew the real story were Horse, Esperanza, Chemehuevi Joe, and Robyn.

When Johnny told Horse about D R Westover, Horse wasn't concerned.

"I've never bought into the FBI's inside job theory. If someone from the Union Pacific was tipping off the thieves, it would have to be someone very high in the company, and the idea a highly placed executive is helping thieves steal random items is ridiculous. I think the gang working the trains hit the guns by pure luck. I also think if they hadn't stolen guns, we'd never have heard a word about these thefts."

"I agree."

"This conductor has a good point. A week ago, Joe and I went out and walked the line again, and we found more seals. The thieves are still at work, but you've never seen anything alongside the tracks?"

"Nope. These guys are pretty smart. Moonless nights and tarps the color of the desert."

"Then the only way to catch them is when they're on the train."

"You're right. I haven't told Westover where I'm from or who I'm really working for, but since he figured this out, I've been running the trains every time we're on Cima grade."

"That's the ticket. But be careful; we don't know anything about these guys. They could be dangerous."

"On a different subject, how's Robyn doing? I mean, I talk to her on the phone, but you see her at work. Is she holding up okay?"

"She's worried about you, sure enough, but she's good. She's a keeper, Johnny."

"You should know, boss," Johnny laughed, "you worked hard enough to get us together."

"I did, at that. Esperanza is still teasing me about it. Calls me 'Captain Matchmaker.'"

"And how's the Tony Alpino project coming?"

"Real good, Johnny. I've been running with him. He's in better shape than I am."

"How about in the sandpit?"

"He's a natural. Real rough-and-tumble kid. Rennie Wrexler is going to think he walked into a buzz saw."

Johnny Quentin's second call was to Robyn. It warmed his heart to hear her voice.

The night of April third, Johnny checked the cargo pockets of his fatigue pants before leaving the caboose. Plastic cable ties in one, coils of thin nylon rope, and a bunch of 40d nails bent just below the head in the other.

There was no moon when he stepped onto the first flatcar as the slow-moving freight climbed Cima grade. *This is the night,* he thought. *I can feel it.* He had often had similar feelings on night trails in the Central Highlands of Vietnam and had seldom been wrong.

Fifteen TOFCs forward of the caboose, he struck paydirt. Trailer doors were open, and he could hear someone moving around inside. He climbed up, eased the doors closed, latched the hasp over the cleat, and inserted a slightly bent 40d common nail where the lock had been.

"Hey!" came a muffled cry, but Johnny was already moving away.

By the time he neared the head end of the train, he had locked five thieves inside the trailers where they were at work. He had subdued two more, secured their hands and feet with cable ties, and left them tied to the landing gear of trailers.

The first thieves to board the train had climbed on closer to the head-end, and the looting of a trailer there had progressed much further. Three men had been working separate flatcars when one of them found a bonanza: a trailer filled with televisions and stereos. He hurriedly recruited his partners to help with the high-value cargo.

Boxes containing televisions and stereos were stacked on the edge of the flatcar. Two thieves were lowering them as close to the ground as they could reach before dropping them to the cinders below when someone pushed one of them over the side along with the box he had been holding. The second rose to his feet and pulled a knife from the sheath on his belt. His reward was a broken wrist and a face-plant on the right of way that knocked out two of his teeth.

The man who had discovered the electronics was inside the trailer when he heard a scream. He climbed down, picked up his bolt cutters, and saw...no one! He moved to the edge of the flatcar. On the right of way, a man he presumed was a train crew member kneeling on one of his partners. The train was moving slowly away from the pair as it climbed the slope.

He jumped from the car, hoping the noise of the train would mask the sound as he landed. He stumbled but regained his balance and stepped down the embankment below the right of way. Guided by the continuous stream of agonized profanity from his partner, he walked through the desert and climbed back up. The crew member was securing the screaming man's feet.

The man crept forward, lifted the bolt cutters over his head, and was moving toward the man when a muffled voice behind him said, "Don't!"

He whirled to see a slight figure in dark clothing, arms extended. Something about the figure's head made it look like an extra-terrestrial life form, an impression reinforced by the glittering starlight reflecting from where its eyes should have been.

"Drop those."

The man hesitated. The slight figure fired into the air, and flames from the gun lit up the night sky. Simultaneously, something slammed into the man from behind, knocking him to the ground. The bolt cutters went flying.

"Don't try to get up," came a different voice. "Stretch out flat and put your hands behind your back."

"Hook him up, Deputy Man," came the muffled and slightly slurred voice.

Johnny stood up and stepped away from the thief on the ground. He motioned woman of the desert moon to follow him and led her off the embankment where he spoke to her in a lowered voice.

"I'd better get back on the train. There might be more of these guys up ahead."

"I doubt it," said woman of the desert moon. "I'm sure they jumped off when they heard the gun."

"Yeah, you're probably right."

"Don't fret. Tracker Man will hunt them down."

"I'm assuming the cube truck is down by Kelso."

"It headed that way after it dropped these men off."

I'm unarmed. I'd like to borrow your gun. Can you do without it for a while?"

"Yes."

"Thanks. I'm going to arrest the guys in the truck. I don't think throwing rocks at the windshield will get the job done."

Woman of the desert moon handed over the gun.

"Got any more ammunition?"

"Just what's in the cylinder."

Johnny examined the weapon.

"Single six. I assume you had the hammer down on an empty chamber?"

"I did."

"It won't be long before this whole place is crawling with cops. Be best if you aren't here when that happens unless you want to meet a whole lot of people."

"Can you leave me out of any report?"

"Yes, and if the guy on the ground brings you up, I'll say I don't know what he's talking about. Thanks for saving my bacon."

"You're welcome, Johnny Quentin."

Woman of the desert moon faded into the night, and Johnny set off at a dead run.

Five minutes later, he was on the caboose, and D R Westover was eyeing the .357.

"I didn't know you carried that."

"Well, D R, I'm full of surprises. I'm Johnny Quentin, on loan from the San Bernardino County Sheriff's Department, working for the FBI."

"I knew I'd figured it out!"

"Yeah, you did. Now, take some notes."

"Why?"

"Because you're going to call my boss."

"Okay."

"Three of the thieves are lying along the right of way. They're secured hand and foot with plastic ties."

"All right."

"There are five locked inside trailers. The trailers have bent nails where the locks used to be, and there are two more thieves tied to landing gear on trailers."

"Let me catch up."

Johnny waited until D R stopped writing, looked up, and nodded.

"When you get to the top of the grade, have the hoghead stop the train and call this number."

Johnny took D R's pencil and wrote out a number on the back of the manifest.

"That will get you the dispatcher at the Smoke Tree Substation. Tell the dispatcher to patch you through to the Captain's home."

"Got it."

"When you talk to him, tell him where the bad guys are. Have him call the feds. Tell him I'm headed for Kelso to arrest the guys in the truck. Have him bring Joe because we might have a couple more to track down. He'll know what that means. Got all that?"

"Need a minute."

Johnny waited while D R wrote. When he was finished, he read aloud what he had written.

"Real good. Now, after you talk to the Captain, take the train down the hill and put it on the siding at Joshua. Wait there for the law enforcement people to show. This whole train is now a crime scene. You and the guys on the head-end are about to get a lot of overtime."

D R Westover rubbed his hands. "I can feel that down payment accumulating."

"And D R?"

"Yes."

"Been a pleasure working with you."

"Likewise, Deputy Quentin. Come visit me in Las Vegas sometime."

"Look forward to it," said Johnny as he went out the door.

The train had been gone for over an hour when Johnny saw headlights crawling up the right of way. He had been thinking about how to proceed and decided the most direct approach was best. He slipped over the edge of the embankment.

Johnny put two rounds through the radiator when the truck drew within fifteen yards. It stopped, and Johnny could hear fluid pouring onto the ground. After a moment, the driver floored it. The truck slewed sideways, rear wheels fighting for traction in the dirt.

Was afraid of that, Johnny thought as he shot out the driver's-side headlight. *Only one round left.*

The driver slammed on the brakes, threw open his door, and bolted across the tracks, leaving the truck in gear. The man in the passenger seat climbed down and lifted his hands over his head as the idling vehicle crawled forward.

"On the ground, face down," Johnny yelled.

The man complied.

Johnny stood. He waited until the cube truck angled off the edge of the embankment and tipped awkwardly onto its side. The rear wheels continued to turn until the engine sputtered and died. He watched to see if anyone came out of the back before moving to the man on the ground.

Johnny knelt with both knees on the man's back.

"Hey! Get off me," the man yelled and began to struggle.

"Hold still," said Johnny, "or I'll smack you with this gun."

He secured the man's wrists with a cable tie, then climbed off his back and put another around his ankles. When he had the man immobilized, Johnny dragged him to the embankment, rolled him over, and pushed him into a sitting position.

"What's your name?"

"Freddie Clemons."

"Freddie, I'm Deputy Johnny Quentin of the San Bernardino County Sheriff's Department, and you're under arrest."

"For what?"

"Nice try."

Johnny recited Freddie's rights under the Miranda decision and asked him if he understood. Freddie nodded.

"Don't just nod," Johnny said, "Say 'yes'" if you understand your rights."

"Yes," said Freddie.

"Good. I'm going to go round up your partner."

Johnny crossed the tracks and headed in the direction the driver had gone.

Northwest of the Union Pacific tracks lies Cima Dome, a massive granitic batholith. Determined to get as far from the rail line and Kelso/Cima Road as fast as he could, the driver ran toward it and started to climb. The dome is steep, rising abruptly from twenty-two hundred feet at the rail line to fifty-five hundred feet at the summit. It wasn't long before the driver slowed to a jog and then a walk.

Despite the profusion of stars overhead, visibility was not good, and Johnny moved slowly up the hillside. There was no reason to hurry. None of the men he had secured were going to get free.

He heard the driver before he saw him. Heard him coughing. The two-pack-a-day smoker was bent over, hands on his knees. Johnny came out of the desert behind him.

"Get on the ground and put your hands behind your back."

He started to turn.

Johnny Quentin pulled back the hammer on the .357. It was an ominous sound that froze the driver mid-movement.

"If I wanted you to turn around, I'd a said so."

Clay Nantz knelt down and stretched out on the ground with his hands behind his back. He was too winded to complain when Johnny put both knees on his back and hooked his wrists together with a cable tie.

Johnny stood.

"All right, get up."

"You have to help me."

"No, I don't. You either get up, or I'll hook your feet together and leave you here."

Clay Nantz groaned as he struggled to one knee and then the other. He got one foot under himself and struggled to rise. Johnny stepped behind him, yanked him up by his wrists, and stepped away. Nantz stumbled and almost fell before he managed to catch his balance.

"You can turn around now. What's your name?" asked Johnny.

"Clay Nantz."

"Clay Nantz, you're under arrest."

Johnny recited the Miranda litany to Nantz and asked him if he understood. Nantz said he did, and the two men began the downhill trek to the Union Pacific tracks.

When they reached level ground, there was a Sheriff's Department patrol car parked on the shoulder of Kelso/Cima Road. They walked past it, climbed to the tracks, and found Horse standing next to Freddie Clemons.

"I just read him his Miranda rights," said Horse when Johnny led Clay Nantz across the tracks. "He said you already did."

"Yessir."

"Well, now he's been double-dosed. Who's this you've got with you?"

"Clay Nantz. Been Mirandized."

"Which one was driving the truck?"

"This one."

"Then Freddie here must be the leader. We'll pass that on to the FBI."

Freddie lifted his head to stare at Horse.

"That's right, boys, you're not dealing with just a Sheriff's Department. The FBI and the ATF are going to land on you with both feet."

"What's ATF?" asked Freddie, craning his neck to see both men.

"Alcohol, Tobacco, and Firearms. You're going to get to know them real well.

Johnny, let's get these two in the back of my car. Andy and Joe are up the road looking for the guys you left along the tracks. At first light, Joe will check to see if anybody came off the train and did a runner."

"I'd like to talk to you for a minute after we get these two in the car," Johnny said.

"Okay."

After they locked Clemons and Nantz in the back of the patrol car, Johnny and Horse walked down the road.

"Before we start, I've got a question for you," said Horse.

"Go ahead."

"I'm assuming you put the holes in the radiator and blew out the headlight."

"I did."

"I didn't know you were carrying a gun."

"That's what I wanted to talk to you about. There are three guys up there, and one of them may tell a strange story."

"About what?"

"I pushed two of them off a car. Didn't know there was a third one still on. He must have jumped off while I was hooking up his partners. He came up behind me with a pair of bolt cutters and might have brained me, but woman of the desert moon showed up and saved my butt."

"And he's going to tell that story?"

"Probably. Woman not only saved me, she gave me her gun. Would've had a hard time with the truck if she hadn't."

"How good did he see her?"

"Long enough for her to fire into the air before I knocked him down."

"And he didn't see her after that?"

"Nossir. He was face down in the dirt, and we climbed to the bottom of the embankment before we talked."

"So, you don't think he could hear you."

"No. Too much train noise and we were too far away."

"Let me think about this for a minute."

Horse put his hands on his hips and stared off to the west. Stars were racing to their deaths with the first glimmers of morning twilight. He turned back to Johnny.

"Tell me what you think he saw before you knocked him off his feet."

Johnny thought for a moment.

"A figure in dark clothes. Had on that high-gloss-black motorcycle helmet with the tinted visor. Couldn't see the eyes."

Johnny paused.

"And now that I think about it, you could see stars reflected in the visor."

"Okay. Must have looked weird. You know, Johnny, I think that man was hallucinating."

Johnny smiled.

"Works for me."

"Good. By the way, I called Darnold at his home, and he should be landing in Vegas soon. The FBI guys will be out here shortly, but Darnold will be around if there's a press conference, which, knowing the FBI, I'm sure there will be. I wanted to make sure they didn't take all the credit."

Johnny smiled.

"Can't have that."

"Now, let's go see a man about a train."

— Chapter 25 —

APRIL 1973
Protecting a Source

*T*wo *weeks later,* the bulk of the investigation into the train robberies was complete. Horse, Johnny, Agent D'Arnauld, and Agent Johns were gathered at the office of the United States District Attorney for the State of Nevada. All four men were seated on one side of the conference room table when the door opened, and the District Attorney came in, followed by two ADAs.

"Gentlemen," said the District Attorney when he was seated across the table with an ADA on each side of him, "thank you for coming today."

"Our pleasure," said Agent Johns. The others on his side of the table nodded, although Horse was less than pleased. This whole thing smacked too much of politics for his taste. After all, he and Johnny had already spent hours being interviewed by ADA Morgenthau and ADA Thompson. What else was there to say?

"I wanted to let you know that I will be the lead prosecutor when this case goes to court. ADAs Morgenthau and Thompson, whom you all know, will assist me."

So that's it, thought Horse. *As usual, the guys who did the work won't get the credit. Come on, get on with it.*

"I've been briefed on the interviews with Captain Caballo and Deputy Quentin, and I've read the transcripts, but I still have a couple of questions. First, there's a man my ADAs weren't able to interview, and I was hoping he'd be with you today."

"You're referring to Joe Medrano?" asked Horse.

"That's the name."

"Joe doesn't do interviews."

"Why not?"

"First, he's not a sworn officer of the law. I hire him to help me track people down. Tourists mostly, motorists, sometimes. Anyone who has disappeared in the desert."

"But those people aren't trying to hide."

"No, generally, they're just dumb."

"But the men who jumped off the train and ran, they didn't want to be found."

"If it doesn't fly, Joe can track it."

"I see. Well, what if I want him to testify in court?"

"He won't."

"Excuse me."

"He won't."

"I can compel his testimony."

"You can try. He'll just disappear."

"We'll find him."

Horse smiled.

"Something amusing, Captain?"

"Sorry. Just had an image of a bunch of city types trying to find Joe Medrano in the desert."

"If we have to, we will."

"But as I said, you'll never find him."

The AG studied the rangy man across the table from him for a moment and then waved his hand dismissively.

"I'll take your word for that, Captain, but please, pass on my appreciation for what he did."

"I will," said Horse, relieved.

"By the way, did he say where they were headed when he caught up with them?"

"Toward the Vegas Highway. Got lost in the Ivanpah mountains near Kokoweef."

"Cocoa leaf?" said the DA.

"Kokoweef. The Lost River of Gold. A mining legend."

"Sounds intriguing. Can you give me a quick summary?"

"1936. A desert rancher named Earl Dorr set out to discover a lost gold mine in the Ivanpah Mountains. Found three vertical limestone caverns. Claimed to have climbed inside and found an underground river of gold but could never find it again."

"And people are still looking?"

"Yes. Scam a minute. The current group is Concave mining. They'll give you a tour for two dollars and fifty cents or sell you a rare mineral specimen. So rare they haul them out of the mine by the truckload. Concave will go bust, and their investors will lose their money. Somebody else will buy the claim and find more investors, who will lose their money, and so on and so on."

The AG shook his head.

"Mysterious trackers, elusive gold miners, you've got some strange folks in your part of the country, Captain."

"That we do, sir."

"Speaking of strange, there's something in the interview with one of the suspects, a"…he consulted his notes, "Colin Crespi, that's puzzling."

Uh oh, thought Horse, *here it comes.*

"This Crespi claims some sort of strange being that looked like a space alien spoke to him and then discharged a weapon before Deputy Quentin knocked him flat. Can you shed any light on that, Deputy?"

"Sounds to me like he was eating magic mushrooms," Johnny said.

"Ah, psilocybin. Yes, that's been showing up in Las Vegas. Well, interesting reading, anyway."

Nice one, Johnny, thought Horse.

"Now," said the DA, "on to something more serious. The leaders of this operation, at least the ground-level leaders, Freddie Clemons and Clay Nantz, won't talk. The gang members rolled over on them, and if that isn't enough, we've got Deputy Quetin's testimony, but Clemons and Nantz clammed up, even when we offered reduced charges in exchange for information. They're obviously afraid, and that leads me to believe the Mafia is involved here."

"I would agree with you on that score," said Darnold. "Those AR15s disappeared without a trace. A lot of guns, and they're just gone. The ATF has sources, but we haven't heard a word."

"And that would square with the little we've got on air cargo theft at McCarran," added Agent Johns. "We know it's going on, but we can't get close to it."

"Just penetrating the Mafia distribution network for stolen goods would be a huge breakthrough," said the District Attorney, "but these guys won't cooperate. Which brings us to a case that went through this office before I was appointed here."

"You're talking about Arthur Ransome?" asked Jules Johns.

"Exactly. If Captain Caballo hadn't uncovered a possible link between Ransome and the theft of those guns, we wouldn't have anything at all. In fact, if it weren't for Captain Caballo and Deputy Quentin, we wouldn't be sitting here today."

"I'm glad to hear you say that, sir," said Darnold. "I like to see the guys who do the work get the credit."

"I agree," said Agent Johns. "I must admit I was a little leary when Agent D'Arnauld suggested involving Captain Caballo, but he and Deputy Quentin broke this thing wide open."

Lord, don't lay it on so thick, you two, thought Horse.

"As you know, Ransome was involved in air cargo theft at McCarran," said the District Attorney. "This was well before the Mafia got involved out there. Arthur Ransome was arrested, but he wouldn't talk. We didn't get anyone but him. Obviously, he was protecting someone. The question is, do you think it was Clemons and Nantz?"

"Could have been," said Agent Johns.

The District Attorney continued. "Ransome served his time in Lewisburg Federal Penitentiary, which is where he had contact with the two men from Smoke Tree who identified him as someone who had pressed them for details about an abortive train heist. And we know that when Ransome got out, he returned to Nevada. The question is, do we think he was protecting Clemons and Nantz, and now they're protecting him?"

"It's a possibility, sir," said Agent Johns. "But he's left Las Vegas, and we can't find him."

"Where have you looked?"

"He told his employer his mother was terminally ill, and he was going home to be with her. Didn't know when he'd be back. Said his mother lived in Oregon."

"Does she?"

"No, sir. She lives in a small town in West Virginia. When I called her, she said she was in good health. She also said she and her husband hadn't seen Arthur since he was arrested for the thefts at McCarran. We put surveillance on the family home just to be sure. No sign of him."

The District Attorney turned to Horse.

"Captain Caballo, what's your take on this? Do you think this Ransome fellow is involved?"

"I do. As you're well aware, criminals often learn things in prison that make them more successful when they get out. Couple the information Ransome picked up from Austin Banner in Lewisburg with access to a distribution network he had before he went to jail, and I think he was right back at it when he returned."

"Do you think we'll find him?"

"I don't think we'll ever see Arthur Ransome again."

"Why not."

"Look at the timeline. Ransome gets arrested back in '65. Won't talk. ADA talks the judge into giving Ransome the max. Seven years. But he doesn't leave it at that. ADA talks the judge into intervening and getting Ransome sent to Lewisburg, a place for the worst of the worst. Mostly violent offenders, which Arthur Ransome wasn't.

This ADA contacts the U.S. Attorney's office in Pennsylvania. Asks them to send an attorney to visit Ransome in prison and offer him the possibility of parole if he cooperates and turns over his accomplices. Ransome still won't do it. So far, it's reasonable enough, but then the ADA stepped over the line."

"How so?" asked the District Attorney.

"He sees to it that the attorney returns every month with the same offer, thereby putting Arthur Ransome's life in danger. I'm surprised Ransome survived for seven years. But he did. Went out max time."

"And returned to Nevada."

"Ransome's a smart guy. I'm sure he did his research and learned the railroads don't report thefts because they don't want to spook shippers," said Horse.

"So," said the DA, "he contacts his old gang, and they start stealing stuff from moving trains."

"Exactly."

"Then why did he leave?"

"That's easy. The guns."

"I don't follow."

"The gang was probably happy with the big score, but Ransome knew it would bring federal heat. I'll bet we never hear from him or about him again."

"What do you think?" the District Attorney asked Agent Johns.

"Well," said Johns, "we haven't had any luck finding him."

"And you Agent D'Arnauld? What's your opinion of the Captain's theory?"

"Since he's the guy who put this together, and I've seen him at work before, I'd take it to the bank."

"Then I guess our only recourse is to continue to work on Clemons and Nantz."

The District Attorney got to his feet. Everyone rose with him.

"Thank you all again for your excellent work. You, in particular, Deputy Quentin. There will be letters of commendation from my office for each of you."

Could boost my career, thought Agent Johns.

Couldn't hurt my career, thought Agent D'Arnauld.

Yeah, yeah, thought Horse.

Waste of time, thought Johnny Quentin.

The four men gathered to say their goodbyes in the parking lot outside.

"Been a pleasure working with you gentlemen," said Agent Johns as he shook hands, "even you, Darnold."

"Hey," said Darnold, "First time you've ever called me anything but 'Agent D'Arnauld.'"

"Getting ready for the new regime."

"What new regime?" asked Horse.

"Acting Director Gray's confirmation hearing didn't go well. He's on the way out. Looks like the new guy will be William Ruckleshaus, and rumor has it he's going to relax standards. Make the FBI a little less formal, so I'm practicing my more casual attitude."

"And calling me Darnold."

"Actually," said Agent Johns, "I think I'll go with 'Darnit Darnold.'"

"Then we'll need a nickname for you. Anyone got any ideas?"

"On the railroad," said Johnny, "they take conductor's first and middle initials and make a nickname."

"Sounds interesting. What's your middle name, Jules?"

"Ulysses."

"J. U. Johns. Got it!" said Darnold. "Jumped Up Johns!"

Johnny laughed.

"Good one, Darnold. I like it."

"Just one problem now," said Darnold.

"What's that?" asked Jules.

"If Captain Caballo is 'Horse,' and I'm 'Darnit Darnold,' and you're 'Jumped Up Johns,' what about you, Deputy Quentin? What's your middle name?"

"Don't have one."

"That could make things difficult."

"Got an idea," said Jules Johns. "We can use his undercover name, make his nickname out of that."

"What was it?"

"Donny Quest."

"Perfect," said Darnold. "D.Q. Quentin: 'Dis Qualified Quentin.'"

"Come on, 'Disqualified,'" said Horse. "Let's get back to Smoke Tree."

— Chapter 26 —

REVELATIONS

Johnny Quentin was enjoying a few days off after his time undercover for the FBI. He drove to the Caballo's hillside home to work with Tony Alpino and was pleased with the boy's progress.

"A lot better with the throws and falls," Johnny said while they were taking a breather. "Horse has taught you well. He learned all that from Burke Henry. And not just learned it, mastered it."

"He told me about him. He must have been quite the guy," said Tony.

"That's what I hear. Saw him around town from time to time but never met him. Wish I had."

"He must have died the summer I came to Smoke Tree. Were you here then?"

"I was in the Army."

"Where did you serve?"

Johnny stood up.

"Enough with the throws and falls. Let's work on kicks."

Later, the two of them were shaking sand out of their workout clothes when Joe walked down the hill from where he had been marking the foundation of the Caballo's new home.

"Hello, Mr. Medrano," said Tony.

"Joe."

"Sorry…Joe. It's hard for me to call adults by their first names."

"Call Captain Caballo Horse," said Joe.

"Yeah, but everyone does."

"Esperanza doesn't."

"Got me there....Joe."

"Johnny," said Joe, "a minute?"

"Sure." Turning to Tony, Johnny said, "Good workout! Again tomorrow, and maybe a run?"

"Sure thing. And thanks."

Johnny and Joe watched Tony walk away.

"Good kid," said Joe.

"He is."

"The boys," said Joe.

"Donny and Danny?"

"Yes."

"Something wrong?"

"Leaving soon," said Joe.

"Have you"....Johnny hesitated, searching for the right phrase... "heard from Charlie Merriman?"

"No. A feeling."

"Okay. Let's go."

When the sun touched the Stepladder Mountains to their west, Johnny, Joe, and the Merriman twins were near Red Rock Falls in the Chemehuevi Mountains.

"Wanted to talk to you up here," said Donny,

"As the sun went down," finished Danny.

Johnny and Joe were used to the boys' unusual speech patterns. One of the twins would begin a sentence, and the other would finish it. It wasn't as if they interrupted one another; they did it so seamlessly it was like one person talking. Usually, but not always, Donny began the sentence, and Danny finished it.

"Joe thinks you will be leaving soon," said Johnny.

"He's right," said Donny,

"It's time," Danny finished.

"The American Indian Movement," Donny said,

"Didn't work out," said Danny.

"We had high hopes when Dennis Banks, Russel Means,"

"And the Rosebud Sioux organized the meeting in Washington."

"Caravans left Seattle, San Francisco, and Los Angeles,"
"Last October sixth."
"The fourth caravan left Oklahoma,"
"And took the Trail of Tears backward."
"Trail that took the Cherokee,"
"To Oklahoma when their land was stolen."
"Seven hundred people,"
"From two hundred tribes,"
"Were supposed to meet with President Nixon,"
"But when they got to Washington, he wasn't there."
"All election year,"
"Lies and promises."
"Things here are,"
"Not going to change."
"And Indians will die,"
"On the Rosebud."
"Time for elsewhere places,"
"In elsewhen times."
"Like Charlie told us?" asked Johnny.
Both boys nodded.
"Can you tell us more?" asked Johnny.
"Hard to," said Donny,
"It's so much," said Danny.
"Best to hold,"
"Our hands."
The twins clasped hands and held up their free hands to Johnny
and Joe. At contact, the two men saw a group of familiar faces gathered
around a campfire deep in a red rock canyon. There was one figure
Johnny didn't recognize. A slender woman facing away from him, long
black hair cascading down her back. The Merriman twins pulled their
hands free. The scene disappeared, and the boys began chattering in
their secret language, incomprehensible to anyone else.

After a few minutes, they turned to Johnny and Joe.
"This woman," said Donny,
"This moon woman," said Danny.
"Pease, take us to her,"

"We have to talk with her."

"Can try," said Joe. "Not sure she will."

"We have," said Danny.

"Our ways," finished Donny.

It was dark when Joe and Johnny left the twins at their home in the Mojave Village.

"How did they know about the woman of the desert moon?" Johnny asked Joe as they drove away.

Joe shrugged. "Mojave twins," he said as if that explained everything. And, of course, it did.

At first light, Johnny, Joe, and the twins climbed the embankment south of the corral below Cornfield Spring. Thirty minutes later, they were at woman of the desert moon's door.

Joe reached around the edge of the rock face to rap on the left side of the heavy door.

"Go away," came a voice. "I have a gun."

"No, you don't," called Johnny. "I've got it. Bringing it back."

"About time! Anyone with you?"

"Tracker Man," said Joe, "and two others."

"Sheriff Man?"

"No. Two little boys."

There was a momentary silence.

"I'm disappointed, Tracker Man. Sheriff Man promised you'd keep my secret."

"He tried to," said Donny,

"But we knew," said Danny.

"The only way you could have known is if one of them told you."

"There are other ways,"

"We can explain."

"What other ways?" asked woman of the desert moon.

"Put your hand against the door,"

"And we will show you."

"If I do, will you go away and leave me alone?"

"If you still,"

"Want us to."

They heard movement on the other side of the plank door.

"All right. I'm touching the door, now."

"What part"

"Of the door?"

"The middle," she replied.

The boys centered their palms on the door.

Woman of the desert moon screamed, and Johnny, Joe, and the Merriman twins heard the heavy iron bars sliding in their brackets. The door swung open, and woman of the desert moon stood there in her motorcycle helmet, rubbing her hands together as if they had been burned.

"Who are you?"

"I'm Donny,"

"And I'm Danny."

"May we,"

"Come in?"

"Not until you tell me why I heard the voices louder than I've ever heard them before when I touched the door."

"The Ancestors are always here," said Donny.

"And we have more to show you," said Danny.

"Please," said woman of the desert moon. "Please, show me!"

"Hold our hands," the boys said together as they reached toward her.

When she took their hands in hers, images cascaded through her mind.

A woman, splashing across a shallow lake, pursued by men on horseback. The Turtle Mountains.

A young girl at Cornfield Spring.

A young woman gathering firewood in the river bottom.

A young Kestrel, alongside a young Resolute, leading a burro laden with prospecting equipment.

Woman of the desert moon staggered, nearly fell, regained her balance, and stepped back.

"People who," said Donny,

"Play with fish," said Danny as the boys followed her inside.

"What?" she asked, backing against her makeshift table.

"What the Mojave call my people," said Joe as he and Johnny entered the cave.

"What's that got to do with me?" she asked.

"You are," said Danny,

"Chemehuevi," finished Donny.

"And that is why."

"You hear the voices."

Woman of the desert moon spoke to Joe.

"Are you Chemehuevi, Tracker Man?"

"Yes."

"Do you hear the voices?"

"Of course."

"Do you..." she hesitated.... "talk to them?"

Joe shook his head.

"We hear them. They do not hear us."

"Have you ever seen them?"

He shook his head again.

"They see us. We do not see them."

"Please, Miss Daryn," said Donny,

"Take off your helmet," said Danny."

"You know my name?"

"Of course. And that of your grandmother,"

"Kestrel."

"And your great-grandmother,"

"Mi'ja."

"Mi'ja is where,"

"The thread was lost."

"So, Miss Daryn," began Donny again,

"Take off your helmet," repeated Danny.

"If you'd ever seen my face, you wouldn't ask me to do that," Daryn said.

"Of course, we have seen your face,"

"And so has Uncle Joe."

"Deputy Man has not," said Daryn.

"Pappa Johnny,"

"Is home from a war."

"He has seen such things,"

"As would make you weep."

"Johnny Quentin is your father?" asked Daryn.

"No, Johnny is the Pappa,"

"Because Father said he was the Pappa."

"And Joe is the Uncle,"

"Because Pappa said he was the Uncle."

"This is all very confusing," Daryn said.

"Someday, Miss Daryn, you will understand,"

"But not just yet."

"So please,"

"The helmet."

Daryn stood swaying before them, her mind reeling from all she had seen and heard from the little boys who seemed to speak with one voice. Finally, she summoned all her courage, lifted the helmet from her head, and stood cradling it in her hands. Her twisted face looked like it was made of the wax dripping from the candles illuminating the cave.

"You are so beautiful," said Donny.

"You take our breath away," finished Danny.

"And your heart,"

"Is so pure."

The boys turned to Johnny.

"We will stay,"

"Until the wedding,"

"As we are to be,

"The ring bearers."

"But soon after,"

"We must leave."

"All this time," said Donny,

"We have been waiting," said Donny,'

"But we weren't sure why,"

"And now we know."

"Miss Daryn will be with us in the elsewhere," said Donny,

"And Miss Daryn will be with us in the elsewhen," Danny finished.

"She completes,"

"The circle."

— **Chapter 27** —

COMBATANTS VIE
A Knot Is Tied

P.*E. was Tony Alpino's* last-period class. On the last Friday in April of his senior year, he and Rennie Wrexler stood facing each other on a twenty-four by twenty-four exercise mat in the center of the Smoke Tree High School gymnasium. Coach Lucas stood between them. The other members of the sixth-period physical education class encircled the mat.

Coach examined the leather work gloves worn by Tony and Rennie and announced they conformed to the specifications he required: no weights or metal objects inside the gloves and no buckles on the outside.

"Okay, for the record, are you willing to settle your differences right now, right here on this mat?"

"Yes," Tony replied.

"Heck yeah," smirked Rennie.

"Then here are the rules you have agreed to. No biting, no eye-gouging, but anything else goes. This is not a boxing match, so there are no timed rounds. The fight continues until one of two things happens. Either one of the fighters raises his hand and says, 'I quit,' or, if I think one of you can no longer defend himself, I declare the fight over. Do you both understand?"

"Yes," both boys said.

"Next, the fight takes place on this mat, and only on this mat. If you get knocked or pushed or thrown off the mat, you have six seconds by my count to get back on. If you don't, you lose. And if I think you stepped off the mat on purpose to catch your breath or stop your opponent's attack, I declare your opponent the winner. Understood?"

"Yes," came the replies.

"Okay, and if you're on the mat and your opponent is off of it, you cannot hinder his return to the mat, but once he gets both feet on it, the fight continues. Agreed?"

Both boys nodded.

"I will not be on the mat as a referee," said Coach. "My role is to count six seconds out loud if one of you is knocked or pushed or thrown off the mat or to stop the fight if I decide one of you is unable to defend himself. Are you clear on that?"

The boys nodded again.

"One last thing. When two boys agree to settle their differences like this, I don't ask them to shake hands before they start. If you liked one another well enough to shake hands, you wouldn't be doing this. But when the fight is over, you will leave your disagreements on this mat and shake hands. Now, Rennie, you go stand on that side of the mat. Tony, you stand on the other side. When I step off and say, 'Go!' the fight is on."

Tony moved to the side of the mat opposite Rennie. He had been thinking about this moment for a long time and was not nervous. He knew he was well prepared as he whispered his mantra: "Float like a butterfly, sting like Ali. Spin, kick, and throw like Bruce Lee."

Coach Lucas stepped off the mat. When he did, one of Rennie's friends shouted, "Fly your freak flag, Wrexler!" Another called, "Take the dork's head off, Rennie." "Flex it, Wrex, the dude's out to lunch," added a third.

"Shut it," yelled Coach. "The next guy who shoots off his mouth is going to be on the mat with me, and I guarantee you it will not be a pleasant experience."

The boys fell silent.

"Go," shouted Coach.

An eager Rennie Wexler charged across the ring to close on his smaller opponent. Tony hit him with a solid left jab to the mouth and slipped away.

Rennie shook his head and laughed.

"Is that all you got, *bambino*?" he jeered.

"Save your breath, big mouth, you're gonna need it," Tony said as he moved.

Enranged, Rennie swung a huge right. Tony ducked beneath it and hooked Rennie in the ribs with his right hand before sliding out of reach again. Rennie pursued him, swinging hard. Tony danced away, unhit.

Rennie changed tactics, trying to crowd Tony without swinging at him. Each time he closed, Tony flicked a left jab with just enough force to keep Rennie at bay. Soon, there were red marks on Rennie's face, his right eye was starting to close, and he was breathing hard.

Rennie changed tactics again. He faked unleashing another roundhouse right, and as Tony moved sideways to avoid the punch that never came, Rennie snaked out his left hand with surprising speed, grabbed Tony by the right forearm, and pulled.

Got you! Rennie thought, expecting Tony to try to pull away. But Tony didn't. Instead, he came willingly and fast and was suddenly almost against Rennie's chest.

Even better, thought Rennie as he tried to encircle the smaller boy with his right arm. But Tony turned his left shoulder into Rennie, got his left thumb under Rennie's left thumb, and wrapped his fingers over the top of Rennie's hand. Using his momentum for leverage, Tony twisted Rennie's thumb backward.

Human beings are blessed with opposable thumbs. That evolutionary advantage makes it possible for them to grasp objects and manipulate tools. But thumbs only bend in one direction, and humans are very protective of the feature that differentiates them from apes and chimpanzees. They react without conscious thought to any potential injury to the thumb joint. Trying to protect his thumb threw Rennie off balance. As he staggered to his left, Tony drove his left knee into the side of Rennie's left knee. Knees bend sideways no better than thumbs bend backward.

The pain was immediate and excruciating. Suddenly, Rennie's left leg would not support him. Tony released Rennie's hand, and Rennie collapsed and rolled off the edge of the mat.

"One," shouted Coach, "two,"

Rennie struggled onto all fours and crabbed forward.

"Three… four," Coach continued.

At "six," Rennie had his right foot on the mat, but when he got his left foot under himself, his left leg collapsed again, and he fell just in time to meet a right uppercut delivered with a full hip turn by a waiting Tony.

Rennie went down again.

When he rolled onto all fours, Tony kicked him in the ribs.

"Hey," shouted Rennie, "that's…."

But whatever he was going to say remained unsaid when Tony's right fist slammed into the side of Rennie's head behind his ear.

Tony briefly considered ending the fight with one final kick, but he wanted Rennie to remember this day for a long time, so he bounced away and allowed Rennie to stand. Rennie's knee was still painful, but it supported him. Tony waited until Rennie raised his fits before he closed on him.

Rennie's supporters had fallen silent, and the only sounds in the gym were from the fighters. Tony Alpino breathed deeply and evenly, his shoes squeaking as he danced from side to side. Rennie Wrexler was barely moving as he gasped for air.

"Come on, big mouth. Is that all you've got?" yelled Tony.

Furious and humiliated, Rennie struggled forward, desperate to hit his taunting opponent, and the fight settled into a pattern.

Rennie would surge forward, throwing punches. Tony would avoid them and pepper the bigger boy with combinations, sometimes ending with a right hook to the ribs or a side kick to the midsection. Then Tony would step back and let Rennie suck in enough air to launch another attack.

Tony wasn't sure why Rennie kept fighting, but he was determined to make Rennie raise his hand and say, "I quit." As Tony continued his barrage of punches and kicks, he got careless, the very thing Horse and Johnny had warned him not to do. Tony lingered a moment too long after a right hook to Rennie's ribs, and Rennie landed a right hand of his own, knocking Tony off his feet.

Tony hit the ground, rolled over, and bounced to his feet, ready to defend himself against a charging Rennie. He needn't have worried.

Rennie stood bent over where he had delivered the punch, hands on his knees. He lifted one gloved hand and waved weakly toward Tony when he got his breath.

"I just wanted to hit you once," he said, "and I did it. But I can't beat you, Triple-A."

"You're no quitter yourself, Rennie," said Tony.

"Yes," he said, "I am," and he lifted his hand again and said, "I quit."

Coach Lucas stepped onto the mat.

"You boys shake hands."

After they did, Rennie looped a big arm over Tony's shoulder.

"This," he gasped, "is the best fighter in this whole school, and you'd best not be lining up to challenge him because if you do, you're going to have to come through me."

On a warm, sunny afternoon the last Sunday in April, there was brunch on the Caballo's patio celebrating Tony Alpino's victory. Johnny was there, of course, as was Robyn. So was Eletheria, who had set everything in motion early that winter by walking into the substation and asking to see Horse. Chemeheuvi Joe had been invited, but it sounded like too many people to him. It was a testament to his desire for solitude that he passed up an Esparanza-cooked meal and disappeared into the hills.

Johnny and Horse demanded a blow-by-blow replay of the event, including Rennie Wexler's description of Tony as "the best fighter in the whole school."

"I owe it all to you two," an obviously embarrassed Tony said when he had finished. "Without your help, I'd a got squashed like a bug."

"And don't you forget it," laughed Johnny.

"That's right," added Horse with a smile.

"Enough with the fighting," said Esperanza. "Time to eat!"

Because the tomatoes in her garden were not yet ripe, brunch was bacon *chilaquiles* with eggs and green tomato salsa followed by *tres leches* cake or *conchas* with Mexican hot chocolate.

When everyone was pleasantly stuffed, Esperanza tapped the side of her water glass for attention.

"Before we let the hero get away, we have something important to attend to."

"What's that?" asked Tony.

"A small matter of corsages and not sticking people when pinning them on."

Horse could have sworn Tony was blushing despite his olive complexion.

"Ah, well," he stammered.

"Come on," said Esperanza, "out with it."

Johnny thought Tony looked like he'd rather be on the mat with Rennie Wrexler than trying to figure out what to say.

"Well, see," he said to Eletheria, "the thing is, I was kind of hoping you might want to go to the prom."

"Is this a suggestion or an invitation, Mr. Alpino?" asked Eletheria, batting her eyelashes furiously and clearly enjoying Tony's discomfort.

"Ah, well, what I meant to say…that is, I would like you to go with me."

"Let me get this straight, Antonio Aloysius Alpino. You want me to dress up in a formal dress and dance with you in a smelly gymnasium that will be decorated as…what is this year's theme?"

"Stardust."

"Yes, that's it. Decorated in a stardust theme."

"Yes, Eletetheria. Yes, that's what I want."

Eletheria clapped her hands.

"Goody! Of course, I want to go. I've always wanted to go to a prom, and I thought I was never going to get the chance."

"Congratulations, you two," said Esperanza, "I'll bet you're going to have a great time."

Later in the afternoon, Tony and Eletheria were out at the corral feeding carrots to the horses when Johnny joined them.

"So, Tony, a question."

"Okay."

"Before we started working out together, I asked you what you wanted to do after high school, and you said you'd tell me when you knew me better. Do you know me well enough yet?"

"I do, but I'm afraid you'll laugh."

"I promise not to."

"Okay, well, Dad's going to close the pizza parlor next summer when 66 doesn't come through town anymore. He's going to go back to New Jersey and buy our old place back."

"I see. Are you going to go too?"

"No. I like it here. There's something about this town, this desert."

"What are you going to do? It's hard to get on with the railroad unless your father before you worked there."

"Nah. Don't want to be a rail. I want to…." Tony paused, took a deep breath, and the next words came out in a rush, "be a cowboy."

"That doesn't make me laugh. Not at all," said Johnny.

"See!" said Eletheria. "Told you, Tony. Romantic dreams of the American West are no sillier than romantic dreams of the attic life in Greenwich Village."

"Yeah, but I'm not sure where to start."

"I know a place that needs a good hand," said Johnny. "John Stonebridge lost one over a year ago and hasn't found a replacement yet. His ranch is in the Pinto Mountains. I'll take you out there and introduce you."

"That would be great, Mr. Quentin, but there's one problem.

"What's that?"

"I've never ridden a horse."

"Well, we're looking at three of them. I'm sure Alejandro and Elena can help you with that. Besides, John and his hands do most the work with Honda ATVs now."

Robyn Danforth stood in the vestibule of the Church of the Highway, peeking anxiously around the open doors into the chapel. In front of the stage stood Jedidiah Shanks, the pastor who would perform the marriage ceremony. Carlos Caballo, Johnny's best man, was to the pastor's left, and beside him, Johnny's groomsmen, Seve Zavala, Andy Chesney, and Danny Dubois.

To Jedidiah's right were Esperanza Caballo, Robyn's maid of honor, and Robyn's bridesmaids, Mary Merriman, Connie Zavala, and the newest waitress at the Bluebird, Randi Clague. In front of all those people stood Robyn's intended: Johnny Quentin.

Elena Caballo, the flower girl, was just inside the chapel door with a white wicker basket filled with red and purple bougainvillea blossoms. Red for love, Esperanza had explained.

"But why purple?" Robyn had asked.

"Because," replied her laughing maid of honor, "you and Johnny are as close to royalty as Smoke Tree gets. You, because you were head cheerleader and prom queen, and Johnny because he will always be Johnny Quarterback. But," Esperanza had added, "there are many more red blossoms than purple because love is ten times more important than fame."

The Merriman twins, Donny and Danny, were also just beyond the doors. They each had one hand beneath a red velvet pillow on which lay two gold bands.

Alicia Winterhaven, a once sightless little girl who was now a young woman with slowly improving vision, was playing a medley of romantic songs on the church organ.

The side of the chapel on Robyn's right was packed. It looked to her like every local she had served in her years as a waitress at the Bluebird Café had come to the wedding. The left side was almost as full because so many people remembered the magic Johnny Quentin had performed playing sports at Smoke Tree High.

The only thing missing from the scene was Robyn, and she was growing nervous. Where was this person who was to escort her down the aisle and respond when Jedidiah asked, "Who gives this woman to be married to this man?" Robyn still did not know who it was. The only clue Johnny had provided was it would be someone as old as her father.

Robyn was suddenly aware someone was standing beside her. Startled, she turned to see a ramrod-straight man with mahogany skin and jet black hair. He wore a World War Two Army uniform. There was a row of colored ribbons above his left pocket and a wool-serge garrison cap with blue trim tucked beneath the shoulder loop of his jacket. His brown shoes were polished to a high gloss.

"Friend of the bride or the groom?" Robyn asked, thinking he was a late arrival to the wedding.

"Groom now. Both, later, maybe."

"Excuse me?"

Almost as nervous as Robyn, Johnny had been looking through the open doors into the vestibule.

Should have known, he thought, *that when I told Joe one o'clock, he took it as thirteen hundred hours sharp; not one minute sooner or one minute later.*

Johnny looked at his watch. The second hand was sweeping toward twelve. When it arrived, he looked up, and Joe was in the doorway.

Johnny turned to Jedidiah.

"Joe's here."

Jedidiah nodded to a waiting Alicia, who launched into Wagner's *Bridal Chorus.*

In the vestibule, former Corporal Joseph Medrano offered Robyn his arm and said, "Playing our song."

Cherry Valley, California
February 6, 2022

Acknowledgments

T hanks to Fran Johnson, Needles High School class of 1961 classmate, Cherry Valley friend Don Sterling, and my son Sam George for reading Woman of the Desert Moon in manuscript form and making helpful comments and corrections.

My thanks also to two former San Bernardino County Sheriff's Department employees. Frank Ruvolo, former Special Deputy and one of the original five pilots with the department's air wing, shared his expertise regarding small aircraft. The liberties taken with his sound advice are entirely the author's fault. A conversation with retired San Bernardino County Sheriff's Detective Harry Hatch gave me the idea for the novel's first chapter. Detective Hatch served in the 1970s in the Needles area.

Also, thanks to Reggie Kenner and James Hutcherson, fellow graduates of Needles High School, for their advice regarding railroad operations.

A request from the author

I f you enjoyed this book, I would appreciate it if you would take a moment and post a review on Amazon or Goodreads. We independent authors lack the resources of the big publishing houses and rely on reviews and word of mouth to promote our books.

Other novels in the Smoke Tree Series

The House of Three Murders
Horse Hunts
Mojave Desert Sanctuary
Death on a Desert Hillside
Deep Desert Deception
The Carnival, the Cross, and the Burning Desert
Walks Always Beside You
A Desert Drowning

Made in the USA
Las Vegas, NV
05 September 2022